Confession

– SHEILA M. BARNES –

Sheila J. Barnes.

UPFRONT PUBLISHING
PETERBOROUGH, ENGLAND

CONFESSION
Copyright © Sheila M Barnes 2008

ISBN 978-184426-553-4

First Published 2008 by
UPFRONT PUBLISHING LTD
Peterborough, England.

Printed on FSC approved paper by
www.printondemand-worldwide.com

Chapter One

H e told me it was much altered but I already knew that. Altered it may be, but in my mind, it will always remain just as it was when the farm flourished and we were children; happy to roam the meadows and chase each other round the cowsheds, the pigsties and the sheep pens. How vividly I recall the three of us running and skipping towards the hills that led to the Chase for Borough Heath Chase is famous. You may have heard of it or even been there. Not as the midland counties of England hold much charm in these days of exotic travel and they held even less in the years between, and just after, the great wars.

The farm house is now a prestigious hotel but however it may be transformed, my memory would instantly convert it to its original bearing. Every brick and roofing slate I can picture just as they were when we were together before anything happened to disturb our tranquil summers. Grey slate roof, so beloved of the Victorians, flint walls and small latticed windows. I was tempted to enquire as to its present condition and ask him what alterations had been made since last I visited. More than likely he wouldn't know. Why should he? Mr.

Lawrence is a mere thirty two years of age whereas I am seventy seven and have every reason to recall it in vivid detail.

He, this Maxwell Lawrence called quite unexpectedly some weeks ago. I, who get so few visitors, had been alarmed when Pan entered my little sitting room and told me that a gentleman wished to see me. Naturally I asked his name and business but Pan had shaken her head and said she had no idea. Well, I can't expect much from Pan although, even after all these years, I still ply her with questions and become frustrated when she merely looks blank and withdraws to her own section of the house. Pan never cares to linger in my domain but I can't tell you why not as I am vague on the subject of her personal limitations.

My visitor, a handsome young man, stepped into my room and shook my hand in the manner of a doctor or someone belonging to the professional classes. I didn't stand, I seldom do since my illness, but I read his card and felt no fear that a stranger stood within a few feet of my chair.

'Only tradesmen carry cards these days,' I smiled at him and asked him to be seated.

'Do they?' he said.

'When I was young everyone had cards. My own mother, an ordinary farmer's wife, always carried a calling card. It was expected.'

'Perhaps I am old fashioned.'

'I hope you are,' I said, 'for certainly I am as you would expect.'

My remark produced no comment. Usually any reference to my age has some idiot declaring that I am nought but a mere girl. Mr. Lawrence said nothing but he sat easily in my Chinese chair, his hands together, his elegant legs uncrossed. Quite taken with his thick fair hair and pale blue eyes almost two minutes elapsed before it occurred to me to enquire as to the reason for his visit.

For Maxwell Lawrence had nothing to say.

'Oh, I do beg your pardon,' he answered. 'I was so busy

admiring your fascinating room that my manners completely deserted me.'

My room, to use his own phrase, is fascinating, but that is almost entirely due to the mural. All that matters at this stage is an understanding of how all this began for the start of a story must be clear so everything that follows can be understood.

'I am writing a play,' he said.

'Oh dear,' I answered. The spell was broken. Annoyance dismissed my appraisal of his fine features and boredom made me long to ring for Pan so that she may escort him to the door.

'You've guessed?' he smiled.

'What else?'

'It's a long time ago.'

'When you grow old, Mr. Lawrence,' I said, 'nothing seems so very long ago. One's whole life appears fleeting and events of sixty years ago give the impression of happening yesterday.'

He sensed my change of mood. I, who had almost welcomed him into my home, became stiff and cold. Not being a loquacious man, Mr. Lawrence hesitated before he spoke further.

'I take it you prefer not to visit?' he commented.

'You would be correct.' A vague answer which I qualified with a thoughtful reply. 'My brother takes an interest but we never discuss it.'

'It would distress you too much?'

'I think not but I see little point in staring at a building that has lost all meaning and might provoke unhappy memories.'

He changed the subject and we spoke instead of the school that stands some two hundred yards from my old home and has become quite a feature of the town. It was founded in the mid seventeen hundreds by an educationalist named Saunders. The Reverent Saunders with his wife Harriet built it to promote learning amongst the poor children belonging to the mining community. They named it Saunders House. When they retired their only child, a daughter by the name of Winfred, continued their work and took over as head mistress. The school escalated as people became aware of the benefits of education and Winifred Saunders was declared a woman of exceptional vision and dedication. My brothers completed their first two years of schooling at Saunders House so it followed that, when the time came, I was sent there to follow in their footsteps.

'Is it derelict?' I asked because I visualised it in ruins. Maybe I have been told so or simply because I couldn't bear to think of children actually inhabiting such a fortress of a place in these days of ultra modern architecture.

'I fancy it is.'

'But you're not sure?'

'Not certain, no.'

Such a fact could be easily verified but I harboured no curiosity as to its present fate. This man, Mr. Lawrence, should have known, he was bursting with curiosity and didn't he say he was writing a play?

'Were any members of the Saunders family still in existence and teaching when you were there?' he asked.

'Yes, one elderly cousin who retired after my first term. I fancy he was quite a good age.'

'And may I ask who took it over after he left?'

'Miss Law. Kathleen Law, a local woman but by that time it was owned by the state or some other governing body, so she was only an employee.'

'How long were you at Saunders House, Mrs. Barry?'

'Ten years. I never attended another school.'

If he were, indeed, writing a play, he should have known such details. In any case I tire easily and, although he was both charming and handsome, I had no wish to dwell on subjects long past. He asked several more questions but when he touched on aspects of my history that I no longer wished to discuss, I politely shifted in my chair, offering him tea as a way of signalling that our interview was over.

Mr. Lawrence was no fool. Without hesitation, he dropped his enquiries and turned the conversation to things of the present. He asked after my health as, I believe there was a small paragraph in The Times, no less, announcing that Mrs. Lavinia Barry of Borough Heath, Staffordshire, had been admitted to hospital after suffering a heart attack. I told him I was quite well, a remark which seemed to give him pleasure for he smiled happily and said he was thrilled to find me looking so radiant. At my age the idea of being termed radiant was amusing but, since I am all too aware of my altered features, I thought him insincere.

'And your maid is your only companion?' he asked when Pan had brought the tea tray and quickly left.

'I would hardly call her a companion,' I said.

'But you have two brothers?'

'Only Teddy now. Dominic died last year.'

'I am so sorry.'

'He was in his eighties so it was to be expected, although I miss him.'

'You were a united family?'

'Of course.'

Mr. Lawrence admired my room. He asked if he may wander round and examine my porcelain and, it goes without saying, view the mural? Of course I told him to do as he pleased; even giving him a short history of some of the pieces. I have a fine collection of figurines, some are extremely old and perhaps very valuable although money is not a subject that enthrals me. Perhaps it did not stir him either for many of the lesser ornaments had him enthusing much more than the obviously priceless examples from the factories of Dresden and Limoges. He asked many questions regarding the mural and I was a mine of information. Not being a member of the brigade of people who declare that they know nothing of art apart from liking or not liking certain works, I indulged him with an informative lecture regarding not only the mural but a history of its artist as well.

Mr. Lawrence, if he was bored, was gentleman enough not to show it.

'May I call again?' he asked.

'You will usually find me at home.' I told him, but added a warning that I would be less than inspirational should he require more intimate details.

'I'll remember that,' he promised.

Before he left, he turned in the doorway to ask one more question. Since I had no wish to prompt further visits, my answer was brief. He must have grasped my reluctance; probably with relief for the young do not relish the prospect of drinking tea with old women whatever secrets and fascinations they may harbour.

'Do you feel any bitterness?' he asked.

'It blighted my life, Mr. Lawrence,' I said, simply. 'How would you feel?

Chapter Two

M y mother was a member of the Grafton-Greatrex family who, in turn, were second or was it third cousins to the Dukes of Somerset? She was what used to be called, 'well connected.'

Father's pedigree was less prestigious. Pa was a Scotsman by the name of MacVee, a Highland man whose own father had been merely a factor on Lord Donington's estate near Fort William. He was the most handsome man I ever knew so his breeding was of little importance when viewed in the context of his looks. I suppose that's why Ma married him. She never said so in so many words but I always noticed how her eyes would follow him around a room and how jealous she appeared when other women showed an interest in him.

Because she was an heiress my father was indeed fortunate in so much as he did not have to burden himself with the pressures of business or the trouble of pursuing a career. As far as I can recall he did very little with his life and amounted to nothing at all. Ma never appeared to mind or begrudge him what was rightfully hers. My grandfather was a baronet and a wealthy one at that so she inherited a considerable legacy on his death. Granted his fortune was left in trust but her actual income was substantial. I think by today's standards it would have been in the region of a hundred thousand pounds a year. Our home was her home, by that I mean it was the house where she was born and where her parents and grandparents had lived and farmed for more than three centuries. Chase Farm was a manor house in the true tradition of such places. It stood surrounded by six hundred acres of forest land and was possessed of a home farm complete with its own dairy and fruit orchards. Idyllic, you might say and I would agree.

My memories of Pa are always connected with the estate. He dressed as a gentleman farmer was expected to dress in the late thirties and mid-forties. Breeches and boots, bowler hat and hacking jacket and, although I never knew him to ride, he usually carried a riding crop. Horses were just being replaced by tractors. Grey Fordson tractors. Not particularly picturesque replacements for the romantic image of the ploughman and pair but efficient, productive and extremely prolific after the second world war.

I was only nine when that war broke out but I remember the atmosphere and the long years of deprivation and turmoil. I remember Vera Lynn singing about the white cliffs of Dover on our wooden wireless set and how disappointed I was when, many years later, I actually saw those cliffs and discovered they were a dirty grey and far from romantic. But, with hindsight, I have to admit that my expectations have always had a leaning towards fantasy.

Strangely enough although we lived only twenty two miles from the great industrial city of Birmingham, Borough Heath was totally unaffected by German bombs. If I remember correctly the nearest bomb which exploded was some eight miles away in the vicinity of Wolverhampton. Queues were a familiar feature of our childhood and, although as I've mentioned, we were an affluent family many of the essentials of life were rationed and many almost unobtainable. I still recall the vague excitement which thrilled us when we heard that supplies of sweets or, better still, chocolates had arrived in the local shops. My brothers and I would join the snake-like procession of people who waited patiently to purchase such luxuries but often by the time we reached the various counters we were told that stocks had sold out.

Disappointment was experienced at an early age.

Teddy, my younger brother was fourteen when the war began and Dominic, sixteen. I adored them both and can't recall any discord between us. In the main I find that brothers and sisters tend to argue and disagree but we three were always the best of friends and generally speaking, despite the disparities in our respective ages, spent our leisure time together. Thank God neither boys were conscripted to fight in that wicked war as both were under age and later in reserved occupations.

Borough Heath, in common with towns and cities all over the country, was cursed with casualties. Many of our own tenants lost sons and Ma never failed to send condolences and visit the bereaved; no doubt praising the Lord that her own sons remained safely within the house each night.

Pa was exempt from active service as, by profession, he was listed as a farmer therefore engaged in a reserved occupation which exempted him from duty on the front line or any other line which would have taken him from us.

Just before the war, at the age of seven, I was the sole member of the family still attending Saunders School, my brothers having moved on. Teddy would have been about twelve and Dominic almost fifteen. After completing a preparatory period at Saunders the boys were enrolled as weekly boarders in a school near Stafford but they came home every Friday night and stayed until quite late on Sunday evening. It was our custom to attend evensong at St. Mary's Anglican Church in the town centre after which Pa would drive them both back to the county town in his Humber Super

Snipe. To this day, I can describe every inch of that massive car for I have had a life long love affair with cars. Even now I own a prestigious Mercedes although, since my illness, my driving is limited.

It was at about this time that Ma told us we were to have a new brother or sister; a startling piece of news which we discussed without a vestige of enthusiasm. I recall Teddy remarking that the baby's gender was of little consequence as whatever it happened to be the age difference would prevent it from interfering with any of us. I worried because, being the only girl, it occurred to me that I might be called upon to baby sit or become mother's little help. Ma was a good mother and, for all her inherited wealth, she never believed in farming us out to a nursemaid or a nanny but, I have to add that neither she nor Pa were what might be termed as engaging parents. By that I mean that they never did much with us. We never had a holiday or a trip to the seaside or any of those outings which, even during the war, were the highlight of many children's lives. Dudley, a small town close by, boasted a well stocked zoo but, as far as I can remember, none of us were ever taken there anymore than we were treated to picnics or birthday parties. I don't think it was because our parents were harsh or unthinking but since we had such extensive grounds in which to play and entertain ourselves, they considered we had pleasures enough.

And how we did enjoy ourselves.

Miles of wild countryside surrounded the farm. Even in later years, when every spare inch of land became obscured by ugly blocks of flats and housing estates, the immediate vicinity surrounding our home remained spacious and beautiful. Teddy told me, not so long ago, that it is protected by an ancient decree that prevents its use as building land. The forests and bracken laden pathways are in every respect untouched by time as is my present house and perhaps even myself.

After the worst winter since records began, the summer of

nineteen forty six was hot and sunny. It needed to be since we had had snow almost every day from the twenty first of January until the sixteenth of March. Farming the rock hard land proved an ordeal for the newly returned labourers who were happy to be home after the ordeals of war. Teddy, Dominic and myself made sleighs and revelled in the powdery snow which drifted across the wind swept fields and made the roads impassable. From early light until past six, when the boys were at home, we skated on the frozen lake and built snowmen; hardly feeling the bitter winds such was our delight in the exceptional conditions.

Gradually more men came home from battle and were returned to the mines and to their families. Those were the days before anyone understood the importance of counselling or the effects of trauma on the human mind. It would have been beneath the dignity of most of those hardened soldiers to admit that they suffered nightmares or felt unable to cope with domestic life. We have digressed since then and most men appear fragile and feminine even though they have never experienced adversity. Our own farm manager had a son who was so traumatised by the horrors he had endured that he couldn't return to his normal duties for over two years. Unfortunately, to add to his woes, his own father declared him a wimp and the town's folk ostracised him when he dared to stroll down the High Street. His story bears no relation to my own but it shows how public opinion has changed so radically. Liberal attitudes, which prevail in this new century, were unheard of after the war and remained buried for some three or even four decades later.

Often men, who had served in far away places, boasted of their exploits and many had medals to prove their bravery in critical campaigns. My brother Dominic used to listen to the estate workers telling tales of hand to hand fighting in Monte Casino and wonder at stories concerning action in unheard of places such as Chittagong and Bangladesh. Two cousins, who were responsible for maintaining our apple orchards, had escaped from the Nazis in Berlin and Dominic was fascinated by their accounts of underground networks and the cruelty of the concentration camps. Ma, in the end, put a stop to his late night meetings with those men because she said war was not a subject to be discussed before bed time especially as Dominic was studying for his school certificate.

Anyone hearing her comments would have supposed the poor cousins to have performed some objectionable or unsavoury act which required censure. Dominic thought them heroes and so did I but that was over sixty years ago and our way of thinking was vastly different.

In due course Ma had her baby. I would like to add that we celebrated the birth of our new brother but Peter, as he was named, seemed to belong exclusively to Ma and conveyed absolutely no interest to any one of us. Whether Pa was thrilled or even mildly pleased with this late arrival, I really can't say. I expect, as Ma was almost forty and he was ten years older, the new baby was not the most welcome member of our family but, whether or not that was the case I have no idea.

Peter was the most gorgeous baby you will ever see. His hair was thick, wavy and as blonde as bleached wheat in August; his complexion, a shade of milky peach. Every part of him, from his flawless features to his amethyst eyes were perfection personified. I could list his attributes for hours and tire myself with the exhaustion of writing but I will spare such effort for it is enough to say that he was truly beautiful.

Beautiful or not, he held no appeal for Teddy, Dominic or myself. We didn't dislike him or suffer jealousy, we just dismissed him as we would had he been a newly hatched chicken. I, who had feared would be called upon to play the part of nurse maid, was never asked to as much as wheel his pram. The boys never troubled to give him the benefit of a curious glance and certainly neither of them ever stopped to smile or rock his cradle.

As far as we were concerned, Peter simply did not exist.

Since our parents were not given to accompanying us to picture houses or any other sources of entertainment, we soon started investigating such places for ourselves, by ourselves. Even, given my vast age, I clearly recall Dominic and Teddy taking me to see 'The Best Years of our Lives' at the Odeon cinema in Stafford Road. That film won an Oscar for the best film of 1946 and, strange to tell, I saw it on my television set only last week in the comfort of my own sitting room. Old, I might be but my memory is sharp and I can name other films we saw at that cinema such as The Razor's Edge and The Jolson Story.

We all three loved listening to the newly purchased wireless which Ma kept in the front parlour. In a rare moment of munificence, Pa relented and bought us our own set which Dominic was allowed to install in his bedroom. It was a Bush and it had little white buttons which we could press and, as if by magic, find a variety of stations which kept us enthralled for hours at a stretch. If you happen to share my vast age you will remember breath taking episodes of Dick Barton Special Agent and The Man In Black.

Teddy loved to tune into Radio Luxembourg and sing along with the latest songs. I don't think there was such a thing as a hit parade in those far off days but our songs were a darn sight better than anything that assaults my ears now and causes me to switch off whichever device is blasting them into my room. We all knew the words to such standards as Lili Marlene and Bless 'em All. My favourite was, 'It's a Lovely Day Tomorrow,' but I speak of a time when singers were taught to enunciate and adhere to the tune not lose the key and become inaudible as they do today. (Which all goes to show that the years have turned me into an old grouch and someone deserving the name of dinosaur!)

Now and again Peter would crawl into a room where we were busy with homework or just sitting talking. Dominic, at this time, was studying frantically for his matriculation as, to obtain a pass, five subjects were required so it was no good excelling in literature and maths if history or a foreign language let you down. Dominic was determined to be a doctor, a desire that had never deserted him through all the years of his childhood and which made the passing of his exams vital. Teddy and I used to spend long hours testing him on subjects as diverse as geometry and modern poetry. Teddy had no need for such dedication himself as his intention was to manage the farm and run the estate when poor old Pa could no longer manage. For myself, well in those days very little was expected from the daughters of wealthy families, so I can not tell you that I paid much attention to my studies.

On the rare occasions when Peter crawled or, later, tottered into our various domains I think we viewed him as a strange being from another planet and, hoped, that by keeping silent, he would wander away in search of more congenial company. If he threatened to linger or, worse still, tried to engage our attention, one of us would pick him up and deposit him outside the door. Writing of it now, we sound harsh and perhaps cruel but we knew Ma was never far away and that she would collect him and bestow cuddles and kisses on his beautiful head.

Peter wanted for nothing except, perhaps, the love of his two brothers and one heartless sister.

Chapter Three

Ninety forty seven saw a vast change in the community in so much as the coal mines were nationalised. The pit owners of old drove their expensive cars away from the collieries and quit their great houses, still wealthy but no longer in charge. The National Coal Board came into being and was controlled from Westminster. Miners, who had been amongst the lowest paid workers in the country with little chance of promotion, were said to be facing a prosperous future with life enhancing opportunities.

Borough Heath is situated in middle England and is part of what is known as The Black Country. The name may have lost something of its true meaning now but, in my day, and for two centuries previously, it was the heart of the coal mining industry. Further north, lie Stoke on Trent and Hanley which are included in the five towns that go to make up the area known as the potteries.

The Midlands are perhaps not blessed with beauty as is much of our island. Just west of Birmingham lie the Cotswold Hills and, if you crave outstanding scenery they are well worth a visit, so too is southern England with its soft downs and placid coastline. Devon and Cornwall possess a rare splendour particularly appealing to lovers of windswept seascapes and quaint fishing villages. There is a popular poem which refers to the Midlands as being, 'sodden and unkind.' It is written by Hilair Belloc but I can not say that I agree with such a dour description. As children, my brothers and I, thought ourselves privileged to exist in such idyllic surroundings. Miles of unspoilt countryside could be freely walked and our summer days were spent in the fields and forests which surrounded the farm but, of course, I speak of a time before motor vehicles caused havoc and turned even simple villages into race tracks and car parks.

We were lucky to have lived in the freedom of such an age. I am vexed to think I am nearing the end of my life but I wouldn't relish a second youth in these evil times. For one thing our pleasures were simple and easily obtained. No computers or TV sets were vital to our happiness and certainly no drugs or sexual freedom were considered a necessity as they are today. I recall one of our own farm labourers having a daughter who became pregnant by the son of the local post man. Hands were held up in horror, the scandal was such that no one could bear to even speak of it. Now, I'm told single mothers outnumber married ones and no one gives a damn. And when do you see young people merry and laughing? Even when I was always out and about I grieved at the lack of joy on the faces of teenagers and considered them addicted to cheap music and material possessions. Few appeared to have steady work and all required expensive toys to while away their time. Now that I am restricted and my outings are few I still gasp at the quantity of young people who spend their time speaking, to God knows who, on mobile phones.

Perhaps I shouldn't criticize such a foul invention for I have one myself. My brother Teddy insisted on presenting me with one some five years ago. I promised to keep it in the car so that I would always have a means of communication should anything go awry. To tell you the truth I have never got to grips with its mysterious workings and, secretly, never intend to do so.

Dominic studied hard for his school certificate and eventually, as was expected, passed in all five subjects. We congratulated him but at the same time feared that it would herald his removal to a higher seat of learning. Dominic, himself, fretted at the thought of leaving but his determination to qualify as a doctor was stronger than ever, nevertheless he promised to come home as often and for as long as possible.

Saunder's School still served me well and, for all that was to happen in the future, I have to say that I was quite content to literally trot across the road to that little Church of England school and gain scant knowledge from my head mistress, Miss Kathleen Law.

Teddy was still boarding on a weekly basis near Stafford and Peter was walking proficiently but rarely making any attempt to communicate. Whether we thought him weird or peculiar, I can not say for it wouldn't have crossed our minds to converse with him even had he been the most loquacious child in the kingdom.

Pa, at almost fifty two, became distinctly taciturn hardly bothering with any of his children but then he had never figured large in our lives so we merely avoided the worst of his moods and treated him with sullen respect. Ma took to complaining that she had grown old and ceased to go out very much preferring instead to concentrate on her needlepoint and her caged birds. I don't know if people are still interested in caged birds, probably not since television sets and computers fill their homes, but sixty years ago many living rooms were considered unfurnished if there was an absence of gilt cages and canaries.

Our home was possessed of three stories and a basement. There was a time, a very long while ago, when I used to find excuses to drive past it or what remains of it. Years after all its traumas were finally over it was sold to a developer and converted into a Travelogue Hotel. Both Teddy and Dominic, out of some kind of morbid curiosity, stayed there overnight and both agreed it had been beautifully re-appointed. For myself, I could not have born to set one foot over its threshold.

The summer of nineteen forty seven was to be our last one together as a threesome. Dominic had won a place at Christ Church, Oxford and Teddy was preparing to become a full time boarder at King Edwards School in Birmingham. Pa never ceased to remind him of the considerable expense involved in furthering his education but Teddy was never an industrious scholar. His future, we all knew, lay in managing the estate not in acquiring academic qualifications.

A child I may have been and uniformed at that but I could see that farming at our present level lacked a future. Even at that time imports from Denmark and the commonwealth were imploding the home markets and the demand for home grown apples and local honey, rapidly diminishing. So we walked the country miles, listened to our favourite radio programs and sometimes took the bus or train to visit nearby towns. As far as I can recall, neither parent queried our absences or enquired where we were heading. How differently they would have reacted today now that we are aware of the horrors of paedophiles and other unsavoury characters!

Dominic, in any case, was almost a man and had grown to a height of over six feet so Ma probably considered him old enough and big enough to protect Teddy and myself from harm. Dominic was handsome in those days, of course that was to change, but as a young man he was sharp featured with blazing blue eyes and a thick mop of glossy black hair that turned many a girl's head. Not that he ever had a girlfriend but I'm sure he could have taken his pick had he been so inclined. Teddy was small for his age and not blessed with beauty but he was fun and an outstanding mimic. Once someone had spoken to him he was instantly able to imitate their speech, caricature it perhaps, but we could always recognise the original and usually we prompted him to entertain us further. He's a very old man now but, when he visits, still he makes me laugh and for that I thank him for our family has suffered a scarcity of humour along with all the other more obvious deprivations which I suppose were inevitable.

Often we would arrive home very late from our various wanderings. In nineteen forty seven British Summertime meant that it stayed light until ten or eleven o'clock at night. The labourers, on the home farm, were kept busy until the last rays of light faded over the fields for in those days men worked hard for little reward. Five pounds would be considered a hefty wage for ninety hours hard grind. Families were large but food was cheap plus the fact that very little was spent on entertainment or clothes. Many years were to pass before such items as designer labels or expensive gadgets were mass marketed and many clothes were home made including men's suits and shirts. If money was really scarce then children went shoeless. I remember girls at Saunders bare footed and shivering with cold for want of a coat or footwear in the freezing weather. In these liberal times they would be aided by government grants and a whole host of fancy allowances most of which I resent for, due to a lifetime of careful living, I am forced to pay the highest level of taxation.

Eventually our blissful summer came to an end and Dominic left the farm to take his place at Oxford. I cried that night. Cried for the loss of a brother who had gladdened my childhood and been the best friend I ever thought to have. Life without him seemed bleak and, although I loved Teddy dearly, he was no substitute for my clever Dominic. In due course, Teddy too, was dispatched to Birmingham so my future was threatened by both loneliness and boredom.

The radio shows, that had once brought such joy and amusement, meant nothing when I listened to them all alone in Dominic's empty bedroom. Once or twice I ventured to the cinema but, sad and lonely, I crept out half way through films which I knew I would have adored had the boys been at my side.

Perhaps you wonder that I lacked the companionship of girls of my own age or had a plentiful supply of school friends? Approaching my mid-teens I was blessed with a pleasing personality and my looks were considered appealing but, truth to tell, we three siblings had been so self contained that it had never occurred to me to seek fellowship elsewhere.

Dwelling on my loneliness, I took to wandering about the farmland or sitting in the parlour staring into space. Any number of local children played on our land and, when I listened from my seat by the sash window, their games sounded jolly but I never ventured out to join them or entered in their fun. Snobbery had something to do with it. Ma and Pa had always intimated that we were above the serving classes and, whereas, we should show them every courtesy, they advised the wisdom of keeping ourselves aloof.

In this remarkable age I would have had the advantage of being able to text or phone both brothers and feel close to them but in the late nineteen forties communications were restricted to weekly letters. When Dominic first went to Oxford, we corresponded every week without fail. I was even guilty of writing twice and on one occasion, three times. After a few short weeks this practise faltered, not on my part, but because his studies and new interests overtook his desire to continually find the time to write to me.

I would read and re-read his letters several times and write back instantly. Poor Dominic must have been plagued by the postman and embarrassed that his little sister pestered him for news when a new life beckoned and time was at a premium.

It was Ma who first noticed my wretchedness and it was she who took me to task over it.

'Nothing stays the same,' she told me. 'You have to make a life for yourself, no one can do it for you.'

'But I miss the boys.' I told her what she already knew.

'They have their studies and careers to think about and you have your school work. Anyway, there's much to do in the house. It's about time you learnt a few domestic lessons. Why don't you go down to the kitchen and ask cook to show you how to make pastry?'

I haven't told you about our servants, have I? No one has servants these days. No one except me that is and I only have Pandora and a man called Bobby Carter who tends the garden and cleans my car. At the time of which I speak we had a multitude of staff. Wages were low and Ma had bags of money, so we had maids, cleaning women, gardeners and a resident housekeeper. Very posh! We were never quite grand enough to aspire to a butler but Pa employed a farm manager who more or less managed him so I always thought of him as a personal valet. Our cook was called Matty and she looked just as a cook should look. Fat and cheerful with a bright red face. Her domain, naturally, was the kitchen but she had a set of rooms on the third floor and, once, she invited me to take tea in them. They comprised of a large bedroom and a fair sized sitting room. Matty had her own bathroom and even a tiny kitchen where she could make cups of tea and prepare the odd snack. Not that she looked in need of extra sustenance; I would have thought our below stairs staff were as well fed as were Ma, Pa and myself but I suppose she had time to herself and enjoyed entertaining her friends.

Pa began to suffer heart problems around this time. Quite what ailed his heart, I don't think we ever knew but he had to travel to Birmingham to see a specialist every month and twice he was detained in Selly Oak Hospital also in Birmingham. Strangely enough, I can't recall Ma ever visiting him during one of those prolonged stays but I do recall his decline in health. His breathing became laboured, his usually brisk movement, slow and a walking stick his constant companion. The farm manager I mentioned, his name was Fred Corbett, became even more of a valet and a permanent fixture by Pa's side. One seldom saw one without the other for Pa took to leaning on Fred's arm as he ambled about the farm. Stairs proved too much and so did any kind of exercise which meant that he habitually hung about the ground floor of the house.

I kept my distance.

Pa and I had never been close simply because he showed such little interest in his only daughter and only slightly more so in the boys For all his amazing looks, I can't think he meant a great deal to Ma at that time. She spent her days in a small room to the left of the hall which we called the morning room and he spent his waking hours in the cavernous sitting room. During the coming winter he was forced to abandon his place beside Ma, in their first floor bedroom, and take to sleeping in his study. All the furniture of business was removed. His mahogany desk, three filing cabinets, the walnut bookcases which housed leather bound books devoted to farming and agriculture, all were disposed of or sent to the sale rooms.

Pa was clearly a very sick man.

I worried about his health and desperately wanted to discuss my fears with Dominic. Dozens of letters I posted to him but Dominic always wrote back telling me not to fret as Pa was simply growing old and we had to face the fact that age and decrepitude were inevitable. Teddy came home that Christmas and lifted the picture slightly as we went out and about together and I was able, for one whole week, to shelve my worries. But he had to resume his studies in Birmingham or, at least, pretend to do so. It came out years later that most of the time he was skipping lessons on account of the fact that, at an early age, he fancied himself a candidate for the Wimbledon tennis championships and spent his time pestering the professional at his local club.

Eventually Ma had to engage a nurse to tend to Pa. I suppose in these days of high wages and shortage of skilled workers, he would have been placed in a nursing home but it was the practise at that time to engage a private nurse in the hope that she would manage the invalid thus minimising undue upset to the rest of the household.

Pa's nurse was called Doris and she seemed pretty elderly to me. I suppose when you are not quite fourteen someone in their mid forties appears ancient although Ma didn't seem so and she was even older. Doris Haywood, that was her name and she began her reign in the February of nineteen forty nine. A severe humourless person, she swished around the ground floor reminding me of Mrs. Danvers in the film, 'Rebecca.' Doris herself adds little interest to my story but her niece, Isabel more than makes amends for that.

It was unusual in those post war days to tolerate unnecessary encumbrances and servants of any kind were not normally employed if they had a child or a dependant in their care. Ma had hesitated for almost a fortnight before agreeing to the addition of Isabel. I forget the finer details but I remember her irritation over the fact that the best nurse she had interviewed should possess the drawback of a protégé. Miss Haywood explained that the girl had no one but herself due to the fact that both her parents were dead. But our house was vast and one more occupant posed few problems so Isabel and her aunt were allowed to move in. Isabel, being seventeen years old herself, proved a capable nurse in her own right. As far as I was concerned she broke some of the tedium caused by the bleak presence of her aunt and also it was pleasant to have a young educated girl about the house.

Pa's illness and the gloom it created was increased a hundred fold when Ma took to her bed with some malady which necessitated a twice daily visit from our family doctor. I expect it was a strain of flu but, truth to tell, I forget what ailed her or what her symptoms were. Matty did her best to cheer me and Dominic came home for a long weekend which was absolutely heaven.

One wet Saturday evening, he took me to Wolverhampton Hippodrome where we saw a play called, 'Ladies in

Retirement.' On the following Monday, we spent a whole day in Stafford where he treated me to a green satin dress, some boots and an expensive dinner in the first hotel I had ever entered. Naturally, having been deprived of his company for so long, I was ecstatic to have him all to myself even if it was only for a few days. Only Teddy had been home that Christmas although why Dominic had stayed in Oxford remains a mystery even to this day. Maybe he felt the need to absent himself from his cloying family once he had experienced the freedom of life without stuffy parents and clinging sisters to survey his every move?

During our dinner, Dominic became serious. The jollity of our day together, the last two days in fact, were forgotten. Ordering a coffee for me and a brandy for himself and, whilst cupping the bulbous glass inside his clever fingers, he upbraided me for developing, what he called, 'a selfish attitude.' Dominic pointed out that although I was a teenager, almost a young woman, he considered me both childish and self centred. My coffee almost choked me as my beloved brother continued his chastisement but, I had to admit, that much of what he said made sense. Never having considered myself self indulgent, I hung my head in shame for every word he said rang true. I wasn't grieving over Pa's suffering as a loving daughter should; I was merely irritated that it inflicted a slight burden on me personally. Both parents becoming ill at the same time, Dominic said, had merely annoyed me and, further more, I had not displayed a vestige of concern or sympathy for either one of them. Apparently I had complained, non stop, that the situation was disturbing my usually trouble free life. Dominic finished his brandy and touched my hand.

'Don't think I'm being unkind, Vinnie,' he explained, 'but it's essential, with Teddy and myself away, that you take some sort of responsibility for our parents.'

'Pa has his nurse and Isabel,' I replied.

'They're just paid employees, Vin. It's love and kindness

from the people who matter that he needs now.'

'He was never very caring about us, Dom.'

'Perhaps not but we don't know what pressures he was under when we were just kids. That farm doesn't run itself you know.'

I don't think Dominic believed that it was hard work which prevented Pa from spending time with his children anymore than I did but what he said seemed reasonable so I promised him that, when he returned to Oxford, I would make it my business to be a loving and caring daughter to both parents.

'And then there's Peter,' he said as an after thought.

'Oh, he's all right,' I shrugged.

'But is he?' Dominic looked thoughtful. 'We've none of us ever bothered with him so he probably feels lonely and isolated with Ma ill and Pa hardly ever putting in a appearance. Take an interest in him, Vinnie, take him out for walks or read to him, that sort of thing.'

Never in the four years of my little brother's life had I given him a serious thought. To be honest, I seldom saw him. That must sound very strange considering that we lived in the same house and shared the same parents. Peter had a grand playroom on the second floor and, I can't recall him leaving it to wander about the farm as we three had always done. When I was his age Pa had given instructions that a swing was to be erected in the orchard and a sandpit built near the stables. Dominic, Teddy and I had spent hours amusing ourselves on that swing plus we had two ponies which I recall with great affection to this day. Mine was piebald and Teddy's as black as night. Quite why Dominic didn't have one of his own I can't say but, of course, we shared them and often he rode mine. They were called Robbie and Rastus. (It's just taken me a good five minutes to recall the name, 'Rastus' but, I'm not quite as senile as I feared for the name came to me as I gazed out of my sitting room window and saw my cat, Angel, washing herself on the terrace. A cat reminded me of a pony, long gone, perhaps I am senile after all?)

But I digress.

Dominic's remarks hit their target and I made up my mind to be more caring. I took to enquiring after Pa's health at least three times a day until he ordered me to get about my own business and leave him to his. Ma recovered but was noticeably weaker. Looking back after all these years I am of the opinion that ill health suited her. Having no desire to do anything more strenuous than her needlepoint and sit, feet up, on her red velvet sofa, she inclined eagerly towards invalidity.

Peter was another matter.

The first time I entered his playroom he threw a wooden horse at me and his aim was accurate enough to draw blood from my forehead. My instinct was to retreat and remain aloof, as had been my practise since his arrival almost five years ago, but Dominic's words rang in my ears so I advanced on him with a smile.

Peter's playroom was truly amazing. I have three children of my own and, when we owned a flat in London, we spent many hours perusing the great toy shops and department stores of the West End. Kit, my husband, was an electric train enthusiast and, luckily, we had two boys so he was able to indulge his own pleasures and feel unrestrained in the matter of buying endless rolling stock. For our daughter Anna, who has always been the joy of my life, I bought all manner of toys as the temptation to resist was pointless. Choosing gifts for the children brought as much joy to us as it did to them and funds were available to delight us all.

Money for toys we may have had but our children's playroom was practically shoddy compared to Peters'. Just after the war, toys were in short supply but, somewhere, Ma or Pa must have discovered an Aladdin's cave of such items. To say Peter had every manner and make of plaything is to exaggerate but I have never, before or since, seen such a collection outside of a well stocked toy shop. Whether he preferred his three enormous rocking horses to his hundreds of cars both miniature and pedal sized, I never fathomed. Teddy bears, boxed games, forts with cannons and armies of lead soldiers, conjuring sets, crayons and paint boxes were piled high on every square inch of the floor. Hand and string puppets cascaded from chairs and the ceiling. Jig Saw puzzles, quite beyond his capabilities, spilled their pieces onto the carpet and stuffed animals with glass eyes peered from every corner making me quite forgot my mission which was to bring entertainment to one small boy who appeared entertained enough.

'Go away,' Peter shouted, breaking the spell which his room had cast upon his only sister.

'What a lot of toys you have,' I said, inanely.

'Get out.'

'Let me see them properly.' I approached him on my way to inspect a post office set which lay near his feet. A stinging sensation accompanied by a sticky feeling in the region of my chin, stopped me in my tracks. Peter had struck again and this time quite badly.

Blood flowed from a deep cut below my lower lip and the pain was intense. A sturdy metal train had caused such damage thrown, of course, by Peter. Shocked as well as hurt, I held my handkerchief to the wound and asked him why he had done such a thing. Peter neither answered nor favoured me with a glance. Furious and injured, I took hold of him fully intending to administer a hard slap. Of course, I didn't. Nasty little brute he might have been but he was still very small whereas I was almost fully grown and therefore strong enough to inflict real damage, so I resisted but admonished him soundly.

Peter stared at me but said not one word.

Slamming the playroom door, I made up my mind to ignore him for the rest of both our lives. My main concern was to rush to the kitchen so that Matty could dress my wound. After that, I burst into the sitting room, where Ma and Pa happened to be listening to a play on the wireless, and I complained bitterly of my brother's wretched behaviour.

Neither parent took the slightest notice of my outburst. Ma, muttered something about Peter being very young and the fact that I should make allowances whereas Pa, as far as I can recall, made no comment whatsoever so I slammed their door in the same manner as I had slammed Peters'.

With hindsight I should have stood my ground and made them listen properly.

Hindsight is a wonderful thing!

Chapter Four

I n nineteen fifty one, Teddy caused a major upset within the family.

At the tender age of not quite eighteen, he announced his engagement to a seventeen year old girl by the name of Dorothea Stephens.

Pa, although growing progressively weaker by the month, rallied enough to curse and condemn the union. He was of the opinion that Teddy was far too young to contemplate marriage and announced that should he pursue such a disastrous course, he would disinherit him. Ma, always keen to boast of her family connections, merely demanded to know the pedigree of Dorothea Stephens.

Considering Teddy had always had his heart set on managing the estate, Pa's talk of disinheritance should have deterred his plans.

Such threats made not a jot of difference!

During the late winter and early spring, Teddy brought Dorothea to the house on numerous occasions. The happiness, which was so apparent on the faces of both my brother and this young lady, was a sight to behold. Towards mid summer, even

Pa warmed to her and Ma, invalid or not, became animated in her presence. It wasn't long before all animosity was put to one side, and Pa actually ventured outside once again where, leaning on Teddy's arm, he took Dorothea on a conducted tour of the farm. Eventually, it was agreed that Teddy should leave King Edwards in Birmingham and take up his rightful position as Estate Manager. Since any lingering doubts concerning his marriage to Dorothea were soon dismissed, a September wedding was planned and Dominic was requested to come home so he could act as best man.

I remember Dorothea Stephens to this day. She was quite petite, no more than five feet tall, small featured with dazzling blue eyes and hair the colour of a wheat field in August. Teddy could span his hands around her waist with ease and her shoe size matched mine as we both wore a size three. She was just as much fun as Teddy and together, they could have found success as a music hall act. Both were blessed with the ability to imitate any accent or person and both were capable of amusing their audience for hours on end. Whenever I saw then together, which was often, I would always be uplifted by their laughter. Theirs was a union which held the promise of great happiness and I applauded Teddy's choice of bride with all my heart.

Dorothea originated from a tiny village in the heart of the Derbyshire Dales. Her father, just like mine, was a farmer although compared to Pa he farmed in a very small way, doing most of the rough work himself. Any feelings of snobbery which Ma might have harboured were dispelled within a matter of weeks, for each one of us learnt to love Dorothea.

Dominic came down from Oxford that summer. Many years of practical work lay ahead but he was well on way to qualifying as a doctor and my pride in him was massive. So, once again, we were a united and happy family. Pa's health, although not good, appeared improved and Ma literally had a new lease of life. This time instead of being just the three of us, we became four. Wherever we went Dorothea came with us, which was to be expected as soon she was to be a fully fledged member of the family. Twice we visited her home in the beautiful Derbyshire Dales and became familiar with her family and friends after which she came back to stay with us in Borough Heath where preparations for the wedding were in full cry. It was decided that, once she and Teddy were married, the west wing of the house was to serve as their living quarters. To this end Pa and Teddy concentrated on plans for an elaborate conversion so that builders could move in and construct an entirely self contained flat. We all took an interest in the work involved and, although it must have cost a fortune, Pa never once complained or tried to cut corners.

At some point Dorothea attempted to befriend Peter for he was an attractive little boy and it was only natural that, as she was soon to be his sister in law, she should gain the affection of the baby of the family. Although she did everything in her power to coax him away from his playroom, he consented only to shake her hand, refusing any further offers of friendship. In the end, just like the rest of us, she abandoned all efforts of companionship and left him to his own devices. Ma insisted that he spoke to her at the dinner table but a curt nod was all I ever knew her to receive.

Although we possessed hundreds of milking cows and calves, several fearsome bulls and fields overloaded with sheep, we did not own a dog. A farm without a dog seems bereft especially as we had two full time shepherds. You would have thought a guard dog or a pack of terriers, to control the rat population, would have been deemed a necessity but obviously not as no puppy or working collie had ever set foot on our land. Dorothea changed all that by pestering Teddy to buy her a dog of her own and, naturally he rectified the omission within the week. The most adorable black cocker spaniel puppy was bought from a neighbouring farmer and given to Dorothea as a pet.

We called him Raq in memory of Romany and Raq, who

were real life characters in a radio program about the countryside. You would have to be my great age to recall either Romany, who was a true gypsy and Raq (pronounced RACK) his dog, but many people still remember the program with affection and some may even recall the sad saga of Dorothea Stephens.

A wet and depressing spring turned into a gorgeous summer. Day after day, sunshine and heat prompted us to forego our indoor activities and rush for the fields where we indulged ourselves with picnics and slow strolls through the woods. During the long warm evenings Ma often brought her needlework out onto the York stoned terrace which adjoined the morning room. Once or twice even Pa joined our happy group and, for a man of taciturn temperament, he became quite loquacious. I remember watching him as he recounted tales of summers long gone when first he and Ma inherited the farm and we were all very young. Once again I thought his looks quite spectacular and understood what Ma had seen in him all those years ago.

Teddy and Dorothea made ideal companions for all of us. Many young couples, so obviously in love, would have preferred the solitude of just each other's company but my brother and, soon to be sister in law, were more than content to remain with the rest of us thus turning almost every evening into something approaching a party.

Home refrigerators were still the prerogative of the rich. Now one would be hard pressed to find a home without such a convenience, but in nineteen fifty one they were still very much a rarity. Naturally we had one. I think it was powered by gas by that hardly matters. It was huge and white and it stood against the wall in the main kitchen. Strangely enough, although Matty was our devoted cook and a clever one at that, it was Ma herself who discovered a unique recipe for making truly delicious ice cream. Almost every evening we waited for her to appear with her latest offering even craving more when the tin was empty. Often she would have Peter in tow and, for a few rare minutes, he would smile happily as she spooned a generous helping into his cherubic mouth. To this day my happiest memories of Ma are centred on those summer evenings and her deliveries of ice cream.

Raq was also included in our nightly ritual and he would bark joyfully when offered his special portion. Although we all adored the little black spaniel, from first to last he was very much Dorothea's dog. She was a natural trainer and soon he was house trained, walking to heel and, to coin a pun, dogging her footsteps. To see Raq without Dorothea or visa versa was rare. The little dog appeared to love us all but he knew she was his mistress and seldom took his golden eyes from hers. Peter, showing considerable interest in the pup, would do his best to pick him up and take him indoors. We chastised him as we thought he would closet him in the playroom in much the same way as he closeted himself.

For once Pa showed a glimmer of interest in his youngest son and suggested to Ma that a dog be provided as a companion for him. Ma shook her head firmly and said he was too young and that he would tease it. I thought the word tease a substitute for a more evil action which he might inflict on some poor animal as the episode of the thrown train still rankled whenever I saw him.

Our merry days in the sunshine were interrupted by two things. Firstly a thunder storm of unusual severity occurred during the third week of July. One of our oak trees was struck and a neighbouring barn, burnt to the ground. Dominic, Teddy and I stood in the great hall watching the fork lightening as if we were being treated to a firework display. I think one of us, and it wasn't me that I do recall, passed a remark concerning the puppy and asked as to whether the others thought he might be frightened by the thunder. Teddy said if Raq appeared scared Dorothea would cuddle and reassure him until he calmed down. It was me who giggled and asked what would happen if it were Dorothea who was frightened and not the dog as she was no where to be seen.

And that was the second thing that happened on the night of the storm.

No one could find Dorothea.

At first it was of little consequence. As I've said, ours was a vast house. If I remember correctly it contained over thirty rooms and possessed three staircases. Even then, when properties tended to be big enough to house large families, it ranked as a show piece; a manor house of exceptional proportions. If such a property existed today no doubt it would either be owned by The National Trust or housing some flamboyant celebrity from the world of show business.

Teddy breezed off between thunder claps to search for Dorothea but returned alone and merely laughed when Dominic suggested that she was, in all probability, shivering under a stair well. As the evening wore on the storm gathered momentum and Pa appeared in the hall to order us away from the window. Dominic argued, saying we were perfectly safe but he was quite insistent and we eventually complied. Joining Ma, in the morning room, we all sat around and complained that the weather had ruined our usual party under the cedar tree on the newly mown lawn.

By nine o'clock the worst of the storm began to abate and a glimmer of daylight showed through the french window which led to the kitchen garden. One by one we deserted Ma and stepped through the door into the fresh air and down towards the delicious scent that was emitting from the rose garden.

There we encountered a soaking wet and shivering Raq. He lay, almost covered by the thorny stems of a group of tea roses, making no move to greet us. Teddy rushed to rescue him and we all gathered around his wet and shaking body.

'Better get him in and give him a rub with a towel,' said Dominic.

'I'll see to him,' I offered.

'But what's he doing out here?' Teddy questioned.

Of course our actual words are lost to my memory but they must have been along those lines. There was no sense of panic during those first few moments, that I do recall although one of us did comment that it was unlike Raq to be far from Dorothea especially as such a violent storm had been raging.

Teddy, clutching the drowned rat that was Raq, led the rest of us towards the kitchen door where Matty met us in the scullery and presented us with a large green towel in which to wrap him and dry his fur.

'Where's his mummy?' she asked. Matty always referred to Dorothea as Raq's mummy.

'Deserted him,' Dominic replied.

'That's not like Miss Dorothea,' Matty frowned.

Whether it was the frown or her general air of concern that made us view the matter in a more serious light, I can not say but our attitude changed from one of vague amusement at the plight of the puppy to one of concern about Dorothea.

Teddy, abandoning his share of the drying, announced that he had better go and see if she was all right. Dominic and I then left Raq with Matty and, we too, spoke of the necessity of finding her as there was a strangeness about the situation which portended worry.

That was in the region of half past nine or maybe even later. Our search for Dorothea started laconically. Both Dominic and I assumed that Teddy would quickly locate her so no desperate measures involving either of us were required. Pa poked his head out of, what was then his bedroom on the ground floor, and asked if the rain had ceased. Dominic assured him it had, adding that no word had come from any of the farm hands which need give rise to concern. Assured that the animals and the buildings were unaffected, I suppose he prepared for bed. Ma was no where to be seen so, looking back, I expect she had retired even earlier.

On the second floor landing we met Teddy who was

breathless from darting from one room to another. Not all the rooms were furnished especially since both boys had been away from home. My own room was on that floor and I rushed to it feeling foolish as I opened closets and searched my bathroom. If Dorothea had chosen to stray into my room it was hardly likely that she would remain there once the thunder had ceased. The room next door to mine was a spare one and, apart from an old desk and some faded portraits, completely bare. Beyond that was a triangular room which stored the newly washed clothes and household linen which awaited the services of a girl called Amy whom Ma employed to do our ironing. Three other rooms housed spare but unmade beds and one large and south facing room had been given over entirely to storage so it was crammed with dusty books, unwanted ornaments and crates containing I knew not what.

Dorothea certainly wasn't to be found anywhere within the precincts of my search.

By this time both the boys had deserted the second floor so I climbed the servant's staircase to the third floor. Matty's quarters were locked although Teddy was trying to force the door.

'Don't do that,' I ordered.

'She may have got locked in,' he said, aimlessly.

'What in Matty's room?'

'Well she's got to be somewhere.'

On that point we all agreed but as, room after room was searched and no sign of Dorothea discovered, the somewhere became more and more elusive.

We returned to the ground floor and went down to the kitchens. Dominic suggested we explore the cellars but I don't think any of us believed she would hide in the underground warren that served as more storage space mainly for wine and winter fuel.

By half past ten there was an atmosphere of panic.

Armed with torches we began a search of the grounds.

Teddy even enlisted the help of one of the farm hands, a young lad by the name of Herbert Forrester who, because he slept in a makeshift bedroom over the tractor shed, was near at hand. Herbert whistled up four other young men and they jumped into their dungarees and came down to the cow yard to see what was wrong.

'We can't find Dorothea,' Teddy explained.

'Is she lost?' asked a lad called Ned Bingley.

And that was the first time any of us had had to admit that, as far as we were concerned, Dorothea Stephens was indeed lost.

My last memory of that terrible evening was of a large group of young people screaming the name of Dorothea and hurling themselves in different directions as they ran across the farm land to seek her out. I recall Isabel was amongst the searchers and, at one point, even her Aunt Doris donned a straw hat and poked her nose out of a first story window to survey the scene.

I wasn't allowed to stay with that search party. Dominic was insistent that I return to the house and go to bed. I protested, saying I wanted to help but both he and Teddy pointed out that as it was dark, damp and cold, I would only present a further liability. Reluctantly, I obeyed. Truth to tell, I was frantically tired and shivering with cold. Even in July when a storm has broken a long heat wave the night can turn icy; this one certainly had and I was glad to return to the warmth of the house. Once undressed and tucked into my bed, I remembered nothing more until I was woken by Matty somewhere in the region of eight o'clock the next morning.

I don't think Matty had ever set foot in my room before and, waking suddenly, I couldn't think why she should be standing by my bed. She was holding a cup of tea and I remember noticing that her hands shook.

'You better get dressed, Miss,' she said, 'your father wishes to speak to you.'

'Whatever does he want?' I asked petulantly.

'That's for him to tell you.'

Matty placed the tea on the night table beside my bed and hastily retreated. As I sat up to drink it, unpleasant memories of the previous evening surfaced, causing my heart to thump. In all my sixteen years my father had never requested an interview at such an hour. Truth to tell I couldn't recall him ever asking to see me for any reason at any time. My behaviour had never given rise for complaint and, in any case, he wasn't that sort of father. Not over interested in his children, neither their opinions nor their welfare would have prompted him to request a meeting.

Dressing quickly I went down to the hall where a group of people were standing in a circle, earnestly talking in an animated manner. Dominic and Ma were engaged in a serious duologue, their heads close together, their expressions fraught. Teddy, Pa and several farm hands appeared to be talking all at once and I thought the noise would make it quite impossible for anyone to hear what anyone else was saying. As I approached the group, Dominic came and took my hand.

'I want you to tell us, Vinnie,' he began, 'when you last saw Dorothea?'

'Just before the storm last night,' I said. 'It must have been shortly before six o'clock when I asked her if she'd like to come with me to the orchard because Ma wanted some fresh apples for the house.'

'Did she agree?'

'No.' I frowned because I hadn't taken much notice of her refusal and had only asked her to accompany me out of politeness.

'What did she say?'

'As far as I can remember, she said she was going to wash her hair.'

'Did she seem upset or not her usual self?'

'Good heavens no,' I answered sharply. 'I wouldn't have left her had I thought her unwell or distressed.'

Pa was audibly cursing which, in itself, was unusual. Everyone swears now. Street language is appalling and people use foul words for which, not so very long ago, they would have been severely castigated. To hear my puritanical parent even using the word 'damn' was mildly disturbing. Everything about the atmosphere that morning was disturbing. Frightening, I think is a more accurate word.

'Lavinia,' he addressed me. 'This girl, Dorothea Stephens, how well would you say you know her?'

He spoke her name as if she were a stranger. Considering his query concerned the young lady who was about to become his daughter in law; a girl for whom he was overseeing the conversion of the west wing of his own home, she might have been an alien from another planet.

'Almost as well as Teddy,' I replied.

'Is she given to moods, sudden flights of fancy, that sort of thing?'

'Not that I know of.'

'Changes her mind to suit herself?'

'No.'

'Reliable, would you say?'

'I would.'

'Not said she's got cold feet about marrying your brother?'

'Certainly not.' I thought he must have a poor opinion of Dorothea to be asking such demeaning questions. 'What's this all about, Pa?'

'Bloody woman's gone missing, that's what this is all about, Miss.'

He turned his back on me and I rushed to the corner of the hall where Dominic and Teddy had their heads together, engaged in rapt conversation. Teddy in particular looked wretched. His usually bright eyes were dulled with exhaustion, his complexion pale and his shoulders slumped. Dominic, handsome but sombre, put his arm around my shoulder.

'As you've gathered, Vinnie' he said, ' we couldn't find Dorothea last night and we're all very worried.'

'What are you doing about it?'

'Well, we shall have to involve the police which is a pity because there may be a quite rational explanation for her disappearance but we daren't let anymore time elapse.'

'Have you contacted her parents?'

'They're not on the phone,' Teddy said.

'Then ring the village post office and ask them to get Mr. Stephens to ring us. She might have gone home although I can't think why.'

'She wouldn't have gone anywhere without telling me first,' he answered.

'She might have had an urgent message that we know nothing about.'

'Don't be silly.' Teddy looked ready to strangle me.

'We've even discussed that.' Dominic kept his arm reassuringly around my shoulders. 'It's most unlikely because, even if a messenger had arrived without our knowledge, she would have told us before she rushed off anywhere.'

'And how the hell would she have travelled, by space ship?'

Teddy was sarcastic and who could have blamed him. He adored Dorothea and her welfare was paramount to him. We were all fond of her and her mysterious disappearance was a crippling worry to the whole family. Ma, I distinctly remember, was sitting weeping on a hard backed bench which stood beside our telephone table. In the early fifties phones were still a rarity. People didn't feel the need for constant communication as they do now and most houses were without such an instrument. As you will have gathered, my parent's affluence provided our household with every modern convenience so, naturally, we were amongst the elite who had one installed with several extensions dotted about the house.

Dominic or Pa, I forget which one, acted upon on my suggestion and rang the post office in Dorothea's Derbyshire village. A request was made that someone fetch her father to the nearest phone where we could speak to him personally. Pa said phoning was much better than sending a telegram as they always caused alarm.

It was quite sometime later before our call received any response and then it was Mrs. Stephens who rang, not her husband. When Pa asked her if Dorothea had returned home she replied that neither she nor any other member of the family had seen her for over five weeks and if any harm had befallen her there would be trouble. Foolishly, in my opinion, Pa did his best to placate her by saying that Dorothea was perfectly all right but had taken a walk and been gone somewhat longer than usual. The poor woman must have thought us a group of lunatics for disturbing her with such trite news.

Except for the inevitable milking, all farm work ground to a halt. Our two shepherds were summoned down from the high fields and every able bodied man was ordered to search for Dorothea Stephens. Dominic and Teddy together with Isabel headed that search and even I was allowed to join in as were several of the labourer's daughters. Children as young as nine or ten accompanied old people in their seventies and eighties as everyone set about the task of finding our missing house guest.

Ma and Pa remained indoors as a visit from the police was imminent. Pa had been reluctant to ring the station but, after the somewhat guarded threat from Dorothea's mother, I think he decided to err on the side of caution.

Everyone asked themselves and their neighbours where on earth she could have gone? I know I tried to reason it out as I took a stout stick and began beating fronds of fern along the overgrown paths. Now and again I espied Teddy or Dominic rushing to and fro as they called her name and searched the hedgerows. We all feared she had strolled across the fields, got caught in the storm and met with some disaster or succumbed to a fall. Rabbit holes were plentiful and it was all too easy to catch your foot and go sprawling. An ankle could be easily broken or even a leg or, then again, she could have been struck by lightening.

The thoughts that ran through my head must have been echoed by everyone engaged in that fruitless search for we all wore expressions of anxiety and each searcher experienced a feeling of foreboding.

At some point towards lunch time I returned to the house. Having been denied breakfast and overcome with nervous anxiety, I remember feeling faint. Almost collapsing in the hall, I was relieved when Ma appeared and escorted me into the morning room. An egg on toast was quickly brought as nothing in the way of a proper meal was to be cooked that day. Even Matty and the kitchen staff were looking for Dorothea, I might add, in the most unlikely places.

But where else could any of us look?

Once the immediate fields and out-buildings had been explored, together with every room in the house, only the far reaching extremities of our land remained. The boys, I know, spent hours searching miles of surrounding countryside and found nothing.

Although the day was a warm one I noticed that Teddy, returning to the hall in the company of Isabel, was shivering. Dominic was dry mouthed and only pretending to be optimistic. Both boys made reassuring remarks presumably to steady Ma and myself but their words sounded hollow and no one responded with a positive reply.

The police were holding council with Pa in the sitting room. Naturally my brothers were summoned to join them leaving Ma, Isabel and myself to ponder the mystery.

'She's out there somewhere, hurt I'm sure,' Ma said.

'But why would she have gone out, Ma?' I asked. 'She said she was going to wash her hair, that was why she didn't come to the orchard with me.'

'She may have changed her mind and followed you. The storm was threatening so she would have looked for cover and probably met with an accident.'

'Perhaps she took Raq for a walk and lost him. Sometimes he runs away and it takes her ages to find him.' That from Isabel.

But non of us placed our faith in such vague explanations. For one thing the thunder storm did not start until gone seven and my trip to the orchard took place before six so she would hardly have run for cover over an hour before the rain fell. If she had sheltered in a barn or stable, we would have found her hours ago. And why was Raq, the puppy, abandoned and straying in the rose garden?

Ma and I waited for what seemed like hours. I know we had little to say to each other for what new theories could be discussed or observations uttered? Isabel, normally a diffident young woman, forwarded even more preposterous ideas as to the fate of Dorothea but, when her imagination failed her she slipped quietly from the room and I have to say Ma and I heaved a sigh of relief for silence was preferable to inane speculation. Pa and my brothers reappeared at about three o'clock and a police sergeant requested a word with me but, of course, I had nothing useful to add to the information he had all ready received.

Not long afterwards a full scale police search was put into operation. Sometimes, when the case has been discussed in recent years, people enquire if such things as helicopters were in action as early as nineteen fifty one? Yes they were. Even now, whenever I hear the familiar drone of a helicopter my heart misses a beat as the sound, immediately, takes me back to those days over sixty years ago when they flew overhead searching for Dorothea.

Their search was fruitless.

She was never found.

Chapter Five

K it Barry completed his internship at London's Chelsea and Westminster Hospital alongside my brother, Dominic. So friendly did the two boys become that they shared a flat in the Fulham Road and Dominic was almost always accompanied by Kit when he came home for short holidays.

I married Kit Barry in nineteen fifty seven when he was just twenty five and I, not quite nineteen. On completion of his lengthy training he set up as a general practitioner here in Borough Heath and I became a busy doctor's wife.

But that was a long time ago and I have been a widow for the past four years. Strangely enough, despite the ill health suffered by Pa, he survived Ma by almost twenty years. After the disappearance of Dorothea Stephens, and the marathon task of desperately trying to find her, Ma suffered some kind of decline.

Dominic, already qualified and Kit equally so, tried every conceivable remedy in an effort to cure her many ills, both physical and mental. Obviously she had her own physician, Howard Richards, who was in constant attendance and a great friend to us all.

Her last illness was of such a complicated and contrary nature that Dr. Richards had difficulty in diagnosing the actual cause of death. In the end the certificate simply read, Natural Causes resulting from Neurasthenia. It has always been my belief that poor Ma just gave up. After the trauma and all the unpleasantness that followed, she simply took to her bed and succumbed to chronic depression.

My life wasn't exactly packed with humour at that time either. Teddy, distraught and changed beyond recognition, farmed the land, ate, slept and kept to the north wing of the great house, offering little company to any of us. Dominic, busy in London, did all he could but his time was limited so I had to wait weeks and sometimes months between his precious visits. Peter grew more beautiful every day but remained difficult and uncommunicative therefore his pretty appearance failed to stir my flagging spirits. At almost nine years of age he still attended Saunders School. It often occurred to me that Pa completely overlooked the existence of his youngest son until he was reminded by the then head master that he must dispatch him to a senior school. Peter was grudgingly sent to Stafford to follow in the footsteps of Teddy and Dominic but no Humber Super Snipe ferried him backwards and forwards as it had his elder brothers. Peter must have considered himself banished for none of us saw fit to send him letters or visit his barracks of a boarding school.

At fifteen, my own education ended after which my life centred around the farm and the care of Ma and Pa. Doris Haywood had suffered some sort of mild heart attack or suspected stroke and, whereas she was still able to care for Pa for a few hours each day, it was her niece Isabel who became his chief nurse.

Quite tall for my age, I was already five feet eight inches tall a height which was considered exceptional in those early days of the fifties but, when I glance from my front window now, I notice the majority of young girls are five ten or even taller and take size nine in shoes. My eyes were sea green and my long hair, light brown. I was considered attractive but, when I occasionally gaze at old photographs taken in our youth, I see only the handsome features of Dominic and the wondrous face of Peter. If, long ago, Lavinia MacVee, who became Vinnie Barry was once a beauty then time has indeed been cruel. The old crone who stares back at me from my mirror makes me shudder.

Such irony awaits us all!

Ma was only fifty four when she died. She was still beautiful with lightly curled auburn hair and bright blue eyes. I grieved for her parting but what could I expect? She had been ill for so long and the prospect of future happiness was not exactly looming large on her horizon.

After her death, I did what I could to comfort Pa. As I have said, we had never been close but at sixty four, afflicted with heart trouble, I feared for his welfare and did all in my power to make his life comfortable. Occasionally I would manage to stir Teddy from his usual apathy and persuade him to sit with Pa during the long winter evenings so he might interest him with accounts of the farm and its progress. Teddy, usually tired and depressed himself, would say it was my job to care for the old man but, now and again, he would plod towards the sitting room and do his best to lift his spirits.

In the early fifties anyone over the age of sixty was deemed very old indeed so I considered it something of a miracle that Pa still survived. Teddy, himself is now over eighty and I am seventy seven but neither of us would be considered candidates for the Guinness Book of Records, for in this new millennium, our respective ages would be considered quite normal.

Dominic continued to visit whenever he could manage to find the time and more often than not he brought Kit Barry with him. Kit's given name was Christian but he had been nicknamed Kit from babyhood so we all followed suit.

Thinking of him now I am tempted to write pages in praise

Confession

of his looks, virtues and skills for, after all, I fell in love with him and became his wife. Kit was tall, taller than either of my elder brothers and he towered above Pa so he was at least six foot three. His hair was that lovely crinkly kind that never seems troubled by wind or a stray hand teasing it's blonde curls. Eyes the colour of a summer sky and a mouth more fitting for a film star than a general practitioner tempted everyone to love Kit for his kindness and patience were incomparable. It was easy to understand why Dominic delighted in his company and why every member of our staff longed to beg his time and walk the fields by his side. Even Peter favoured him with mild interest and although it didn't last it was considered quite an achievement whilst it did.

For myself, I had difficulty taking my eyes from his fine-looking face or my attention from his wonderful speaking voice. Dominic and Teddy spoke perfectly, as of course did I, but Kit had a slightly throaty tone, husky I think it would be termed, and it added a fascinating resonance to his words. People are said to possess clever hands. I suppose that's a figure of speech for hands in themselves have no claim to skill but to watch Kit manipulate his long fingers and observe the elegant display of those hands never failed to thrill me. Later, when we became lovers, the gentleness of his caress was almost unbearable. Patients often remarked on his healing touch and for me it was the most sensual of all his actions. In old age, I miss those hands almost as much as I miss his physical presence and loving care.

At sixteen years of age, I worshiped him. Matty, growing old herself, would tease me, telling me I had a crush on Dr. Barry which made me blush because, although her words were true, my feelings amounted to much more than a mere a crush. I literally adored him and continued to do so for over half a century.

In nineteen fifty two, well bred young ladies knew very little about sex and, certainly didn't engage in acts of an

- 47 -

intimate nature. Kissing and hand holding were considered the ultimate in any courtship and perhaps that is why couples married earlier. Frustration and desire hurled them towards the nearest altar so that their passions could be gratified in a seemly manner.

How very stuffy that sounds but age dictates decorum!

Had I been privy to the finer facts of life as, today even a child of eight or ten appears to be, then I would have understood Dominic's devotion to Kit for he too loved him and not as a brother or a best friend. But a story worth the telling must turn its pages slowly so the reader is not distracted by extraneous issues.

After Ma died Doris Haywood's own health began to decline to the point where she could no longer nurse Pa but Isabel more than made up for her aunt's absence. She and I took care of him and made sure that his life was as comfortable and trouble free as was humanly possible. Teddy, working from dawn to dusk on the farm and Dominic preparing for an illustrious career in medicine prompted me to fill my own time with the maximum of effort. Thankfully, Peter posed few problems. Still a solitary boy, I must admit to having little connection with him. Once, when he was sent home from school with a bad dose of flu, I was forced to tend him and found it strange to be in close proximity with the one brother who, by rights, should have been my constant companion. I might add that, once he was partially recovered, he dismissed me as though I represented no more than a necessary evil to be banished at his will.

Pa rallied yet again when Teddy announced that modernization of the farm had become not only necessary but essential. To this end, new buildings were planned including a state of the art milking parlour. Many of the old barns and shelters were falling into disrepair so Teddy contracted a firm of builders who set about renewing most of the out-buildings. Outdated machines were replaced and new equipment ordered. A combine harvester and two brand new tractors were agreed upon and Pa, excited by the prospect, took to rising early and walking, unaided, to the yard to oversee the progress. I was pleased that he was well enough to enjoy watching the improvements take shape but my real delight lay in knowing that Teddy was filled with an enthusiasm, which since the disappearance of Dorothea, had been lacking.

Poor Teddy had suffered so much more than the rest of us which was inevitable. Of course it was, he had adored Dorothea. Their wedding day was booked, their apartment completed so his future promised perfection. No one could have dreamt that such a dramatic event would deny him a lifetime of happiness. For that matter, no one could have imagined such a mystery occurring to anyone, anywhere. Occassionally, I read or hear on the news, that a child has gone missing and I grieve for the parents but seldom can I recall a story to equal that of Dorothea Stephens.

Considering the advances in forensic science and computer technology, modern methods must be a hundred times more sophisticated than they were all those years ago but, nevertheless, the police search was thorough and impressive. Seventy two days the police hunted for her. Tracker dogs, helicopters, officers with metal detectors and even mounted police combed miles of surrounding countryside. Not only that but it seemed that the entire able bodied population of Borough Heath had joined in the search. Old and young, some just school children, beat back the undergrowth and dived into the dirty depths of canals searching for clues. Our farm was at a standstill for days on end whilst every hand forsook his tasks to look for the pretty girl who had become everyone's friend.

Dominic and Teddy hardly allowed themselves time to eat, so desperate was their need to find her. Dominic in particular wore himself out through lack of sleep and neglected meal times. In the end he developed a dreadful cough and cold and was forced to remain in bed for two days. Teddy was little better but refused to give in and I feared they both would die if she were not found soon. Matty told me that I must be brave, adding that she was sure the mystery would be cleared up but that I was to expect the worst. People who disappeared for such a length of time, she told me, generally turn up dead.

We all though that.

That Dorothea was dead, I mean.

No one actually voiced it but we all believed we were hunting for a body rather than a living person. One of the worst aspects of the whole affair was the arrival of Dorothea's parents. Mr. and Mrs. Stephens were, as you would expect, devastated, but unfortunately, due to their wretchedness, they blamed us for neglecting to take proper care of their daughter. Naturally Teddy told them how much we had all loved and cared for her but their accusations became quite violent as the days went by. It has always been my belief that their attitude exacerbated Ma's decline almost as much as did the actual loss of Dorothea.

After the first three days, I ceased to join the search parties. The weather, which had been perfect, suddenly turned sour and rain accompanied by gale force winds swept across the sodden fields. Teddy particularly begged me to remain indoors. I think the Stephen's beastly accusations made him over cautious when it came to the treatment of young women.

Mostly I stayed close to Ma, trying to comfort her for she reacted badly. No soothing words on my part prompted her towards bravery or helped to calm her shattered nerves. Quite the reverse, within a week she began to suffer bouts of hysteria, loss of appetite and despite barbiturates, prescribed by Howard Richards, she spent her nights either in floods of tears or pacing the floor of her room.

As one would say today.

That was all we needed!

Day followed day and, in a way, time stood still. Police procedure was consistent and gruelling. Many officers began to look haggard as disappointment and bad weather took their toll.

I might add, that several of them shed tears as their efforts failed and their fears heightened.

National newspapers carried the story as did the suddenly ubiquitous television. Radio news bulletins were plentiful and, as far as I can recall, the docks were searched as were airports and railway stations.

I suppose I was living in a personal nightmare but, strange to say, I found the ability to switch off. Tending Ma and keeping a watchful eye on Peter, I made every effort to ignore the mayhem which surrounded me. Peter, himself, was completely oblivious to the turmoil which, considering his tender years, was almost unbelievable When my own children were the age he was then, I was pestered by thousands of questions every minute of every day. Why this and why that from morning until bedtime but Peter, just a school boy, on no occasion showed either interest or curiosity. Even the helicopters and the mounted policemen, which would have captured the imagination of any other child, failed to attract his attention.

Since everything suffered disruption, we mostly took to eating our meals in the kitchen. That he disliked intensely, saying he wouldn't eat his dinner if he couldn't sit at the dining room table. His crass remark made me wild and I chastised him for not sparing a thought for his distraught brothers or for Dorothea who was lost and probably in peril for her life. Peter merely shrugged his little shoulders and threw his apple pie on the floor.

Eventually, Mr. and Mrs. Stephens returned to the Derbyshire Dales. Seeing them pack their car and drive away, I cried. Beastly as they had been, Dorothea was their only daughter and the youngest of their four children so their hearts must have been broken. Mr. Stephens had his own farm to see to and what more could he do on ours? No fresh reports arrived and there was no where else to search. Even the police began to cut down on manpower and the helpful town's folk returned to the normality of their daily lives. Dominic needed to continue his medical career and Teddy had a much neglected farm to set to rights. Pa took to staying in the sitting room and Ma predicted that the events of the summer would kill her before Christmas.

Poor darling was proved correct.

Chapter Six

P an calls everyone by their Christian names.

Old as I am, and having lived my life in a bygone age when servants knew their place and respected their betters, I cringe when she calls members of my family by their given names.

'Michael's here,' she's just announced.

Michael MacVee is Teddy's son and my only nephew. Part of my devotion to Michael I put down to the fact that he reminds me of a young Teddy which, apart from his many other attributes, I find quite captivating. Of course he's is in his mid forties now and already showing signs of middle age. His once black hair is turning grey and his shoulders tend to stoop.

Don't grow old. It's demoralising!

'How are you Aunt?' he enquires.

I kiss him and accept his gift of a box of chocolates. I tell him I am well which is true even though, only last year, I suffered a heart attack. At seventy seven, I doubt it will kill me, I intend to survive into my eighties just as Pa did.

'How's work?' I ask because Michael is an actor and his profession is precarious.

'Not bad,' he smiles his Teddy smile. 'I might have landed a part in Coronation Street. I've done the audition bit and met with the casting crew so keep your fingers crossed.'

'I will.'

Personally I can't stand soap operas but I understand that most people adore them. The actors who tediously portray the characters, week in and week out, are notably well paid and achieve a sort of fame so my fingers will be crossed.

'How's Tim?'

'Well,' he pauses, 'actually, Aunt Vin it's Tim I want to talk about.'

I've already hinted that my brother Dominic was drawn to his own sex but that was long ago when such liaisons were never spoken of. Two men of my acquaintemnce hanged themselves rather than, as we say today, come out. Homosexuality has always struck me as an alien condition. An illness, a perversion; but I am old and the world has changed. This boy, my beloved Michael is gay and Tim Watson his partner. Teddy and I used to brood over the matter into the small hours when first we learnt of it but neither of us gained a jot of understanding. Teddy used to blame himself believing that he must have failed as a father. I, being more enlightened, argued that it is quite impossible to turn anyone into something they're not.

Michael was born that way and it must be accepted.

'How is Tim?' I repeat because Tim Watson is amongst the most likeable of men and I am inordinately fond of him.

'Oh, he's fine.' Michael smiles and then looks at me in earnest. 'He's been offered a part in a TV documentery.'

Tim is an actor. That's how the two of them met. Both had parts in a West End revival of the 'Importance of Being Ernest' at The Haymarket. Teddy and I went to see the show and fell over ourselves with pride. We attended the first night party and it was there we learnt that Michael and Tim were lovers. Neither of us knew what to say but, after all the bizarre events which our family had endured, we decided to accept their news as though it were the most normal of events.

'Good for Tim.'

'You may not be so pleased when I tell you the programme is a rehash of the Dorothea Stephens saga.'

'I'm not pleased at all.'

'Trouble is, Aunt Vin, Tim can't afford to turn it down. Work's been patchy since the Ibson thing closed so he's grabbed it with both hands.'

'I see.'

'A fellow called Lawrence has written it. I believe he came to see you.'

'You believe correctly.'

'You're offended.' He senses my change of mood.

'It's a bloody pity these things can't wait until your dear father and Peter, not to mention myself, are dead and done for. It's cruel to rake it all up in what's left of our lifetimes. I suppose there's money in it?'

'If you really feel that strongly, Aunt, Tim will turn it down. He's already said he will but I told him I would speak to you first.'

'Then go and tell him the old bitch wishes him well. If he doesn't play it someone else will, so what the hell?'

'Dad said much the same thing.'

'Poor Teddy.'

'Dad should have been an actor himself, he's still the best mimic I know.'

'He always was.' It was on the tip of my tongue to add that Dorothea was equally gifted but mentioning her name only brings heartbreak so I reverse. 'Who is he playing?' I ask.

'Peter,' says Michael

Chapter Seven

When most girls of my age were out on the town, enjoying their youth, I was tied to the house looking after Pa and Peter. Lonliness became my friend or, perhaps I should say, my enemy. All day, Teddy was out in the fields or away tending stock auctions. Pa, spending his days closeted in the sitting room reading either the Times or studying accounts, for he took an active interest in the day to day running of the farm, meant that I was bereft of company.

Peter, even more taciturn and aloof, was little trouble as he kept to his room during the school holidays and days would go by when I hardly caught a glimpse of him. Matty kept me up to date with the local gossip and taught me to be a first rate cook into the bargain but I lacked humour in my life.

What you would term, good old fashioned fun.

Of course, on the rare occasions when Dominic and Kit came home, then I was in seventh heaven but they were dedicated to climbing the ladders of their chosen careers so their visits were infrequent. Dominic was specialising in cardiology and Kit aimed to be a G.P., but an exceptional one.

Especially during the winter and in bad weather, I had very

little to do. Once my household chores were completed, Peter either away at school or locked in his second story lair, I had only Matty for company. Three girls helped in the house but non of them appealed to me nor, I should think, I to them. They were rough, caring only for superficial pleasures and their respective boyfriends whereas I liked to think I was something of an intellectual so when Matty announced that she was to leave, the blow was severe and I was deeply depressed.

Apparently her only sister, whom I heard about over the years, was suddenly widowed and the sisters had long agreed that, should such a circumstance occur, they would share a house and keep each other company in their old age.

Her news upset me to the point where I couldn't sleep and, now and again, I found myself weeping. Without Matty, I would have no one. Writing to Dominic, I tried to make light of it but I know he read between the lines because he and Kit came home the following weekend to discuss the matter with me.

'We shall have to replace her,' Dominic told me.

'Why?' I asked, disconsolately.

'To keep house and see to the meals.'

'That's my job,' I retorted. 'It's the only job I'm likely to have. I can't leave the house whilst Pa is alive nor while Peter is still so young.'

'I won't have you being a drudge either,' Dominic said.

'What Vinnie needs,' Kit chipped in, 'is a younger woman, younger than Matty who can do all the hard work but be something of a companion as well.'

'A companion to whom?' I asked him

'To you,' he explained. 'Matty's a jolly fine cook and I know the two of you are good friends but the woman's in her late fifties. What you need is a friend, someone nearer your own age. A pal as well as a servant.'

'Where do I find this friend in need?'

Both boys looked blank, it was Teddy, making one of his

rare appearances round the kitchen tea table, who simply said, 'Why don't we give the job to Isabel. She's getting paid for damn all at the moment and we're housing and feeding her into the bargain?'

'But she's Pa's nurse now that Doris is too ill to look after him,' I said.

'Pa no more needs a nurse than I do,' he replied. 'She's been here all these years and with most of us away or out all day, there's not a lot for her to do.'

For some reason, which I was unable to explain, Isabel Haywood had never appealed to me. Not to say that I didn't like her or that there was any friction between us, just a negative feeling that amounted to indifference. Dominic and Kit continued to sing her praises and, it was true, that with Pa's upturn in health, she was in need of further work to justify her keep.

'It's not as if we do any entertaining,' Teddy reminded me of our solitary existence. 'No dinner parties to cater for, no young children in the house and many rooms shut up now Dom's away. I think she'll fit the bill to a tee.'

'And she's only a few years older than you, Vinnie,' Kit smiled. 'You're bound to have things in common. She'll cheer you up.'

The idea of Isabel cheering me or anyone else come to that seemed absurd but the boys seemed insistent that she should take over from Matty and I must admit I didn't care enough to argue. Isabel was offered the position of cook housekeeper and we all thought she would jump at the opportunity. It must have occurred to her that, in view of Pa's partial recovery, her job had become tenuous particularly as she and her aunt had no home awaiting their return. Teddy paid them both a living wage but since they were housed and fed I thought it unlikely that either one of them would have savings to fall back on. In the fifties and early sixties all these benefits and allowances, which are so liberally handed out today, were meagre and difficult to obtain. Our offer should have been seen as a gift from the Gods.

But Isabel turned it down.

Kit even stayed on a further two days in an attempt to entice her to fill the vacancy and Dominic suggested an increase in wages but she told them both that, if she was no longer required to nurse Pa, both she and her aunt would leave within the month.

Teddy, exasperated, asked me to step in and talk to her. He said there must be a valid reason why such an excellent opportunity should be shunned and, apart from anything else, he was personally intrigued as to why she wouldn't accept.

'P'raps she doesn't like us,' I suggested.

'Course she likes us. Look how loyal she's been and how helpful when we were searching for Dorothea.'

'Everyone was helpful then.'

We both sighed and the sadness in Teddy's face persuaded me to humour him by attempting to win her over. I agreed to talk to Isabel before the day was out and do my best to discover why she refused such a beneficial and simple job as housekeeper to a solitary farmer, his elderly father and one undemanding sister. With Dominic away from home and Peter seldom in evidence, the work would be minimal and her home secure.

Trotting off to find her I tried to drum up enough enthusiasm to convince her that our offer would be better than winning the football pools but, quite frankly, I couldn't have cared less whether she changed her mind or not. Matty had been with us since I was born and I was still devastated that she was to leave, neither did I see any reason why she needed replacing. What was there to do now that we were hardly a family any longer?

When I finally found Isabel she was sitting on a five barred gate looking moody and anything but the friend in need suggested by the boys. Had I been asked I would have said it was she who suffered acute depression and I the person sent to cheer her.

'Teddy says the job's still yours if you change your mind.' I could have put that trite remark in a dozen more appealing ways but, again, my heart wasn't in it so I just made the comment and prepared to turn round and go back to the house.

'Vinnie,' she called me back. 'Sorry, I should have called you, Miss MacVee.'

'Not necessary,' I shouted.

'It's a very kind offer and I wish I could take it.'

'You must have your reasons.' I said, not particularly interested as to what they may be.

'I do,' she answered, looking so dejected that I stopped in my tracks, returned to the gate and smiled at her.

'Is there anything we can do to make the job more appealing?'

'The job's perfect,' she said. 'It would mean Aunt Doris and I could stay here and I'd feel I was justifying our keep. It's just that something's happened that makes it impossible for me to accept.'

'Nothing horrid I hope.'

'For me it is.'

'Well I won't pry but, as I've said, Teddy really wants you to change your mind and stay on as our housekeeper.'

'Thank him for me, Vinnie.'

'I wish I could tell him why you've turned us down but I'll say you were grateful.'

Again I turned to go but something in her expression compelled me to linger. Isabel was not a beautiful young woman but she was what people termed, attractive. In her youth she had a fine mane of chestnut hair which shone with the brilliance of strong light hitting steel. Her eyes were the colour of English honey and her complexion flawless. Men probably found her irresistible but I had never viewed her as anyone other than Pa's nurse. A hired hand due only the consideration given to any other member of our staff.

'Perhaps your brother would be kind enough to make up my wages,' she said.

'You mean you want to leave right away?'

'I have to.'

Her comments started to intrigue and far from not caring I remember being overtaken by curiosity. Poor Isabel looked so utterly wretched and also, somewhat selfishly, I was suddenly struck by the fear that Pa, at some point in the near future, would suffer an undoubted relapse causing us the trouble of finding a new nurse at a moments notice.

'Of course you don't have to,' I almost shouted. 'You've been with us a long time and you should stay put. Stop being such an idiot and take the damn job. If you've got problems then tell me or Teddy what they are and we'll help you solve them only please don't run away.'

After that, I did turn sharply and head for home. Trying to persuade Isabel to see sense turned into a bore and, as is the way with all very young people, the problems of others were of no interest to me.

But, within a few short weeks we were all to hear and, to a certain extent, worry about the problem that beset Isabel. Teddy came into Pa's sitting room quite late one evening and sat in one of the many armchairs which had become obsolete now that so few of us remained at home.

'That bloody girl's gone and got herself in the family way,' he announced.

I don't recall Pa showing any interest but I certainly did. Gossip served as entertainment in those bleak days before soap operas provided the fictitious variety that soon became more intriguing than reality.

'What girl? Who?' I asked, alive with curiosity.

'Isabel Haywood.'

'My nurse?' Pa then showed a morsel of inquisitiveness himself.

'That's why she wants to cut and run,' Teddy went on. 'Fool of a girl. How's she going to cope if she leaves here?'

'Her aunt's not up to caring for her,' Pa said, 'neither could she afford to.'

'Did she tell you, Teddy?'

'Pretty well. I found her crying in the top field and, good Samaritan that I am, I went to see if there was anything I could do.'

'And that's when she told you?'

'More or less. At first she just said she was leaving for personal reasons but one look at her belly and it was me that told her come to think of it.'

'That's because you're around cows in calf all day long.' Such a remark from Pa was unusual considering his lack of humour so was the fact that, pleased with his joke, he added, 'And pigs and sheep not to mention cats with kittens and the woman who sees to the washing and has a new baby every spring.'

'Quite,' agreed a tight lipped Teddy. 'Trouble is I'm not sure what to do about it.'

'It's not our worry.' That was the extent of my compassion.

'Of course it's not our bloody worry but I'd hate to think of her ending up in the poor house and that's what it'll amount to.'

Remember I speak of a time when illegitimacy was categorised as a sin. Unmarried mothers were mentioned in the same breath as criminals. The disgrace was enormous but you will have to take my word for that because attitudes have changed to such an extent in these days of state benefits and liberal hand-outs that it is almost unbelievable.

Pa was not only in the best of humour that particular evening but was also apparently brimming over with a hefty dose of humanity and kindness. It was he who suggested that we persuade Isabel and her aunt to stay on despite the horrendous offence she had committed.

'We've plenty of room and food enough,' he said in his best Scots accent. 'Let the lassie have her bairn in comfort.'

So it was that Isabel took over from Matty in the role of housekeeper and, in due course, her baby was born; a girl whom she named Rose. We took to that baby just as if she had been our kin. Whenever Dominic or Kit came home for a weekend or a whole blissful week, they spent time with Rose. As she grew and turned from baby into toddler we all vied for turns to play with her. I never warmed to Isabel but the baby I loved with all my heart. Losing Matty had proved a heartbreak but, with Rose in the picture, gradually our house took on a lighter aspect and the agonies of the past became slightly blurred.

Strangely enough we never troubled Isabel with questions regarding the father of her child. Maybe the boys made enquiries but either she wouldn't say or perhaps even they didn't bother. It was my opinion that one of the farm hands was responsible but, quite honestly, what did it matter? Pa was happy with her prowess in the kitchen, praising her steak and kidney pies and looking forward to his meals as he had in the old days but the greatest joy of Isabel's reign was the transformation it brought to Teddy. Daily he began to revert to his old self and appear happier than I would have believed possible. For myself, overpowered by my love for Kit, I considered all our troubles were over and we could look forward to a trouble free future which would compensate for the dreadful events of the past.

Almost fifteen months after the strange disappearance of Dorothea I was even more convinced that Isabel held the key to Teddy's future happiness and when he happened to mention that they were planning to go and see a film together, I immediately viewed them as sweethearts.

'You don't mind us going?' he asked.

'Good heavens, no,' I said and meant it.

'But it means you will have to look after Rose.'

'That will be a pleasure.'

But Teddy and Isabel's outing to the cinema turned out to be anything but a pleasure after all. Having plenty of time in which to amuse Rose before putting her to bed, I had anticipated a happy evening enhanced by the knowledge that Teddy was enjoying himself for the first time in ages.

Rose slept in a small room adjoining Isabels' which was half way along the second floor landing. My own room was also on that floor although at the very end and several corridors removed. Two doors from Rose's bedroom was Peter's playroom and over the years I had avoided entering that particular sanctum.

We were playing hide and seek; a wonderful game to play if you have a house as big as ours was at that time. Little alcoves and recessed doorways made excellent hiding places and the wide landings invited a chase. Some of the doors were open so Rose was able to totter into various rooms and hide behind crates of apples or piles of books abandoned to disused spaces. Thoroughly absorbed in our game, we were suddenly disturbed by a piercing scream which came from the direction of Peter's playroom. Grabbing Rose, for I couldn't leave her to wander and fall, I rushed to see what had happened.

Peter, I quickly judged, had been playing a game which involved stacking furniture against a wall, to represent a mountain. No doubt he had imagined himself an intrepid mountaineer climbing a treacherous peek to thwart some gruesome enemy. Unfortunately his expertise in the simulated mountain department left much to be desired as his flimsy edifice had, apparently, crumbled beneath him as he neared the top. Two chairs, which he had placed precariously on top of an old sofa and pushed haphazardly against the wall, had toppled under his weight causing him to fall heavily and twist or sprain his right ankle.

Lying on the floor and crying copiously, I found him clutching his foot which was obviously causing him great pain.

Placing Rose on a small seat near his desk, I advanced to see what I could do to help. Peter, at that time was tall and slightly over weight so assisting him to his feet proved difficult. Failing to move him, I suggested ringing for a maid but he clung to me, as if we were all in all to one another, insisting he would allow no one but myself near him. After a monumental struggle, I managed to get him to the foot of his bed where I unceremoniously dumped his heavy body, allowing it slump onto the counterpane. After that I hurried to the nearest bathroom and fetched a wet flannel which I bound round the swollen ankle in the hope that I might quieten his screams and give him some relief. To see him in such distress was pitiful and, although I had never felt affection for my youngest brother, at that moment I did.

Grabbing Rose, who was wide eyed and deeply upset herself, I went down to the hall and rang Howard Richards, our family doctor. Howard, thankfully was at home and spent at least five minutes on the other end of the phone assuring me that he would be round as soon as possible. I remember feeling frantic. There must have been at least two maids somewhere in the house but neither of them was visible and Pa, I knew, would not wish to be disturbed by such an irksome event. Teddy and Isabel, having so recently departed, obviously would not return for some two or three hours so I had my first taste of responsibility in so much as two children, one of whom was badly hurt and the other not yet two years old, were dependent solely on me.

Dr. Richards, of course, made light of my little drama. Diagnosing a strained tendon, he said Peter was to stay in bed, with a cold compress covering the offending ankle, and a couple of aspirin tablets to relieve the pain. After he'd gone I managed to put Rose in her cot but I couldn't wait to rush back to Peter who was still fretting and screaming for my attention.

Almost unbelievable but, in all our years together, I had scarcely heard him speak my name. We may have been complete strangers, so distant was our relationship. The evening of the damaged ankle an onlooker would have supposed us to be the most devoted brother and sister on the planet for every time I moved as much as three feet from his bed, he screamed my name and wound his arms around my neck when I approached. Twice little Rose, disturbed by all the commotion, tottered sleepily into his room and on both occassions he screamed and even swore until I removed her.

Peter wanted only me.

The sister he had, only a few years before, assaulted by throwing a toy train at her head, was suddenly his champion. That night was spent beside his bed because, although I was exhausted and only half awake, he wouldn't hear of my leaving. Teddy and Isabel came home at around half past ten o'clock whereupon Isabel offered to take over his care but Peter would have non of her and, impolitely, told her so. Teddy remonstrated with him calling him a big baby for making such a fuss over a sprained ankle but, ignoring the criticism, he clung steadfastly to me. Teddy shrugged and advised me to go to bed just as he was about to do, so whether or not the trip to the cinema had been a success, I did not, that night discover, but later events proved that it had.

The next day Pa was told of Peter's accident but he showed little in the way of sympathy only commenting that, at Peter's age, he was already helping his father on Lord Donnington's Estate and certainly not playing with toys in a nursery. I was ordered to leave my brother in his room and only attend to his meals and the administration of the aspirin tablets an order which pleased me for I was fractious from lack of sleep and completely perplexed by the situation. How Peter, an obnoxious child in my eyes, could have changed so rapidly just because of a swollen ankle, I found bewildering. Understanding the emotions and actions of others has never been my strong point and, at that time, I was hardly more than a child myself.

Once Peter found himself deprived of the company of his suddenly beloved sister for some perverse reason he turned his attention to Rose. Although the little girl was hardly more than a baby he, to use a modern expression, bonded with her. Whenever I passed his bedroom door or Isabel searched for her, she was to be found sitting on his bed. More often than not he was to be heard reading stories out loud or else showing her how to put simple jigsaw puzzles together. As his foot became less painful, he hobbled to and from his playroom to fetch an endless supply of toys to keep her amused. Isabel, being busy and myself totally uninterested in his progress, meant that we both delighted in this unlikely attachment if only in so much as it kept both children out of our own hair.

Naturally Peter's ankle injury healed quite quickly but his attachment to Rose, if anything, grew stronger. Teddy was the only one who took the slightest notice of this newly formed friendship.

'He'll have to start helping me out there,' he pointed to the cow yard. 'He's strong enough now to pull his weight. Why a boy of his age wants to play nursemaid to a baby is beyond me.'

'Oh, as long as they're both happy, who cares,' Isabel said.

'But it's not natural,' Teddy insisted.

Pa said much the same thing but when I asked him to have a fatherly word with his youngest offspring, he hurried back to his room and closed the door.

Dominic and Kit came home soon after the sprained ankle debacle and Kit and I started walking out together; generally thinking of ourselves as a couple. As it was harvest time, Dominic helped Teddy in the fields and Isabel was everyone's friend.

The matter of Peter and Rose faded into insignificance as happiness, conspicuously absent since the mysterious disappearence of Dorothea, returned in abundance. Picnics under the cedar tree delighted our evenings and splendid meals, presented by Isabel, were enjoyed throughout the day.

Once again Teddy made us roll about with laughter at his jokes and mimicry.

The good life had returned.

Until history repeated itself and Rose went missing.

Chapter Eight

On Christmas Eve, nineteen fifty nine, Kit Barry and I
were married at St. Mary's church, Borough Heath.

Often, over the years, people have asked why we chose such
an auspicious day to pledge our vows. In a way it was
unintentional as we had intended to opt for a Spring wedding
but, in the early part of December, Pa's precarious health quite
suddenly took a turn for the worse and we feared that further
delay might deprive him from attending the ceremony.
Another factor was Teddy's marriage to Isabel Haywood which
had taken place in late August. That event had, as it were, taken
our slot, but we were more than prepared to wait until, during a
tea party at the farm, the vicar of St. Mary's almost jokingly
announced that he was free on Christmas Eve. I remember we
all laughed thinking it slightly absurd until Kit jumped up and
shook his hand declaring that it would be the most wonderful
way to celebrate both the festive season and the start of our
married life.

So that is the only explanation I can offer.

I was nineteen years of age and Kit was twenty five. His
internship completed he was then a fully qualified doctor and

we were both set on his becoming a general practicioner here in Borough Heath. Pa, by way of a wedding present, helped us to buy this house and he also gave us five thousand pounds to enable Kit to set up his practise.

There were several doctors in the vicinity; established men who were favoured by the town's folk but, within seven or eight months, Kit had built up an astonishing reputation and patients began to flock to him. Young, handsome and married to me, whose family they had known all their lives, he had many advantages the finest of which being his medical expertise. Kit from first to last was an exceptional doctor. Whether it was his proficiency or his charm and kindness that so endeared him to everyone, it is difficult to say but, so popular did he become that, for the first few years of our marriage, I must admit that I seldom saw him. Those were the days when doctors were on call seven days a week, twenty four hours a day. Locums and night services were not popular in the early years of the National Health Service so if your chosen profession was healing the sick then you did so every minute of the day and night.

Kit was strong but I've seen him struggle to get to bedsides whilst suffering severe colds and once when hardy recovered from a severe dose of chicken pox which he caught from one of our children. Weather never deterred him from turning out in the middle of the night neither did festive occassions or auspicious personal events. When our first son was born, and Kit delivered him in this very house, he held surgery as normal within half an hour of the birth although he had attended me throughout the entire night.

In all we had three children. Two boys and our daughter, Anna. It's unbelievable to think that John, our eldest, is almost sixty and Philip, fifty three. Anna, my baby, is a mere forty eight but I still tend to treat them as I did when they were in the nursery and find myself severely reprimanded when I attempt to dish out orders or proffer criticism.

My marriage was wonderful. Words to describe our happiness are plentiful but unnecessary, for what more can I add? Happy and blessed as I was my joy in knowing poor Teddy was equally so, provided extra special delight. After the tragedy of his loss of Dorothea I viewed it as God given justice that he should find contentment for, although I thought him fond of Isabel and happy to take her out and about, I had doubted his fondness extended to marriage.

But I was wrong: we all were.

To this day I clearly remember the evening when an excited Teddy rushed into the sitting room where Dominic and I were taking it in turns to read out loud to Pa. Wreathed in smiles he told us that he had proposed to Isabel and she had accepted. Even Pa, who seldom showed a trace of emotion, was overjoyed. Dominic grasped his hand in joyous approval and I had to be physically removed from his neck as I couldn't stop hugging and kissing him. An engagement party was celebrated in late May and an August wedding planned to take place just prior to the harvest. Somewhere in my heart I knew Isabel would never quite take the place of Dorothea but she was what many people would term as 'nice' and she was certainly a hard worker. Perhaps the use of such a trite word as nice proves me baron when it comes to the art of description but more exotic adjectives just wouldn't fit someone as bland as she. At the time of the marriage, Isabel was pleasant and capable but interesting or possessed of great substance, she was not.

Of course she and Teddy remained at the farm. It was a ready made home but, I noticed that Teddy strictly avoided the wing which Pa had converted when Dorothea was thought to be his bride. With Pa inhabiting only the sitting room and the down stair's cloakroom, which was then replete with a bath, Teddy and Isabel had the run of the house. Not quite the whole house as Peter had, more or less, commandeered the third floor where he had secured several of the doors with heavy padlocks. Teddy told us that he kept his old playroom intact and believed it still housed all his childhood toys. Since no one was ever allowed near enough to check, I have no idea if that was the case or not.

Although very busy assisting Kit during those first years of our marriage, for I acted as his telephonist and some time nurse, I spent as much time as possible with Pa who was then approaching his seventy fourth birthday. Isabel was attentive and usually on hand should he need her but she also took an active part in the running of the farm and looking after anyone who favoured the old home with a visit. Dominic was very much in the habit of staying there during holiday periods and, later on of course, she and Teddy had a child of their own; Michael.

At first we thought that Isabel shied away from bearing further children. Kit and I often discussed their childless state and he was of the opinion that Isabel, having lost a beloved baby, couldn't face the thought of giving life to another. Teddy never mentioned the matter of children so we kept our opinions to ourselves. Three or it might have been four years into their marriage I remember Teddy coming to the house and asking if he might speak to Kit in private. Since we were the closest of siblings, I must admit to being intrigued. Teddy always confided in me so why, on that occasion, he seemed consumed with embarrassment, I couldn't imagine.

Since doctors take an oath of secrecy where patient's problems are concerned, I was somewhat surprised when Kit told me the reason for Teddy's visit. Actually I ought to add that Kit did not act as physician to any member of my family as we thought it inadvisable, although I may say that I personally never consulted anyone but my beloved husband and seldom even him for my health was robust. At my present age I am a fixture in my doctor's waiting room but that's a very different picture. It's called 'old age' and the less said about that evil the better.

Had Teddy been his patient I doubt Kit would have

grinned and told me that my brother and Isabel were desperate for a child but as non was forthcoming the poor chap had been forced to ask for advice. He said that Teddy had blushed and stammered in his effort to gain help but, of course, to Kit it was the most natural of medical problems.

'What did you advise?' I asked.

'To go home and make love to the woman,' Kit laughed. 'What else?'

'Any fool could have told him that.' I remember feeling vexed. 'Presumably that's the problem, she can't conceive?'

'Presumably giving her a kiss once a fortnight doesn't help.' Kit was still laughing.

'But Teddy wouldn't come to you if he wasn't doing what he should be doing.'

'Well, he did.'

On that ambiguous note, Kit had to leave as he was summoned by some poor soul in ditresss but our chat concerning Teddy and Isabel left me feeling uneasy. Surely, I reasoned, my brother could not think babies were found under gooseberry bushes as Ma had hinted all those years ago? In any case, Isabel had already born a child so I assumed her to be adept when it came to the business of procreation. With that in mind I made it my business to visit her as soon as possible and find out for myself what problems, if any, they were experiencing.

'Oh, Teddy's never really loved me,' Isabel said, when I tamely enquired, if they were happy. 'I knew that when I married him. That girl, the one who went missing, was his only love but he was fond of me and I of him so I thought we might find some sort of happiness.'

'But Teddy does love you,' I said, for I believed it to be the case.

'No, not loves,' she corrected, 'is content. Quite content but not in love.'

Slowly I guided my questions. Assuring her that I had never

thought to see Teddy so at peace and cheerful, I asked if they had ever thought of having children?

'After Rose,' she looked at the floor in the way I seen her look a thousand times, 'I didn't think I'd ever want another baby but now I want one more than anything else in the world.'

'But Teddy does not?'

'Oh, yes he does.'

'But not quite yet?' I prompted.

'To get babies you have to have sex,' she said simply, 'and Teddy thinks once is enough. I conceived Rose after only one miserable encounter with a man who had no use for me but with Teddy I did not and he seems to think I should have done.'

'But that's ridiculous,' I almost shouted.

'Tell him, not me,' said Isabel as she turned and left me but not before I noticed a tear in her eye.

By the time that conversation took place, Kit and I already had our first child. Dominic, I was pretty sure would never marry for, as Kit and I both knew, his romanatic interets lay in other directions. My only feeling concerning that discovery was one of extreme sadness for life is quite trying enough without the added burden of being different. The world, I knew would misunderstood and ignorant people would revile him for his difference. Kit, although Dominic's orientation was alien to him, was non judgemental and it made not a jot of difference to his feelings of friendship for my eldest brother. Once I asked, out of nothing more than lurid curiosity, if Dom had ever made a pass at him when they shared the flat together in London. Kit was emphatic that no such thing had occurred and was of the opinion that Dominic would remain celibate if only because of that archaic law which remained in place until nineteen sixty seven. In those dark days, practising homosexuals were imprisoned, now they are to be found in every profession and are accepted by so called normal people everywhere.

Times they are a changing!

If Teddy and Isabel were to remain childless and Dominic without a female love interest, then our children, for we intended to have six at least, would be bereft of cousins and Kit and I would be denied the pleasure of becoming an indulgent aunt and uncle. Perhaps that's what motivated me to speak to Teddy for the subject was not a topic which I would normally have broached over tea and cherry cake.

Teddy, at first, was furious thinking Kit had primed me. In the first instance he was correct but it was because Kit had mentioned it that I had approached Isabel. This I told him and, bit by bit, he calmed down and listened to his little sister giving him a lecture on conception and the wonders of intimacy with the person one loved best in all the world .

One year later, I congratulated myself on offering such expert advice for Isabel gave birth to a healthy boy whom they called Michael Christian. Kit was flattered that his given name was bestowed upon his nephew and I, delighted merely to have such a relation, celebrated for over a month.

Teddy, for obvious reasons, was the most diligent of fathers. After the tragedy of Rose, poor Michael was hardly let out of his sight. As the years went by, Kit and I intervened yet again and, gradually, he began to grant his son a freer reign. Kit was of the opinion that Michael became gay or queer, as he always termed it, because he was protected almost to the point of suffocation. My own feelings, then as now, tend towards the belief that such anomalies run in families but my days of dwelling on the family of my youth are almost over.

I have learned to banish my memories as one discards bad dreams or unpleasant experiences. Working on this narrative opens the memory chest that lurks in the darkest recesses of my mind and evil, like trapped insects, flies everywhere.

I shall ring my bell and summon Pan so that she can bring tea and toast.

My fire and her administrations will aid sleep otherwise my

night will be plagued with ghosts and who can honestly swear that they are unafraid by ghosts?

Chapter Nine

S ometimes, now that so may years have passed, I can bring myself to think of that awful day over half a century ago when poor little Rose was drowned in the cow yard. It was a Thursday, that I recall distinctly and it was during the late afternoon. Isabel had been out collecting blackcurrants as we were preparing to make jam in the outer kitchen and both of us presumed Peter was tending Rose.

As I waited for Isabel to gather the fruit, one of the hands came in which in itself was unusual as the farm labourers seldom entered the house. Seth, his name was. Seth Pondesbury, a name I shall never forget. Seth startled me because I was engaged in deep conversation with one of the maids but I remember we stopped chatting and stared at him wondering what business had brought him into our domain.

'Thought I better tell yer,' he said. 'Yon youngster is all over the place and all on her own at that.'

'Which youngster?' I asked.

'Yorn baby.' He pointed at Isabel who had finally returned carrying a basket of currants.

'Rose?' I asked, as if she were the mother of half a dozen

babies.

'I'd a brought 'er in me sen but me 'ands is filthy.'

Seth Pondesbury displayed a pair of the dirtiest hands imaginable making Isabel and I laugh.

'Never mind.' I smiled at the gangling boy who stood hiding his hands behind his equally grimy back. 'I'll come at once and bring her in.'

'Will you?' Isabel busied herself pouring the fruit into the brass jam bucket and, apart from expressing mild astonishment that her tiny daughter was roaming freely in the yard, she appeared quite unconcerned.

Seth and I headed for the back door and parted on the outer steps. Running in the direction of the cow yard I quickened my stride as heavy rain began to fall. In my mind, I was already castigating Peter who should have been minding the baby as, indeed, we presumed he was.

First of all I ran to the enclosure where the cows were waiting for milking time. It was five o'clock and like all animals they knew the time to a second. The thought of Rose mingling with the great beasts made my heart jump so I was relieved to find she was not entangled with our Friesian herd. Next I went into the milking parlour where Teddy was cleaning the machines.

'Have you seen Rose?' I asked.

'Rose?' He repeated the name as though it were alien to him. Of course the thought of Rose toddling about amongst the machinery and the animals would have conjured up a bewildering picture to anyone.

'If Peter's brought her out in this downpour I'll be after him.' Teddy enjoyed reprimanding our little brother it was the nearest any of us came to confrontation which, secretly, we all longed for.

'I think she's wandered off on her own,' I said.

'Well make haste and take her in; she's no right to be wandering about on her own it's dangerous out here for a little one.'

With that remark, I deserted the parlour and raced across the cobbled path towards the new stable block. Heavy rain sprayed my back and my velvet house shoes caused me to slip and slide in the mud. At one point I wondered if I should return to the kitchen where, I was sure, Rose was now to be found. Surely, I reasoned, somebody would have had the sense to pick her up, dirty hands or not, and take her indoors. Two girls who worked with Teddy in the milking parlour passed by on their way to herd the cows and I asked them if they had seen her. Neither girl had so I continued my search heading down towards the tractor shed. Most of these buildings were either newly renovated or in the process of reconstruction.

The tractor shed was only half finished. The idea was to extend the existing one and build onto the back of it so that a weather proof extension could house the new combine harvester which Teddy had recently ordered. Foundations had been laid and a partial wall erected but it was open to the skies and no builders were in evidence due to the torrential rain.

I jumped over planks and half finished joists avoiding the water logged cavities which had formed in the foundations. About to abandon my task and return indoors I caught sight of something red. Remembering that Rose had been dressed in a red romper suit that morning my heart stood still.

Stood still and then beat so rapidly that I feared it would burst.

Considering my discoverey it might have been merciful had it done so there and then so that the agony of the following six months could have been averted. Rose must have wandered from Peter's side and toddled into the half built shed. Being in the precarious state which it was she would, all too easily, have lost her balance and fallen between the joists into the deep foundations some ten feet below. Weeks of stormy weather had caused water to collect, resulting in deep pools which, in turn, had submerged the lower regions of the structure. On that depressing afternoon, I may well have been staring into the depths of a neglected swimming pool.

Rose was already dead when Teddy and the farm hands jumped down to rescue her. I remember screaming for help for even I, a fully grown and strong young woman, could not reach her body without falling in myself. Somehow, even as I shrieked, I knew it was too late. Just gazing at her tiny frame from my lofty position on the high timbers told me the little girl had drowned.

It is pointless to attempt a written account of the reaction which my discovery caused for the ensuing distress can surely be imagined. Distress is by far too mild a word when much more dramatic ones come to mind but a child of barely two years old dead from such an avoidable cause defies description.

Our grief resembled physical pain and was boundless.

Isabel, we considered, an example to us all. If she endured heartache, and surely she must have done, she kept her dignity. No hysterics from Isabel only an outward show of calmness and a stoicism which cast shame on the rest of us. I, for one, took to my bed for over a week and cried most of the time. Dominic came home from The Royal Heart Hospital in Surrey, where he was studying open heart surgery, and Kit was granted five days compassionate leave from The Chelsea and Westminster in London. Teddy tried to keep going, for a farmer must but, in six weeks, he lost over a stone in weight and fear gripped my heart when his agonised eyes met mine. Over night he seemed to have aged and worn thin. Poor Teddy must have thought himself a victim of the Gods now that tragedy had struck again.

Someone had to tell both Peter and Pa. We feared for Pa's health and, for once, we pitied Peter for he had made a special friend of the little girl. Pa was badly affected but Dominic, simply shook his head and told him that many families had to suffer even worse misfortunes adding that, in the course of his work as a heart specialist, he witnessed such disasters weekly, sometimes daily.

Peter was another matter.

As I have said, my youngest brother and myself were not close. No one was close to Peter. But he had thought the world of Rose and, as far, as he could relate to anyone, he had related to her. It may have been an unlikely friendship but, like many such attachments, it was sincere and her loss hit him hard. Isabel did her best to comfort him and Matty made a brief return to help us in our time of crisis.

As the weeks turned into months and memories of the funeral together with the worst of the nightmares began to fade, gradually we all regained some sense of normality. Pa was never to be quite the same again in fact only a few weeks later he showed the first warning signs of dementia. Peter seldom appeared, even for his meals, so trays were taken to his old palyroon and left outside the door as he declined to answer any knock. Since the circumstances causing his withdrawal were understandable and, to some extent expected, we indulged our own misery and left him to his.

Dominic, although shocked and grieved himself, became our rock. He spent hours trying to comfort poor old Pa. With me and, up to a point with Isabel, he spent even more hours trying everything in his power to divert our minds from the horror and the guilt. Of course we all suffered guilt. Our constant cry was, 'Why did we leave her in the care of a mere boy when we weren't even certain she WAS with him?'

Such simple queries haunt the suddenly bereaved for there was no doubt about it, Isabel and I had been negligent. Kit once admonished me quite rigorously for harbouring such guilt, reminding me that since she was Isabel's child and not mine I should not be expected to shoulder the burden of blame which I carry almost to this day.

Finally, because of the enormity of what had happened, Isabel and Teddy appeared much much closer and, almost because or in spite of the tragedy, they decided to get married.

A decision which cheered everyone as it helped to erase a very small corner of the sadness. As a family we started to believe we could look forward to a trouble free future.

Lightening had struck twice but we were all still young and surely we had suffered enough for several lifetimes?

Chapter Ten

P eter, showing little or no interest in Teddy and Isabel's
wedding, was not present at the ceremony. Considering
the sadness which had preceeded it, no one anticipated a jolly
affair but, never the less, it turned into a quite a joyous occasion
even though we had to force our smiles.

Isabel looked truly lovely in her peach bridal gown and
Teddy, never the handsome hero, managed to compliment her
in a silky grey morning suit. Dominic, I shall never forget for
he looked like a latter day pop star. Strange that I should
compare my handsome brother with a modern celebrity but,
when I view these never ending photographs in glossy
magazines of today's pin ups, I think Dominic would make
them all look very ordinary.

Tall, sleek, with the blackest of black hair and eyes the
colour of lapis lazuli, he was sensational. I doubt a female,
married or single, present at that wedding could take her eyes
from his perfect form. I was proud of him that day. Not only
did he look beautiful but I knew him to be brilliant, charming
and the most caring of men. Kit was smart in a grey three piece
suit and, although I say it, I was pleased with my own

appearance which comprised of a two piece blue organdie dress complemented by a large black hat trimmed with dyed blue ostrich feathers.

Pa was pushed in, what used to be called a bath chair, by our ever faithful Matty and he showed every sign of enjoying himself. The harvest was about to be gathered so the fields were resplendent in a golden haze waving in a warm breeze. If the Gods had been unkind in the recent past they apologised that day and offered us a present of perfection.

I know that at some point during the evening, Peter favoured us with one of his rare visits to the dining room. Teddy and Isabel had booked a brief honeymoon in north Wales but planned to remain at the farm during the whole of their wedding day so we were altogether as a family during the evening. Matty and I, assisted by the farm hand's wives, had prepared a magnificent feast. At least six of us had helped to spit roast a whole pig and half a side of beef and every manner of cake and pudding you could name had been lovingly baked. That was in the days before people dreamt of eating what was then referred to as 'foreign food' so our menu might be considered boring now that more exotic dishes are favoured.

Peter's appearance gave me little pleasure as he was dressed in his old corduroy trousers, a crumpled shirt, odd socks and badly worn slippers. I remember glancing at him and then at my immaculate elder brother and making an odious compasison.

Kit and I, as yet unmarried, stayed at the farm whilst Teddy and Isabel had their few days by the sea. Often I laugh when I think back to those last days of the fifties; how narrow and restrained everyone was! So full of happiniess that the wedding had been such a success, not to mention the amount of unaccustomed champagne we had consumed, Kit suggested we do the unthinkable and sleep together. I was shocked, thinking him quite a rascal to have even contemplated such a daring deed.

My daughter Anna brings her men friends to stay here with me every so often and they always share a bed. I used to fuss, now I accept it. It is the behaviour of the times and I am an old woman who clings to the past as, one day, so will she.

It is the way with every generation!

When our newly weds came home the harvest had began in earnest so Isabel and I seldom saw Teddy. He was out working in the fields at just gone five each morning and it was often gone ten when he returned. Isabel made piles of sandwiches or packed home made pies to sustain him through his arduous days but I was comforted when she told me that before he set foot in the fields he also ate a hearty breakfast at a time which, to me, seemed the middle of the night. At some point Isabel began to help out in the milking parlour as the house no longer required the labours of two women. Pa kept to the old sitting room which was now his only domain; even my efforts at keeping it clean distressed him as he preferred to be left to his own thoughts whatever they might have been. Twice a week I insisted on using the vacuum cleaner to rid the carpet of crumbs but the noise and my unwelcome presence made him quite vindictive so keeping the room respectable was a job in itself. But my head was full of my own wedding and my heart full of love for Kit, so his declining health and failing grasp of reality had little or no affect on my romantic state of mind.

In late October my present house, in the centre of Borough Heath, came on the market and I phoned Kit, who was still in London, telling him that I wanted to buy it. Kit couldn't get leave for over ten days but he knew the house as it stands prominently in the middle of the High Street. I was terrified it would be snapped up instantly as our local wine merchant had his eye on it and said so after church one Sunday morning. Discussing anything with Pa was out of the question as his concentration was limited and so was his understanding. Before the tragedy of Rose he had promised to buy a house for Kit and I and also make us a present of a lump sum but now, due to his advancing senility, I was worried that he wouldn't remember such promises.

Teddy suggested that I ask the bank manager or our solicitor to come to my aid but, in the end, neither person was needed as Pa, miraculously, recalled his promise and offered no resistance to my plea for cash.

The house was bought and I spent the hours of my days measuring, cleaning, engaging and instructing decoraters and imagining my life as a doctor's wife. At every opportunity, Kit visited and purred over the wonders of our newly acquired property. I bought furniture from the big stores in Birmingham and began to fill each and every room. Sometimes I would spend a night under, what was then my own roof, and luxuriate in my luck at having procured the house of my dreams.

Once the gas and electricity were switched on I prepared meals in my ultra modern kitchen, (which is now outdated and scorned by my children) and spent my time exclusively at the house. I missed the farm and the family atmosphere but the thrill and novelty at being mistress of my own establishment outweighed any lingering sentiment.

Kit arrived whenever he had a free day or weekend and plans for our Christmas Eve wedding were in full cry. His visits being infrequent meant that most of the time I was alone so Teddy suggested I bought a dog for company and also for protection. Crime, although not so violent nor so prolific as it is today, was still a major issue and both my brothers worried for my safety.

After Dorothea's disappearance her parents took her dog, Raq, home to Derbyshire with them, which was a blessing as reminders of the heartbreak were plentiful enough without the presence of a grieving animal to further distress poor Teddy.

My dog, when Teddy convinced me it was a sound idea to have one, was a Jack Russell terrier whom I called Robbie. He was the first in a long line of 'Robbies' for I have a thirteen year old such terrier even now. It is one of my constant prayers that this Robbie dies before I do but he is a great age and, according to my new and forward thinking doctor, I am merely a woman of mature years.

Seventy seven is the new sixty according to him.

(He should try living with my back and knees if he believes that!)

With the Jack Russell lovingly installed and new furniture arriving almost every day, I was, more or less, living permanently in my new home. A decorating firm from nearby Walsall were busy wallpapering and painting. Carpenters, electricians and other workmen laboured tirelessly to convert rooms to my liking and two gardeners laid a large lawn and crafted flower beds where only an old air raid shelter and some derelict sheds had stood. Teddy visited and so did Isabel. Both complimented me on my ingenious home making abilities but the person I least expected to visit turned up at the back door one bitterly cold morning in early November.

It was Peter.

'Came to see your new place,' he said as he brushed past me and strode into the hall.

'I'll make you some tea,' I said, because, opening my door to such an unexpected guest had been something of a shock, and I hardly knew how best to greet him.

'Bit bare, isn't it?' This said as he stared at the blank walls in my living room.

'There's some more furniture on the way.'

'There's enough of that,' he sneered. 'It's the walls that are big and bare.'

'We shall hang some pictures.'

'What sort of pictures?'

'Well, I haven't really thought.'

'Why don't you have an original mural?'

'Of what?'

'Of anything you like.'

'And who would paint such an exotic thing?' I asked.

'Me,' said Peter.

Peter, who had never had anything to offer in the way of conversation, suddenly began to expound on the joys of an original painting which would stretch across several square yards of plain wall. He spoke of landscapes, seascapes, reproductions of famous places of animals and architecture.

'But not people,' he said at last, 'I'm no good at drawing people.'

'I didn't know you drew at all,' I replied tartly, for I knew hardly anything of this tall blond brother who remained a stranger even then.

'Done a lot back at our place.'

'What on the walls at home?'

'Yes.'

'May I see them?'

'No.'

'Then how do I know if you're any good?'

'If you don't like what I do you can get your lackeys to wallpaper over it.'

'You can paint a landscape on that far wall.' I pointed to a long expanse of bare wall that stretched between the french windows and the main door. 'Something local. Deer in the forest perhaps.'

'I'll start tomorrow,' said Peter who turned and walked away without as much as a goodbye or a backward glance.

To be honest I have to admit that his visit and proposal upset my entire day. A mural held no appeal and his presence left me feeling uncomfortable. The thought of him spending hours, days even, painting God knew what, on my majestic wall quite frankly horrified me.

But he had shown an interest and made an offer which could be interpreted as helpful and I knew I must not turn him away. By this time, although no one was over interested in problem children or prone to place labels on odd behaviour, I think we all knew Peter suffered some mysterious disorder.

Totally lacking any social graces, he found even simple conversation difficult and his school work was appalling. I think we termed him, 'backward' but since he caused us little trouble, we dismissed his perculiarities and made light of his secluded life.

The very next morning my back door bell rang at just gone six o'clock. The early hour together with the fact that I was still in bed, unnerved me. Wondering who on earth would wake a lady at such an hour, I hastened to the back landing to peer through a window. My intention was to shout down to whoever was troubling me and tell them to go away at once. Robbie, just a puppy, joined in the intended abuse, yapping loudly.

My wakener was non other than Peter.

Peter the painter!

'Can't you come back later?' I shouted sleepily. 'I don't get up until seven thirty.'

'No.'

So it was that, reluctantly, I threw my robe around my shoulders and trudged down the stairs to let him in. Laden with a large black case plus a huge canvas carrier, which weighed heavily on his right shoulder, my young brother marched past me, heading for the living room.

'Now I'm up,' I said, grumpily, 'I better make some tea and breakfast. What can I get you, eggs or cereal ?'

'Nothing,' said Peter.

Eating a poached egg in the kitchen and feeding some puppy meal to Robbie, I thought long and hard about Peter. When my simple fare was finished I decided to go and see what he was up to and make some suggestions of my own. First I marched Robbie into, a still dark garden, as house training was a priority but nearing the french windows, I couldn't resist peering in. For quite five minutes I watched whilst he donned an artist's smock, stirred paint, a lot of paint, pots of which stood in rows on a long trestle table. No such table had I seen before so I concluded that it must be of the collapsible variety which could be carried in one of those heavy bags. After a while, the movement of either the dog or myself drew his attention causing him to look straight at me and I, of course, smiled and waved in his direction.

By way of response, Peter turned his back and looked away showing no sign of having noticed me. Suddenly I was cross, another inadequate word. I wasn't just cross, I was furious. My living room was to be the centrepiece of the house. It was to be the room where we would entertain. A room I would furnish exquisitely, make comfortable and elegant. If pictures were required to enhance those graceful walls, then I would search galleries and auction rooms until I found paintings which suited my taste. A huge mural daubed by a half wit did not rate amongst my immediate requirements!

Literally racing indoors, I hurried to the room and turned the doorknob determined to halt his progress even before it began. If he wanted to paint anything I decided to let him loose in one of the spare bedrooms where his handiwork could be hidden but any defacing of that wall I was not going to tolerate

The door was locked.

Shouting his name, I demanded entry but my pleas and knocks were ignored. Trying another method, I returned to the garden and rattled the french window. Peter didn't so much as favour me with a glance. To annoy me further, he turned both his back and the table so he could block my view entirely.

Out of temper and upset, I rang the farm to ask Teddy if he could find the time to come down and throw him out but one of the maids said he was busy in a lower field and wouldn't be in until dusk. Isabel rang later to see what I wanted but, by that time, I had calmed down so I decided not to trouble her with my petty problem. As Peter, himself had said, if I didn't like his mural, I could simply paint or paper over it.

That day proved busier than expected. The G.P.O., who owned the telephone system in those days, had more extension sockets to install in what was going to be Kit's surgery. Robbie needed attention, the new cooker developed a curious fault and the chimney sweep arrived a week early thus I was engaged with the business of the new house until late afternoon. At six o'clock precisely, Peter emerged from the living room and walked out through the back door.

Not a word did he say nor was he carrying his heavy bags.

'Finished for today, have you?' I almost screamed.

No answer was forthcoming so, using a firm tone, I added 'By the way, I don't want that door locked. I will not have it.'

But I may as well have spoken to the breeze as he was already half way down the garden path. To add to my frustration, when I hastened to the living room to inspect his work, the door was still locked. Obviously he had secured it and pocketed the key. Kit rang later and I poured out my misery concerning Peter and the unwanted mural at length.

'Oh, let him do whatever he wants,' he advised. 'Poor chap, he probably thinks he's doing his sister an enormous favour and it might turn out to be okay.'

'Have you ever seen anything he's painted?'

'No but we do tend to ignore him. He probably wants to give you something in the way of a wedding present and this is all he can think of.'

'But he's brought half a paint shop with him and a table.'

'I'll be home the weekend after next so I'll sort him out then,' Kit assured me. 'Don't fret, if he does anything really awful we'll soon get rid of it; in the meantime try and encourage him to chat, he's such a blasted loner it would help us all if he learnt to have something to say for himself.'

There was nothing more I dared to say on the subject of Peter or murals. I could see that Kit admired him for actually doing something for once and Teddy, when told, was also thrilled that he was out of the house and busy.

Ten days elapsed in which I was woken every morning, including Sunday, at six o'clock on the dot to let Peter into the locked living room. Happy still with my lovely house, persevering with Robbie's training and visiting Pa, I decided to push all thoughts of him and his dreaded mural from my mind.

Even into the late fifties central heating was still in its infancy and most households were still reliant on fires. Living in the heart of the black country, I had three tons of coal delivered and employed a workhouse inmate called John Grant to shovel it into the cellar. In those days coal was dumped in back yards or on pavements, neither bagged nor put away, so John was a Godsend. The old workhouses still survived although they started to disappear rapidly once the welfare state took responsibility for the poor and homeless. Many people in Borough Heath employed the inmates at a shilling an hour and those men and women performed all sorts of menial tasks to earn their keep. It was John Grant who, excitedly, came to tell me that he had seen a man painting in my big room and had taken a look through the window to see what he was doing.

'It's the most wonderful thing I ever see'd,' he told me. 'Just like stepping into our forest up yonder.'

'How did you manage to see it?' I asked, for I had almost ricked my neck trying to squint through the same window and failed.

'Lad, left glass door open for 'alf a tick and I poked me 'ead round.'

So one person at least granted a vote of approval.

Kit came home the following Friday. I hadn't seen him for nearly three weeks and his homecoming was a double celebration. Naturally we were thrilled to be united once again and Kit had the added delight of viewing the new house complete with fittings and furniture so it really did look like the home of both our dreams. It was whilst we were sitting at our kitchen table on the Saturday morning, drinking Camp coffee, that Peter suddenly appeared.

'I've finished,' he said.

Kit stood up to shake his hand and effect a proper greeting

but Peter merely heaved his canvas bag higher on his shoulder and, grasping his enormous case, marched out of the kitchen door without uttering another word.

'I hope he's unlocked that damned door,' I swore mildly and took Kit's hand. 'Let's go and take a peek.'

Now I really do need words.

A whole dictionary of them to try and convey the masterpiece that was Peter's mural. As I'd requested or half heartedly suggested, the painting portrayed a woodland scene. The trees were real, I swear you could have climbed them or imagined yourself seated under their branches. The leaves, spring time green, showed veins and contours as in life. Animals were dotted about but discreetly as is their way when roaming the forest. Rabbits, fur wet from recent dew and deer, elegant but watchful, were delicately painted in both the foreground and background. Suggestions of a rainbow were visable but not intrusive or overdone.

Magnificent!

Kit and I, hand in hand, side by side, stood with gaping mouths for words eluded us. At last Kit said something along the lines of, 'Can't belive it.'

And I echoed his disbelief only a thousand times more so.

Peter wasn't just a painter, he was a genius!

Chapter Eleven

In the last few days I've started to worry about this play or documentery that Michael told me about. The one penned by Maxwell Lawrence where his friend Tim is going to portray Peter. Old age, together with the loss of my darling Kit, has increased my capacity to worry by, at least, a thousand fold.

I rang Teddy yesterday and told him of my fears; he agreed that it was most disturbing news and has promised to visit before the week's out. Now I'm worrying that Mr. Lawrence will pester me for further interviews before Teddy arrives. I must calm down or else I shall suffer a further heart attack!

Unfortunately any reminders of the past are always accompanied by nightmares and vivid recollections of people and incidents I would far prefer to forget. All morning I have been beset with images of the Bonnington family. They are as clear to me now as on that first day when Samuel Bonnington came to our front door and announced that he, his wife and two daughters wished to register with Kit as they had recently moved into the town and were in need of a doctor.

'I've heard good reports of your husband,' he told me, 'and I have an invalid daughter so I must be sure we're covered in case she needs emergency treatment.'

'I'm sorry to hear that,' I told him.

Samuel Bonnington, a large impressive man, stepped into our hallway and further, on my invitation, into the living room.

'Good God' he said, staring at Peter's mural. 'What wonderful work. Whoever did that?'

'My younger brother.' By then I had grown accustomed to such comments and had begun to feel pride when announcing that the painter was my own brother.

'Never seen anything like it.' My guest and Kit's, about to be, patient donned a pair of spectacles and spent a good three minutes studying the mural in close up.

'Unbelievable,' he announced. 'Wish he'd do one for me but chaps gifted enough to do that sort of thing don't hang around waiting for business, I expect he's in great demand?'

So many people had admired Peter's mural expressing admiration in the most elaborate of terms but, strangely enough, Samuel Bonnington was the first person to show an interest in possessing one of his own.

'If you really would like one,' I said, wondering if I was saying the right thing, 'I could ask my brother to come and see you to discuss it.'

'Not local is he?'

'Oh yes, the whole family are.'

'Thought a chap with that kind of talent would be living in London or abroad.'

Soon after that conversation had taken place, Kit came in from the surgery. Handshakes were exchanged and Samuel Bonnington registered himself and his family with us. When Kit enquired as to the nature of his daughter's indisposition he explained that she was malformed; a midget in fact with a hump back who was mainly housebound.

'Why doesn't she get out?' Kit asked, somewhat curtly I thought.

'Best not.' Bonnington replied, but gave the impression

that personal embarrasment on his part rather than his unfortunate daughters' was to blame.

'Your own health is good,' Kit asked, 'and that of your wife and other daughter?'

'Very good indeed Doctor Barry. I am seldom unwell although I mustn't tempt fate by bragging about it. My wife, Eleanor, is fine and my younger daughter Laura is as fit as a flea.'

With that Kit, as usual, made for the door for his time was always at a premium. Samuel Bonnington and I resumed our discussion regarding the mural and I promised that I would ask Peter to call on him. Bonnington had just been newly appointed as general manager of the Mid-Borough Heath Colliery and his house was well known to me. Like my old home it was a prestigious building, very large, imposing and, although owned by the National Coal Board, he must have been a man of substance to have procured such a position and such a house.

I remember wondering how I could possibly persuade Peter to make that call. He who hardly ever went out, found conversation next door to impossible and lacked any semblance of social grace, how would he react to an invitation involving a strange house complete with an unknown family?

Kit told me to accompany him.

'With his talent he could make a fortune, Vinnie,' he said over dinner that evening. 'People would be prepared to pay vast sums for what he can do. It's a gift from God; the strange thing is none of us ever knew a damn thing about it.'

'He's not exactly gregarious,' I commented.

'I'll come with you when you ask him and, if necessary, we'll take him in the car together to see Bonnington.'

We had our first car by that time. Naturally a car was vital to Kit who covered miles of local territory but, there again, it was Pa's money that provided it. In the years to come we had such a thriving practise that Kit was able to buy a new car every eighteen months and eventually I had one as well but, at that time, we were dependant on Pa's cash although we repaid his loan in the form of two pounds a month. That first car was a wine coloured Singer Vogue and it was bought, almost brand new, for the enormous sum of three hundred and fifty pounds!

The first snag we encountered, when we visited the farm to put the matter of the mural to Peter, was the fact that he was no where to be seen. Isabel came to our aid, telling us he would be in his old playroom but that he kept the door locked and was unlikely to open it. Kit's reaction was one of exasperation and he strode up the sweeping staircase, that always so impressed visitors, and banged on the playroom door only to find that Isabel was correct. Although Peter was inside, and Kit could hear his wireless playing, no amount of banging and shouting his name persuaded him to open the door.

'Blast.' Kit screamed in annoyance as he returned to the kitchen where the three of us stood in a circle looking, I'm ashamed to say, completely hopeless until Teddy appeared.

'I'll get the bugger out,' he said. Swearing had become a habit with Teddy and, I regret to say, it remains so to this day. 'I make him work you know. Lambing time I had him up on the hills helping Jock and Brian. If there's money to be made I'm not having him shirk.' We had already told both Teddy and Isabel of Samuel Bonnington's interest in the mural and they had expressed both surprise and delight. Teddy particularly so as, being such a hard worker himself, it must have irked to think of our strong younger brother hiding away in an old playroom.

It took time but eventually Teddy reappeared with Peter, head down, trailing after him.

'Your sister's been good enough to find a gentleman who might put some work your way,' he said to Peter. 'You should be very gratful.'

Peter said nothing.

'Teddy's right,' I hardly knew how to coax him. 'A man

called Samuel Bonnington has just come to live in that big old house on Durrant Hill. He works for the coal board and he's a new patient of Kits'. He loved your work Peter and I promised I'd take you along so he could discuss the possibility of your doing one for him.'

'I don't draw people.'

'I know but I don't think he wants people. I think he wants one just like ours.'

'Go and put your jacket on and wash your hands,' Isabel intervened. 'Vinnie and Kit are going to give you a lift to see the gentleman.'

It was then that I noticed that Peter's hands were covered in blue paint. So that's what he did in the old playroom now. He painted. I recall desperately wishing I could view his work but all our efforts, at that particular moment, were devoted to getting him ready to go and see Bonnington. Strangely enough, considering his controversial nature, Peter trotted off returning in less than five minutes with clean hands, carefully brushed hair and wearing a smart black jacket.

'Good boy,' I said; a childish remark which won only a scowl by way of reply.

Peter said not a word on the short journey across town but when Samuel Bonnington cheerfully welcomed us at his door, he was reasonably pleasant and quite talkative. We all trooped into a large room which was impeccably furnished with old fashioned but quality furniture. Almost every square inch of wall was adorned with magnificent oil paintings save the south facing one which Bonnington obviously intended for his mural.

After making us all comfortable and instructing a maid to bring tea, Mr. Bonnington turned his full attention to Peter, enthusing on the subject of our mural. His words were effusive and his manner somewhat deferent as though, finding himself in the presence of such genius, he was overawed.

'What did you want?' Peter soon fell back into

monosyllable mode.

'A sea scape,' said Bonnington. 'Old time galleons, high waves, plenty of action. A battle scene perhaps.'

'Turneresque?' Peter actually smiled.

'Yes, if you could.'

'I'll bring my portfolio if you like and you can see some I've already done.'

'Wonderful.'

If Kit and I were amazed or even stunned to think Peter possessed anything as grand as a portfolio, we neither of us moved a muscle. His next question had us squirming slightly because, although it was a reasonable one, it was entirely out of character for Peter.

'How much did you intend to pay?' he asked.

There was something of an awkward pause before Bonnington replied during which Peter never took his eyes from him.

'That would be up to you, I suppose,' he said at last.

'Then to cover the whole area.' Peter stood up and swept his elegant hand along the length of wall, implying by the action, the vast expanse he had to cover, 'It would be in the region of a thousand pounds.'

Remember I am writing of a time when an average workman, such as our own farm labourers, earned little more then eight pounds a week. A doctor, like Kit, was considered priveledged and extremely rich since he made upwards of fifteen hundred a year and a bank manger no more than a thousand.

'It's a great deal of money,' Bonnington voiced what Kit and I were thinking. 'But I suppose artwork of your calibre is priceless. I must think about it you understand but bring your portfolio by all means because I think we can come to an understanding.'

'There won't be any understanding,' Peter said, curtly. 'That's the price if you want one.'

'Then I must agree but bring it anyway.'

I thought Bonnington was annoyed. Perplexed by such an extraordinery price but not wishing to look small in front of his new doctor and his doctor's wife, he agreed but the decision embarrassed us all.

After that, Peter announced that he must leave at once as he had much to do. Kit and I sprang to our feet as though we were merely the great man's chauffer and secretary and Bonnington hastened to open the door for us. Before we could make our exit a young lady stepped into the room, saw we were all engaged in conversation, and made to depart on the instant.

'Laura,' Bonnington called to her, 'come and meet Doctor Barry, he's to be our new G.P.'

Laura, whom we took to be his daughter, shook hands with Kit, smiled at me and nodded to Peter who stood across the room.

'Pleased to meet you,' she said in the time honoured way.

Laura at that time was about seventeen, pretty as a picture and beautifully spoken. Peter, whom I had feared would ignore her, smiled back and almost rushed across the deep pile carpet to shake her hand. Together they stood for what was not longer than a minute but what a handsome pair they made. I doubt Kit nor Bonnington acknowledged it but I cetainly did particularly as it was the first time I had seen my reticent brother make any attempt at civility. I was entralled.

Peter's blue eyes sparkled as they met Laura's honey hued brown ones. He held her hand for far longer than was either polite or necessary and, just for that fraction of a second, it was if the two stood alone while the rest of us vanished into thin air.

During our trip back to the farm I commented that Mr. Bonnington had, indeed, a very pretty daughter. Peter said not a word and Kit only made comments regarding his opinion of Peter's charge for the proposed mural. On arriving at my old front door, Peter leapt out of the car almost before Kit had halted it; not a word of thanks or a goodbye were spoken and I told Kit to drive home as the hour was late and our mission completed.

So it was that Peter obtained his first commision.

Within a week Samuel Bonnington had officially agreed to the extraordinery price of one thousand pounds for his Turner like sea scape and Peter was installed in his drawing room embarking on the masterpiece. Twice Kit was called to the house in the following month to attend the hunchback daughter and both times he came home out of temper and miserable.

'It's damned wicked,' he told me. 'Poor girl's only twenty one. Okay she's deformed but sharp as a needle up here,' he touched his head. 'Brute keeps her caged like an animal, she should be out having some sort of life not stuck in doors specially in this weather.'

'Why were you called?' I asked.

'She has a cough.'

'Perhaps that's why she's staying indoors.'

'No it's not. She told me she never goes out.'

'Did she seem unhappy?'

'No, but how would she know the difference, she's always hidden away from the world?

'Is she terribly deformed?'

'Well, she's a midget with a hump back. Her condition's called Achondroplasia so, yes I suppose she is.'

'You see, darling, you're a doctor and used to all sorts of human peculiarities but it maybe that Bonnington feels she's safer indoors than roaming round the town where there's a risk of ignorant people shouting after her in the street.'

'If she were my daughter and anyone called her names I'd wring their neck.'

Dearest Kit could be quite violent at times but then he had to witness much hardship in his capacity as a family doctor and usually vented his frustrations on me when he came home. Not that I minded, I understood his dismay when he saw patients ill treated or maimed due to someone else's carelessness or ignorance.

'What's her name?' I asked.

'Rose,' he said, making me shudder.

We turned the conversation to Peter and Kit brightened up. He said, that whilst visiting the poor daughter, he had enquired if Peter was giving satisfaction and Bonnington had shown delight at his progress.

'Did you see Peter?' I asked.

'No but apparently the Bonningtons see a hell of a lot of him what with his daily painting sessions which, by the way he won't let them look at, plus the fact that he also spends a great deal of time courting Laura their younger girl.'

'Never?' I couldn't belive it.

'So you see, Vinnie darling, 'he's human after all. Just like the rest of us.'

Kit laughed.

That night I prayed that Kit's prophesy was right.

Chapter Twelve

T he painting of the Bonnington mural took place just after our first son, John, was born and my happiness knew no bounds. A perfect baby son, a husband I adored and a home which thrilled me more and more as the months passed by.

The practise was thriving even Pa seemed quite well considering his advanced age and the nature of his illness. Dominic, although seldom able to spare the time to visit, was working his way through the ranks of cardiology and looked set on becoming a consultant within five years. Teddy and Isabel appeared content if not madly in love and the farm was a tribute to all Teddy's hard work.

The added bonus was Peter.

Peter, who had worried us over the years with his introverted personality and numerous oddities, had presented us with evidence of an enormous gift which none of us realised he possessed. Not only were we staggered by his brilliance but by the change which had overtaken him as a person. At this point in my narrative my youngest brother was just over sixteen years of age and had lived most of his years as almost a total recluse. Of course he had attended school but had not made even a single friend or joined in any social activities; suddenly he seemed set to earn a thousand pounds and, what was more, he was courting a pretty girl who was teaching him to laugh and enjoy a normal life.

Laura Bonnington, slightly older than Peter, was a gem. We all loved her and vied for her company. She adored the farm, quickly becoming a mistress in the art of milking and driving the tractor; a feat which was permissible in the early sixties. Like everything else it's now against the law to allow anyone under the age of eighteen to drive a farm vehicle as the nanny state forbids such dangerous activities. (And interferes with our pleasures!)

Laura, still engaged in high school studies, would rush home to rescue Peter from his labours on the mural and together they would cycle back to the farm where she would play nursemaid to any sick sheep or herd the cows so she could spend time in the milking parlour. Peter would accompany her and join in any quest which she made her own. I longed to ask her opinion of the mural but resisted in case he kept it secret even from her.

So normal and down to earth had Peter become that he often brought Laura to our house for tea. It thrilled me to be able to be able to use the word 'normal' because, in Peter's case I never thought it would apply. These teatime visits were popular with Laura because they gave her the opportunity to play with John. She simply adored him and told me she couldn't wait to be grown and have a baby of her own.

'Don't wish your life away.' I used to tell her, for I was a very sophisticated wife and mother all at the great age of twenty three.

Laura would laugh and help put him in his cradle. Sometimes Peter would sit with us as we watched long lashed eye lids close over wide blue eyes and sleep make him appear even more idyllic than when awake.

'Would you like a baby?' she asked him one such evening.

'If he was perfect like John I wouldn't mind.'

'You have to get married first,' I joked.

'Only because society says so,' he answered.

'Because it's the right way round,' I corrected him.

Laura and Peter were so besotted with each other at that time that I worried in case my brother was taking advantage of her. After all he was a robust lad with no parent to check him and oceans of time and opportunity to do whatever he pleased. I determined to speak to Kit on the subject but an occassion never arose.

'Why did you say that him being perfect?' Laura asked.

'Healthy, I meant,' said Peter. 'Not a sickly child or a fractious one. Perfect just like my nephew.'

We laughed it off but I wondered if his remark had its roots in the fact that Laura was possessed of an imperfect sister. Whether that sister had had any effect on Peter I had no idea. Had he, in fact, ever met her? Deciding it was inevitable considering the amount of time he spent at the Bonnington house, I dismissed any worries on that score.

But I was wrong to have done so as, in the past, I had been in grave error once before. When Peter had thrown his train at my head all those years ago I should have made Ma and Pa pay attention. I should have complained to anyone who would listen and maybe someone would have taken him in hand.

Weeks went by and there was no sign of the mural. Now and again Kit or I would ask him how it was progressing and Peter would smile and say he, "was getting there but these things took time." Kit worried that Samuel Bonnington would become impatient but neither of us had heard any complaint on the subject so why we worried I can not say.

Once the harvest of nineteen sixty four was safely gathered in as the good hymn says, Teddy invited us all to a party at the farm. All the hands were dressed in their best summer clothes and Pa, resplendent in a straw hat, sat in his chair under the cedar tree. Isabel even managed to persuade her Aunt Doris to join us as she had grown into something of a recluse herself. Several families from our church were invited as was the vicar and his wife plus Laura's parents and her sister Rose.

Two days before the party Samuel Bonnington telephoned Teddy, saying that he was delighted to accept the invitation but although he and his wife, and obviously Laura would be present, his daughter Rose was not well enough to attend. When Teddy told Kit the news, Kit was furious.

'Damn the man,' he said. 'A simple family party with people the chap knows and should trust. Just a picnic in a secluded garden and still he can't bring himself to expose the poor creature. What does he think she is, a deformed monkey?'

'Perhaps she isn't well?' Teddy was alarmed at Kit's fury.

'Of course she's well,' Kit retorted. 'If anyone should know it's her doctor.'

For myself, I was looking forward to the party far too much to worry about Laura's poor sister but Kit, indignant in the extreme, would not be silenced on the subject.

'I'm going to see him,' he said.

'See who, darling?'

'Bonnington.'

'But it's not our business, Kit,' his remark worried me. 'I know how you feel but presumably the girl's as happy as she can be and he probably knows what's best for her.'

'He knows nothing.'

'How do you know?'

'Because however deformed she might be it's no reason to turn her into a Cinderella figure and leave her in the blasted kitchen whilst they and her beautiful sister go to the party.'

'You never know, Kit,' I reasoned. 'She might prefer to stay at home. Those people can be very sensitive .'

'Those people,' he shouted. 'What d'you mean by 'those people.' Rose is perfectly normal except for her outward appearance and that's not her fault and shouldn't be of interest to anyone else either.'

I had seen Kit in such a mood before over a mentally retarded boy who was also closeted by his family. Such instances of injustice upset my loving husband and, to a certain extent, I could understand his exasperation. Times, as I keep saying, have changed so dramatically that now we are educated to except accept all manner of perculiarities in our fellows and taught to treat the less fortunate with kindness and compassion. In the fifties and well into the early sixties many so called freaks were still to be seen in circuses. Another thing, thanks to modern medicine, fewer malformed people are in evidence although, when I was staying with Anna at Brighton just before my illness, I noticed several unfortunates brought by coach to enjoy a day by the seaside and no one paid them any attention. Perhaps it's all part of this political correctness I hear so much about or maybe people are more tolerant and accept differences in others as a matter of course.

For, in diverse ways, are not we all different?

The evening of the harvest party, was perfect. In England that, in itself, was amazing. It had rained on St. Swithen's Day, July 16th, and we had all feared it would continue to do so for the rest of the summer. That last day of August allayed our fears. From six in the morning until almost ten at night, the day was hot, sunny and completely dry. We were blessed indeed!

I know we took John with us but since, like Ma before me, I had never contemplated employing a nursemaid, we could hardly have left him at home. Our baby was familier with the farm anyway and his behaviour that evening was impeccable. Even Aunt Doris, who as far as I can recall was recovering from some illness, managed to join in the fun as there was a great deal of laughter and good natured jollity. Teddy, full of his usual mimicry and jokes, had us in fits although, I might add that the various wines brewed by he and Isabel, were a great assistance in the laughter stakes. For some reason, as I surveyed the familiar outline of Borough Heath Chase glowing purple in the setting sun, my thoughts turned to the tragedy of Rose. So real were my memories that I had to push them away as I feared they would ruin my evening. That sounds selfish but I wanted, not only myself, but everyone else to be happy that night for our party was too perfect to be marred by sorrowful reminiscing.

Peter and Laura sat slightly apart from the rest of us, presumably so that they could hold hands and whisper one to another. Whether Samuel Bonnington was aware of his daughter's infatuation with Peter I can not tell you. Probably not because, as later events confirmed, he would almost certainly have objected violently. It was my opinion that he judged the two young people to be just good friends and, being of an age, have much in common.

Kit, for once was off duty, a minor miracle in itself. In those long forgotten days the majority of doctors worked alone. No six or eight handed practises, as we see today, were fashionable and a general practitioner usually worked from home and saw to every patient himself. I say, 'himself' for I can not recall a single lady doctor working anywhere in our area. Kit held surgery in what should have been our dining room and my beautiful square hall had to serve as a waiting room. Surgery took place every morning, except Sunday, between the hours of nine o'clock and eleven and resumed at five through to seven or even eight o'clock in the evening. The time in between was reserved for house calls so you can imagine how hard dear Kit worked. It was always his intention to grant himself a free evening or even a free afternoon but illness and childbirth are not sympathetic to such wishes so many of our plans for eating out or theatre trips had be cancelled, often at the last minute. The harvest party, being a special ocassion, I wished with all my heart that he could join in the celebrations with John and I and remain, undisturbed, throughout the entire evening. Kit agreed but we both knew it would depend on whether or not he was summoned to a sick bed as our phone would have to be switched through to the farm. It was Dominic who prevented that unwelcome occurrence as, much to my delight, he was paying us one of his rare visits at the time. When Teddy told him of his intention to throw a party, Dominic insisted that he stay at our house and stand in for Kit.

'But you're not a G.P.' Kit had said.

'I am still pretty nifty when it comes to a dose of flu or a belly ache,' he answered.

'And you don't know my patients.'

'They don't need knowing, they need curing.'

'You'll miss the party.'

'And you won't.' Dominic insisted that he act as locum for Kit so that we could go to the farm without the worry of switching phones or dreading the prospect of Kit being called away. Kit was hesitant so we pulled his leg, telling him he was jealous that his beloved patients would prefer Dominic to himself. After consulting his records, and deciding that no female was on the verge of giving birth and no particular case presented a specific worry, he eventually agreed that Dominic should stand in but only if he promised to telephone should anything untoward crop up.

'I promise,' Dominic had said, winking at me.

For my part, I had every faith that my clever brother was more than qualified to administer to Kit's patients and my mind was completely at ease during the entire eveing.

We were almost through our first course of smoked salmon doused in lemon on crisp bread when Samuel Bonnington and his wife, Eleanor, appeared. I knew Kit had visited Bonnington and I had a feeling he had expressed his feelings concerning the deformed daughter, Rose. No word of the outcome had been discussed between us for which I was thankful for, whatever my personal views on the matter may be, I respected the right of a father to act as he thought best when it came to the welfare of his child. So it was that the introduction of Rose to our party came as a huge and very pleasant surprise.

Certainly she was tiny and exceedingly round shouldered

but her face was quite beautiful and her smile enchanting. Particulary, I noticed her hands and wondered if she was a gifted pianist, so elegant and long were her fingers. Complexion wise she was stunning and, as the evning wore on, she contributed more and more to the conversation. Her knowledge of world affairs, in a time when news was restricted to infrequent bulletins on the radio, was amazing and her repartee of amusing stories outdid Teddys' which was saying something. As she blended so perfectly with our family and friends I too cursed Samuel Bonnington for not allowing her more freedom for she enriched our evening and endeared herself to everyone present.

Peter and Laura remained oblivious to the rest of us but when Isabel began to serve all manner of cold meats, great dishes of home grown salad and luscious dairy ice cream with strawberries, the two young people rushed to the trestle tables which Teddy had set out along the west wall of the farmhouse.

Plates were filled and so were glasses. A barrel of beer, in fact more than one, were brought down from the house by several of the hands and the men filled their tankards, drinking to the success of the harvest. I was happy to notice that Rose, whatever other health problems she may suffer, possessed a vigorous appetite and twice her plate was replenished. Peter also pleased me by exhibiting a show of graciousness towards his beloved Laura. Time and again he fetched food and more strawberries to her seat under the cedar tree to save her the inconvenience of rising. For a boy who we had all deemed unable of passing the time of day with his own family, the improvement was astounding. Once or twice, he glanced in my direction and I raised my hand in acknowledgment but I quickly realised that it was not me who took his attention but Rose Bonnington.

Rose was sitting in a comfortable chair which Teddy had insisted in fetching from Ma's old morning room. Samuel Bonnington had been most gratful as, no doubt, that deformed back must have given rise to pain if a seat was unsuitable. Her chair was placed next to my upright canvas one as, I too, was favoured with a special seat so that I could nurse John. The look on Peter's face was far from joyful, rather reminiscent of his old scowl but, thankfully, it was replaced by a smile when he turned back to Laura.

At ten o'clock we had to bow to a cool breeze which heralded the coming night but we couldn't complain, our evening had been sublime. Special thanks and farewells were given to Teddy and Isabel and a veritable queue of people waited to shake Rose's hand as her presence had added much to our harvest celebration.

Once home, and John safely tucked up in his cot, we were relieved to hear that Dominic had nothing of a worrying nature to report. Streched out on our sofa he laughed and told Kit he wouldn't mind a cushy job such as his. No phone calls, no emergency operations or sudden deaths, just perfect peace. Kit had just made a point of telling him that he had hit the jack pot when it came to peaceful evenings as, usually by this time, he himself, would have been called out upwards of six times, when the phone rang.

'See what I mean?' Smiling, Kit went to answer it.

Dominic wanted to know all about the party and I remember feeling slightly guilty that he had unselfishly missed it so that we shouldn't. I cheered up when he assured me that down in Surrey life wasn't all hard work and many parties were thrown in country houses and meals taken in fashionable London resturants. Just as he was about to elaborate on these fancy affairs, Kit, grave faced, returned.

'Don't tell me you have to turn out again?' I said, crossly.

'No, it wasn't a patient,' he said. 'That was old man Bonnington.'

'What did he want?'

'To scream at me it seemed.'

'Scream at you?' It was Dominic's turn to sound angry.

'What have you done to him?'

'Not me. Apparently young Peter's upset him. Only asked Laura to marry him and the silly little girl's accepted. Seems Bonnington holds me responsible.'

'They probably had too much elderberry wine at the party and Peter lost his head,' I said, adding, 'They're both still children with no money and no jobs, it's too absurd. Bonnington shouldn't worry us at this hour with that kind of nonsense.'

'Well he has,' Kit replied. 'He says he wants Peter out of his house mural or no mural and he's banned Laura from ever seeing him again.'

'Storm in a bloody teacup,' Dominic chipped in.

'I'll speak to Peter in the morning,' I told them. 'But I think Bonnington ought to let him finish the mural but just make sure Laura sees less of him.'

'Couple of kids keeping us up.' Kit looked at the clock on the mantlepiece. 'Good God it's gone midnight and I've got surgery at eight.'

With that we all went to bed but I was worried. My earlier delight at the success of the party was forgotten as I lay, wide awake, wondering why any thoughts concerning Peter always unnevered me?

Peter and problems were joined at the hip as far as I was concerned.

Chapter Thirteen

T eddy has spent most of the day with me.
We reminisce, of course we do, but only about pleasant things. We laugh at some of the ideas that our beloved old Ma held so dear and he talks about the farm and Michael quite a lot. For a man of his age, he looks remarkably well and so he should as he still drives a fancy car and takes holidays abroad.

'Michael phoned to say he's got a job doing something called 'voice overs,' he tells me. 'What are they, Vin?'

'Adverts, Teddy. You know when programs break off and we have to endure all those commercial breaks?' Teddy nods. 'Obviously he's landed a job explaining the wonders of the products.'

'Should get himself a proper job.'

'Oh, he's happy enough.'

'Still comes running to me when he's short of cash.'

'You can rest assured he's content and doing exactly what he wants.' I say because the subject of Michael's acting carreer has long been a bone of contention as far as Teddy is concerned, a fact which doesn't stop me rushing to his defence before we drop the subject completely. 'He'll surprise you one day and land a leading part in the West End.'

'He's surprised me quite enough already,' says Teddy and I know just what he means.

We chat about this documentery that Tim is doing and I mention the Lawrence man who is the author of this latest misery. What can either of us say? Dramatic events occurring in your immediate family unfortunately invite interest and no one can rewrite history.

'Do you think we ought to have gone abroad, Vinnie?' he asks.

'I wouldn't have minded but Kit wouldn't hear of it.'

'Dear old Kit.'

We talk of Kit and the wonderful work he did here in Borough Heath. Since his death only last year, Teddy doesn't harp on Dominic and his troubles but sometimes I wish he would for I loved Dominic with all my heart and think of him almost daily. My children nag me to let go of the past so the saga of Uncle Dom is seldom discussed.

Teddy says I should go and stay with him for a week or two as he fears I'm becoming house bound. He misses the farm but still clings to the country and owns a fine cottage in the Derbyshire Dales. I often wonder if he chose that particular county because Dorothea's home was in the dales and still he wishes to be reminded of her?

'I go out more than you think,' I tell him.

'So you should. You're five years younger than me.'

'Yes, but I've had a heart attack.'

'It's a wonder we haven't both had hundreds of those considering all we've been through.' He smiles, but Teddy's always sweet and I hate it when consults his watch and decides it's time for him to leave.

After he'd gone I thought back to the Bonnington affair. It wasn't a subject we had discussed for we seldom mentioned names or events from that particular time but, when I'm alone and I'm sure when he is alone, we both think a great deal about what happened.

As soon as he was free, Kit went straight to the farm on the morning after Samuel Bonnington's outburst on the phone. For one thing I think he was somewhat agrieved that he had been dragged into the unpleasantness as, since Peter lived with him, he saw him as Teddy's responsibility. It was my opinion that Bonnington decided Kit and I were more suited to dealing with the situation as we had started the ball rolling in the matter of the mural.

Peter, as was to be expected, was livid when he heard that he had been denied access to his mural and immediately started raving that he would sue Bonnington. Kit tended to agree but wanted to know why he had taken it into his head to propose marriage to a seventeen year old girl when he himself was only sixteen? Peter said it was all a mistake, that they had talked of staying together but not as a married couple.

If I remember correctly, it took over a week to clear the air. Kit had several long discussions with Teddy and Dominic and the three of them began to resemble a council of war. We all thought it unreasonable of Samuel Bonnington to cancel the mural without parting with a penny piece for Peter assured us that it was almost completed.

The men voted to go and thrash the matter out with him but Isabel and I, being women and therefor much wiser, suggested that the two of us visit Eleanor Bonnington whom we thought must have an opinion of her own and, hopefully, a more reasonable one. To that end we met in the town and then, discussing strategy, we walked to the Bonnington house.

It was Rose who responded to our knock and opened the front door, a fact which eased our passage no end. Seemingly happy to see us she smiled cheerfully as she ushered us into a cosy side room where her mother was watching television. Those were the days when programs like Emergency Ward 10 gripped the nation but already Coronation Street was in evidence although almost a decade would pass before the advent of colour television.

Eleanor Bonnington was more than pleased to see us, at one point I thought she was going to kiss us such was her delight in our arrival. Rose rang the bell so that the maid could bring tea and we discussed the harvest party for a good ten minutes. I can't quite recall when maids became a rarity, as I've mentioned, I have Pan but she is a dying breed as I know of no one else who keeps a full time servant. I suppose, after the second world war, young girls discovered the financial benefits of working in factories and serving in shops; a circumstance which forced married women to manage their own households. Eleanor's maid, I distinctly remember, still wore the full costume of her calling unlike my Pan who wears a perculiar assortment of clothes which she calls, 'charity shop chic.'

After we had drunk the tea and eaten home made cake, Isabel broached the subject of Peter and Laura.

'If Peter has upset you, Eleanor,' she began, 'we are truly sorry. He's only sixteen as you know and there's absolutely no question of he and Laura being anything more than good friends at the moment anyway.'

'I know that.'

'But we all think he should be allowed to finish his mural,' I added, 'because he tells us it's almost complete and we don't think it's fair that he should be banished without a penny for his efforts.'

'I agree,' she said.

'So do I.' That was from Rose.

'Laura's devastated,' Eleanor said. 'I hardly know what to do with her.'

'She'll survive, Mummy,' Rose was smiling.

'Why is she devastated?' I asked, because I understood it was Samuel who was enduring that particular emotion not his daughter.

'Because Peter's ditched her.' Rose supplied the answer.

'I suppose she's been told to see a little less of him since your father's so upset?' I offered.

'Oh, she doesn't care about daddy, he always makes a drama out of everything and we're all used to it.' Rose was still smiling but suddenly her expression changed making her appear grave. 'It's just that she didn't expect Peter to refuse to see her any more.'

'Surely he hasn't taken this mural business out on Laura?' I was amazed.

'Oh yes he has,' Rose continued. 'He wrote her a short letter and popped it through the letter box. It was most curt, a note more than a letter. He told her that he had no intention of seeing her ever again and that she had caused him nothing but trouble. It broke her heart.'

'But they seemed so happy at the party,' I was incredulous. 'He knew he had to apologise for upsetting your father but surely he could have explained that it was all a misunderstanding? Anyway there's no need for him and Laura to part and you never know, ' it was my turn to smile, 'in years to come, when the time is right, they might yet marry.'

'Laura says she hates him now,' Rose continued.

'Yes, well that's teenagers for you,' Isabel added. 'I shall speak to Peter though, he had no right to hurt her feelings no matter how upset he felt.'

The subject of what we all called 'puppy love' took us through the next half hour. I wondered where Laura was and if she knew we were with her mother and sister. Perhaps, in her eyes, we too, were considered enemies because of our association with the now, much despised, Peter. Just as I thought some progress had been made we heard the front door open and close and Samuel Bonnington appeared in the room. Now, a fully fledged doctor's wife, I immediately diagnosed him as suffering high blood pressure for his face was as red as a newly picked apple.

To give him his due, he showed Isabel and myself every

courtesy. Towards his wife and daughter, he was sweetness itself and I forgave his outburst concerning the bizarre behaviour of Peter on the instant.

'I was hasty,' he explained. 'I shouldn't have rung your husband especially at such a late hour. It was the shock of being told your seventeen year old child is about to be wed. I worried she might be in- er- difficulties and over reacted.'

'You mean you thought she might be pregnant?'

'To be honest, yes.'

'But there's no question of that?' I, too, had to be sure for my own peace of mind.

'Oh, no. As you say, Mrs. Barry, the youngsters drank too much home made wine, which was pretty potent by the way, and made some sort of pledge to each other. I, like a fool, saw red and took it out on your brother. My apologies for the misunderstanding.' He almost bowed, inclining his head towards his extended belly.

I desperately wanted to tell him that he had caused untold trouble himself, that his misunderstanding as he mildly termed it, had upset not only Peter and Laura but our whole family as well. Luckily, having reached an age where I had learned restraint served better than recrimination, I accepted his apology and soon after that Isabel and I took our leave of all three Bonningtons and walked back to my house.

'I wonder why Peter was so harsh?' Isabel asked when we some distance away.

'Because of the mural, I expect. He's worked so hard and probably assumed he wasn't going to see a penny piece for his trouble so he took it out on Laura.'

'That's strange,' she said.

'Oh, he's just a boy and bit perculiar into the bargain. I think he sees things differently from the rest of us.'

'But to break Laura's heart specially as he seemed so fond of her.'

'It's weird but then Peter can be weird.'

'So he didn't love her after all?'

'Seems not but, then again, he might have writen that note out of spite just because he got into a rage about the mural.'

'And not meant it?'

'Probably not.'

'I shall still get Teddy to speak to him,' Isabel said. 'He can't go through life breaking hearts, it's so unfair.'

'Bonnington was the one who was unfair,' I reminded her.

After that we decided to drop the subject and hurried home to see Dominic who was spending far longer with us than I had dared to hope. Isabel made tea and I went to see if many patients were waiting for Kit. Only one elderly gentleman was seated in our square hall which was just as well as Kit hadn't returned from his rounds. Dominic wasn't about either so Isabel and I took our tea into the garden and admired John who had been deserted during our visit to the Bonningtons'.

'The boys can't be far away,' I commented. 'Kit wouldn't leave John on his own even if he had an emergency call out so Dom must be nearby.'

'Perhaps he's in the greenhouse?'

We called his name but no one appeared.

'If I find out that Kit and Dominic have left John on his own in the pram out here where anything could have happened to him, I shall be furious,' I said and meant it.

'Nothing could happen, surely,' said Isabel who, after the tragedy of Rose, should have known better.

'A cat could have jumped on his pram and smothered him or he could have fallen out,' I told her.

Our tea was then drunk in silence as I was boiling with indignation over my neglected baby. Isabel, sensing my mood decided to leave but, she too, was upset. Assuring me that Peter would be spoken to, she made her way towards the garden gate and then on to the farm.

Within the next half hour the hall filled with anxious patients but of their doctor there was no sign. I apologised to everyone saying that Doctor Barry had been called away to an urgent case and would be with them as soon as he returned. Where he was and what he was doing, of course I had no idea, but I had to tell them something.

In this day and age we would all have been in possession of mobile phones enabling me to contact my errant husband and brother within seconds. For either of them to have abandoned John was not only out of character but it was irresponisble and could have resulted in catastophe.

By eight o'clock and still no sign of either one of them, I panicked and rang Teddy. He was tired from yet another hard day but he advised me to banish the waiting patients and contact the police in case Kit had met with an accident. Taking his advice I told over two dozen coughing and genuinely sick people that the evening surgery would have to be cancelled and I worried as I watched them file miserably out into the street, untreated.

I didn't ring the police. Don't ask me why but I couldn't bring myself to do anything quite so dramatic. Deep down I felt only annoyance. The idea that both men were in desperate trouble never occurred to me; I just thought them irresponsible and uncaring.

Once John was safely put to bed, I merely sat in the living room and counted the minutes. I was right to do so for at almost ten o'clock the front door clicked open and both Kit and Dominic appeared looking sheepish and slightly drunk.

It was to be the following day before I discovered that their absence was due to a trip to nearby Wolverhampton where, unbeknown to me, Dominic planned to open a private heart clinic. Kit had accompanied him to inspect some premises which both men considered could easily be converted into a small hospital. For once Kit had skipped surgery and deserted his son due to the excitement of the project and, to some extent, I understood why.

Dominic was set to become a self employed cardiac

specialist with his own operating theatre and private hospital. My heart swelled with pride as I visualised a future where he would find eminence and total fulfilment. Earlier problems concerning teenage lovers and furious fathers were dismissed as was my rage at finding John deserted.

We all celebrated that night and why not?

Our dear Dominic was on the road to success and prosperity.

Chapter Fourteen

S ix weeks later Samuel Bonnington threw a really splendid party of his own and half Borough Heath were in attendance. The reason for such an elaborate celebration centred on the unveiling of Peter's mural. We, as a family, found more joy in the fact that a reconciliation between our young brother and Bonnington had taken place than in the fact that it signalled an approval of the painting.

Rose was present, mingling and chatting with everyone. If her father found her form and disfiugerment offensive, it bothered her not a jot for she was charm itself. Eleanor was equally pleasant and made much of our whole family. By this time Dominic had returned to Surrey so little John, resplendent in his carry cot, lay peacefully beside my armchair in their spacious living room. Kit was on call but his patients must have remained healthy that evening as no calls disturbed our enjoyment.

Samuel Bonnington was an attentive host who made up for any past unpleasantness by personally refilling our glasses with fine champagne and expressing, a somewhat overdone, interest in every remark passed by Teddy, Isabel, Kit or myself. I looked for Peter for, obviously, the occasion belonged to him. No sign of my brother did I see so, at just gone nine o'clock, when conversation lagged and everyone was impatient to view the mural, Samuel decreed that we would wait no longer.

The west wall was covered by four enormous white sheets which concealed whatever lay behind them. The sheets, being loosely tacked to the wall, meant there was no regal ceremony involving the cutting of a ribbon or the graceful unfolding of a blind. Samuel and Eleanor had to physically remove the studs and haul down the sheets before we could see Peter's masterpiece.

I was slightly disappointed only in so much as I thought his exquisite work to be a direct copy of Turner's 'Battle of Trafalgar' with an extra serving of battleships which, to my mind, robbed it of originality. However the painting was breathtaking and after a moments hesitation, everyone clapped and gasped in admiration.

Samuel raised his glass to the artist, whom he referred to as a genius, and people shouted words such as 'Bravo' and 'Hurrah' but it needed Peter to compliment the moment and he had apparently changed his mind about appearing.

One by one we inspected the mural, hardly daring to get too close in case we damaged its perfection. Isabel and I studied it for quite half an hour as did everyone else. Kit and Teddy seemed amused by all the adulation perhaps because neither one of them were connoisseurs of art nor did they care over much for galleons on high seas. Never the less, although Kit was on call, he joined Teddy and Samuel in appreciation of Peter's splendid work by drinking his share of a bottle of finest claret.

Whether Samuel Bonnington noticed, or anyone else was aware, I do not know but on one of the imposing ships, manning a cannon, stood a dwarf with a hunch back. I spotted the figure quite quickly and felt embarrassed, praying that it wouldn't offend Rose or her family. I comforted myself that the original Turner, from which it was copied, portrayed such a person. After all, dwarfs have always been amongst us for hundreds of years and Rose was far from the only one residing in Borough Heath but I wished with all my heart that Peter had not included the figure. Since he never tired of telling us that people were not his strong point I wondered why he had bothered to include the dwarf in the first place.

At some point towards ten o'clock, irritation set in. Tired and upset by Peter's absence, I desperately wanted to leave but Kit seemed oblivious to my existence. Throughout the evening John had been much admired but the room was noisy and brightly lit so his snatched moments of sleep were fitful and quite soon I knew he would start to cry in earnest. Invitingly, our car stood but a few yards away in the Bonnington's drive and I was on the verge of escaping, with or without Kit, when Laura suddenly appeared. I wondered if she had discovered that Peter was nowhere in sight for it was my understanding that any fond feelings which had bonded them in the recent past were well and truly forgotten and likely to remain so.

I remember how pretty she looked and how charmingly she behaved. My heart went out to her for I understood love and how soul destroying its loss could be. From time to time and, particularly at that moment, Kit could be infuriating but, had he forsaken me, I would have mourned as though experiencing a death. Young as she was, I knew her feelings for Peter had been deep and her life, after he had so unceremoniously dumped her, would have been shattered. Looking at her pretty face and watching her mingle with her father's guests, I consoled myself that the worst of her woes were fading.

But Laura's heartaches were to resurface that night for at just gone ten thirty, Peter walked into that vast living room and surveyed his mural.

'Where have you been?' I whispered, crossly.

'What's it to you?' he asked, his breath smelling of drink and his manner proving that more than one glass had been taken.

I chastised him. The married sister pulling rank on the youngest member of the family: I ordered him to go home at once. Desperately, I wanted to protect Laura from further upset in the shape of a partially drunken Peter whom, I knew would ruin not only her evening, but the atmosphere of the entire party.

Too late, Samuel Bonnington spotted him and grabbed his hand.

'This young man is my artist,' he shouted, for, he too, was full of good wine, 'Raise your glasses to a genius.'

Then John did begin to cry. Not so much cry as bellow. The buzz of conversation rose to a crescendo as everyone offered strident congratulations in praise of the mural. When loud applause followed the verbal adulation, I went in search of Kit who, together with Samuel Bonnington, was no longer in the room.

It took quite a time to locate him and when I did it was only because a door, leading to a small closet just off the main hall, was slightly ajar. Kit was inside, engaged in rapt conversation with Bonnington. I halted at that doorway because, much to my horror, something approaching a full scale row was taking place within the room.

'Two fifty and not a penny more,' I heard Bonnington tell Kit.

'A promise is a promise,' said Kit.

'The lad's lucky to get anything,' Bonnington continued. 'I nearly threw him and his blasted painting out of the window when my daughter told me he'd asked her to marry him.'

'But she accepted.'

'Only because he'd filled her head with tales of how rich and famous he was going to be. How they'd live in a mansion in London and have all the money in the world.'

'Whatever he said, remember he's just a boy and she's a mere school girl. I still say you accepted his price and now you should pay it.'

'Go to hell,' said Bonnington.

That was when I decided to interupt the less than pleasant conversation and demand that Kit drive us home. Of course I'd got the gist of the disagreement and I agreed with Kit, Bonnington had agreed the fatuous price even though the rest of us thought it excesive. The idea that he was now backing out on his promise was unfair and unjust.

I said so.

'Blasted lad hardly bothered himself to come and see if I was satisfied with his daubing.'

'What?' I was furious. 'It's a stunning success and you know it.'

'For which I shall pay him two hundred and fifty quid.'

'A quarter of the price' said Kit.

'A fair price for a boy who thought to steal my daughter.'

'Your daughter has nothing to do with the promised payment.' I said for I have always detested unfairness. But my desire to return home and get John into his rightful bed outdid my defence of Peter. If a blazing row was in the offing then I decided to leave my young brother to fight his corner. With this in mind I grabbed Kit by the arm and led him away from our red faced host.

Returning to the living room to pick up John, I was surprised to see Peter seated next to Rose; the two of them engaged in animated conversation. Of Laura there was no sign but that was to be expected. Peter's obvious pleasure in chatting to Rose would, normally, have been intriguing but the evening had turned sour and all I could think about was quitting that house in the hope of avoiding further sightings of both the mural and Samuel Bonnington for a very long time.

Kit, enraged by the unfairness of the reduced payment continued to rage for what was left of a very long evening and we both agreed that it was unjust. Peter had been greedy but the fee had been approved by Bonnington and he must have known that the finished article warranted much more than two hundred and fifty pounds.

'Do you think Peter would suceed as a painter if someone discovered him?' I asked my husband.

'Of course he would,' Kit told me. 'He would probably make a fortune.'

As all art lovers will know, Kit's words came true with a vengeance.

Chapter Fifteen.

D ominic's plans for opening his own hospital signalled an end to his work in Surrey.

Naturally, I was delighted when he wrote to say that he had quit his present post and would be taking an interim position in the cardiology department at Stafford Infirmary whilst he finalised his plans. The short letter I received one Tuesday morning pleased me no end for it meant that, with Dominic working in nearby Stafford, the whole family would be reunited. Kit was not so optomisitc.

'Stafford hasn't got a specialist cardiac department,' he said.

'They must take in hundreds of heart attack victims every year.'

'Probably do but there's no clinic or surgery carried out there. Stenting and angiograms are done in Birmingham.'

'Perhaps they're opening a new department.'

'Haven't heard.' Kit hurried out on his rounds.

By this time, Dominic had achieved considerable success in the world of open heart surgery. Teddy and I had followed his career with enthusiasm, reading everything we could find that as much as mentioned his name or the Surrey Hospital where he worked. I rang Teddy and asked him if he had heard the news?

'What's up?' he asked when I mentioned Dominic's name.

'Sounds as if he's got a post at Staffford, I'm thrilled.'

'Oh goody,' said Teddy. 'He can come and give me a hand on his days off.'

'He'll be able to visit regularly. Pa will be delighted.'

'He can keep an eye on Pa's ticker too,' Teddy reminded me. 'Poor old chap's been getting a lot of chest pain lately.'

'Kit says there isn't a cardiac department in Stafford.'

'I hope not. If there is then I've been wasting a hell of a lot of time driving Pa to bloody Brum for check ups when I could have popped him seven miles up the road to Stafford.'

'I expect they're opening a new facility and that's why he's been appointed.'

'All will be revealed,' said Teddy, but we both agreed that it would have to be something prestigious to bring our elder brother nearer to home even if it was only on a temporary basis.

But that was not to be the case. Three weeks after the letter arrived so did Dominic. He looked tired but seemed well enough, telling us that he intended to stay at the farm. Of course Pa, Teddy and I were delighted to hear it and his old room was set to rights immediately. The weeks went by and we heard nothing about his new position neither did he stir himself to take an interest in anything around him. Once I asked if he would locum for Kit so that we could celebrate a wedding anniversary but he refused rather curtly.

'Don't worry him,' Kit advised. 'He's probably got a lot on his plate specially as he's planning this private consultancy into the bargain.'

Nevertheless, we did have out night out. It was one of the few occassions when Kit employed an outside agency to deal with his calls. (A procedure which I was not anxious to repeat as he fussed and fretted during the entire meal in case any of his patients were inconvenienced!) My own worries continued for the following two months because it became increasingly obvious that no new post, interim or otherwise, awaited Dominic and neither did any prospects of a private hospital. Nothing was said and all my questions remained unaswered.

He did his share of work on the farm and wheeled Pa about in his bath chair but, apart from a succession of unexplained weekend absences, he hardly left the house. Isabel and I discussed the problem from time to time but neither one of us confronted Dominic as it seemed rude or, at best, intrusive.

What we did discuss, almost with relish, was Peter's involvement with Rose Bonnington. The most unlikely pairing caused more tongues than ours to wag. Borough Heath centred its attention on my younger brother's attachment to the hunchback daughter of the new colliery manager and people openly asked questions about it.

Kit, always cautious in any circumstances, suggested we keep out of it. When I brought up the subject over dinner, or in the nursery as we put John to bed, he would place a finger against his lips signifying that the topic must be dropped.

'We never heard the outcome of Bonnington's two hundred and fifty pound offer for the mural,' I said, impatiently one morning. 'I thought he had a nerve going back on his word.'

'Not our business,' said Kit.

'And what must Laura think of Peter hanging around poor Rose.?'

'Not much,' he grinned, 'but she must think herself well rid of him. I don't want to be unkind, Vin, but as brother's go, Peter's a non starter.'

'At least he's giving Rose a few outings. Mrs. Mills says she saw them in Walsall High Street last week.'

'Who's Mrs. Mills?'

'Only one of your patients,'

'Oh, I know. She had twins last year and she's pregant again. She should keep her eye on her husband not spy on Peter or Rose.'

'She wasn't spying.' I snorted. 'Anyway, other people have seen them at the pictures together and walking on the chase.'

'Nice to know Peter has some purpose in his life after all.' With that acid remark, Kit, as usual, rushed out of the house.

So I worried about two brothers.

Dominic took priority as I couldn't make any sense of his solitary life holed up in the old farmhouse. Peter's relationship with a deformed lady some five years older than himself seemed odd to say the least of it and why was Samuel Bonnington allowing him to take Rose out when he had played the over protective father all her life?

There's something to be said for being an only child, don't you think?

Kit always used to say that one crisis overtakes another and my brother's problems faded into insignificance as a new anxiety invaded our lives. As a family, we had never experienced the burden of money worries. Ma, as I have already mentioned, was heir to a considerable fortune and after her death her income reverted to Pa. Teddy, working from dawn to dusk, made good money from the farm and I always viewed us as financially comfortable if not actually rich. But times change and cheap imports from the continent began to tell their tale.

In the middle sixties the inovation of the supermarket was well underway and with it came cut price food products. Milk, which Teddy had been selling for a shilling a pint could be bought from the super stores at ninepence. Butter, imported from Denmark and New Zealand was bulk bought and again our farm products could not compete. Teddy cut prices so that the big mulitples would buy but that meant a drop in profits and, coupled with wage increases, ever popular at that time, he complained that his bank ballance suffered.

Ma's will had stated that the farm was to be divided equally between the four of us with the capitol deposited in Pa's account during his lifetime. Dominic, Teddy, myself and Peter were equal share holders in both the property and the land. Pa, we knew would be comfortable for the rest of his life as he needed little money for his personal use; even new clothes were unnecessary as he seldom set foot ouside. Isabel was frugal and so was Teddy but Dominic was certainly spending.

Teddy visited us quite late one evening which, in itself, was a surprise considering he would have been farming since dawn.

'I'm worried,' he told Kit and I. 'This has got to be ironed out.'

'What has?' I asked.

'Dominic's spending,' he said simply.

Naturally Kit and I showed amazment because, as far as we knew, Dominic had turned into something of a recluse so, to be told he was over spending when he rarely left the farm, seemed illogical.

'He's got bad debts,' Teddy explained, 'brought them with him from down south. Not only that but he's forever ordering things from those catalogues that come through the post.'

'What sort of things?' Kit wanted to know.

'Clothes mainly but he's bought a brand new TV and a record player. Isabel says, when she cleaned his room the other week, she counted over three hundred records.'

'Good God,' said, an over careful, Kit.

'What would he want all that stuff for?' I asked.

'We think he's been earning serious money at the hospital and now that he's not working anymore he can't get out of the habit of spending.'

That comment invited speculation as to why he had quit such a wonderful job and forsaken an equally wonderful income. Further more it led the three of us to question why no salary and no new position were forthcoming now that he was back home.

'We'll have to ask him outright,' Kit said.

'I've tried,' Teddy told us, 'but he always says there's been a delay and it will be soon but not quite yet.'

'What won't be not quite yet?'

'His new job,' Teddy said.

'And he's borrowing from you Teddy, is he?'

'From me and Pa. I've put a stop to it but of course Pa couldn't care less about money and gives him whatever he asks for. Isabel says we should take the cheque book away from him.'

'Oh, you must,' Kit agreed.

'Do you think there really is a job round the corner?' I asked.

'No,' Teddy shook his head and looked grave. 'If you really want to know, I think he's disgraced himself and he's been either suspended or struck off.'

That remark was followed by a horrified silence. I must admit that the thought had occurred to me on and off during the preceding weeks. Qualified cardiac surgeons don't have to go out begging for jobs, they are in great demand and Dominic, we all knew was considered one of the best. So why was he sitting in an old farmhouse twiddling his thumbs when the country was crying out for good men and what had happened to the exciting plans for his own practise?

'But Dom wouldn't do anything untoward.' I defended my favourite brother.

'How do we know what he would or wouldn't do?'

'Because we know him,' I almost shouted.'

'He wouldn't carry out an illegal operation or willfully kill anyone,' Teddy agreed, 'but he could have got involved with drugs or stealing NHS supplies.'

'Drugs?' Then I did shout.

'Whenever I pick up a blasted newspaper,' Teddy went on, 'all I seem to read about is this drug culture that goes with pop stars and flower power lunies. Dom would have had access to all sorts of stuff working in a hospital so I just wondered.'

And so it went on late into the night. The three of us trying to work out a reason why our clever brother should be spending money he did not have, idling his time away and not engaging in his beloved work.

Teddy and Kit came up with more and more bizarre explanations but I had my own thoughts regarding Dominic and they were concerned with what would now be called his sexual orientation. However the meeting produced much needed support for Teddy because Kit promised to speak personally to Dominic as, having trained and worked with him, he felt in a better position to do so than any of us.

Teddy apologised for inflicting his troubles on Kit and I and we assured him that we were only too happy that he had. With that we all took a small whisky and Teddy departed sometime after midnight.

Deeply worried we looked in on a sleeping John and then hurried to our bed as the evning had had a shattering effect on both of us. No sooner had Kit switched off the bedside lamp than the phone rang and we both sighed.

'Blast,' he muttered.

'Don't go out unless it's a real emergency,' I whispered as he lifted the receiver.

But dearest Kit had no option.

The call was from Samuel Bonnington to say Rose had been taken very ill and Kit was needed post haste.

Chapter Sixteen

Rose Bonnington, partly because she was frail and, at the best of times considered something of an invalid, was transfered to Stafford Infirmary. Kit had stayed at her bedside for over an hour but had not been able to diagnose her complaint, the symptoms of which were violent sickness and stomach pain.

Whereas, he told me, he was pretty sure she had merely fallen foul of a bug or, at worst collected a dose of food poisoning, he was not prepared to stand by whilst she worsened as people affected by Achondroplasia were prone to acute illness and even sudden death.

'How dramatic,' I said laconically, for the Bonnington family were of little interest to me.

'Old man Bonnington's out of his mind with worry,' Kit said.

'But you think she'll be all right?' I atoned for my previous lack of concern for Rose, unlike her father for whom I had nothing but contempt, was a kind and caring person.

'I'll ring the hospital later and find out what they've come up with.'

Just after Kit had begun morning surgery, Peter arrived. After the fiasco of the night of the mural party, I had not seen him only heard tales of his various exploits with Rose.

'I rang Rose this morning,' he said, without wishing me good morning or glancing at John, 'her dad says she's in hospital.'

'So I understand.'

'What's up with her, Vinnie?'

'They don't know for certain,' I explained. 'Kit couldn't make a diagnosis so he sent for an ambulance and she's undergoing some tests.'

'Oh,' said Peter.

Typical of him, after ascertaining some sort of explanation and realising no further information would be forthcoming, he turned on his heel and made for the door.

'Wait a minute.' I grabbed his broad shoulder and turned him towards me. 'I want to know what happened when we left the house that night. Did you get your money from Bonnington?'

'Yes.'

'How much?'

'A thousand pounds.'

'He told us he was only going to give you two hundred and fifty.'

'He told me the same only I wasn't having it.'

'How did you persuade him to part with such a vast sum?'

'It was agreed.'

'I know but he reneged.'

'No one reneges on me.'

Once again he turned tail and threatened to depart but I still had my hand on his shoulder.

'Peter,' I asked, 'what's Rose Bonnington to you?'

'My friend.'

'But you dumped Laura because of problems with her father so why did you make a friend of Rose when it must have been awkward?'

'Why must it have been?'

'Because, as you'd already fallen out with two members of the family, I wouldn't have thought you'd want to hang around with the rest of them?.'

'Not my fault if Laura tried to make me look daft and old Bonnington wanted to short change me. I like Rose and I hope she gets better soon.'

And that was that. Any further finger hold on his strong frame was of no consequence once he made up his mind to leave.

I watched him stride down the garden path and open the back gate. Peter never used the front door and never knocked. On the rare occassions when he visited, it was always by way of the kitchen door and that was also his means of exit.

During the morning I wondered if, in reality, he really had asked Laura to marry him or whether she had had too much wine and romanticised about the proposal? The idea that she had willfully lied seemed pointless unless she wished to antagonise her father. Never having understood Peter, I still thought it highly unlikely that he would make such a proposal either in jest or in earnest. As a mere schoolboy the idea of his marrying anyone would have been out of the question except that silly things are said at parties especially after a few glasses of Teddy's home made wine!

Then the thousand pounds he said he had received from Samuel Bonnington intrigued me. If he was being honest then what had he done with the money? Perhaps even more treasures filled his old playroom. Thinking of the catalogues that Teddy said arrived by post and tempted Dominic made me wonder if they caught Peter's eye as well? No doubt he would need to buy paints and canvases, art books and all sorts of accessories.

But one thousand pounds!

Kit didn't appear until much later that afternoon and I

immediately enquired after Rose.

'She's oaky,' he told me. 'I rang the hospital and they said they'd done several tests all of which pointed to food poisoning and nothing more sinister. They're going to keep her in for a couple of days just to be sure and then she should be fine to go home.'

'Well, that's good news.'

'Yes, she's a nice person.'

'Have you spoken to Bonnington?'

'No, but the hospital said he'd rung, so he knows as much as I do.'

'Do you think you ought to make a courtesy call?'

'No, but I'll visit when she's home just to show what a caring chap I really am.'

Rose came home the following Wednesday and Kit kept his word, going straight up to the house to check on her wellbeing. Arriving home he was out of temper because he said Peter had been hanging about trying to see her and Bonnington had blamed him for the intrusion.

'Nothing to do with me if the little sod persists in pestering the family.'

'He seems facinated with them.'

'Well he can unfascinate himself as quickly as he likes. Bonnington doesn't require any school boy intruders.'

'It's a strange relationship.'

'It's wierd.'

Kit and I then discussed the thousand pounds allegedly handed over by Bonnington as payment for the mural, but Kit didn't believe it. It was his opinion that Peter was merely bragging just to save face.

'He would have had no option but to take whatever was offered,' he told me. 'There was no contract and everyone knew it was a joke for a lad like him to ask so much.'

'I'll admit he's strange but I've never known him to lie,' I said.

'I think lie is too strong a word,' he answered. 'He just didn't want to look a fool in front of his big sister.'

But there was a follow up to the saga of the mural. Samuel Bonnington, being such a big noise in the National Coal Board, had many visitors. Most of the people who called at his house were either politicians or men of business and the majority came from London. One such man, a baronet by the name of Sir Marcus Delray, was highly impressed by Peter's work. So impressed, in fact, that he asked if it would be possible to meet the artist. I can not say whether his wish was met with any enthusiasm by Bonnington but it was certainly granted as Peter met with Sir Marcus in this very house the following week. The reason for my house acting as the meeting place lay in the fact that the farm was some way from the centre of Borough Heath whereas this house lies in the middle of the town thus it is easy to locate and, being a doctor's home, everyone can point it out.

Lighting a log fire in the sitting room, I made sure I presented my visitors with a welcoming arena for winter was particularly bleak that year. I also went to an enormous amount of trouble baking scones and a variety of cakes so that a lavish tea could further tempt the titled gentleman.

Peter appeared at the appointed time which was three thirty on the afternoon of the eighth of November. I distinctly recall how handsome and prosperous he looked, wearing a new light grey three piece suit, a patterned emerald tie and soft brown leather shoes. It was with great pride that I escorted the baronet into my sitting room to meet him.

The upshot of my hospitality and my brother's attention to dress was rewarded by an invitation for Peter to go to London to paint a mural for Sir Marcus at his home in Chelsea. Of course it wasn't a matter of Peter simply accepting as, still just a school boy, Teddy and I had to be sure that proper arrangements would be made for his stay whilst away from home.

Peter had been protected all his life so the prospect of him leaving the farm and travelling to the capitol had to be thoroughly discussed. Sir Marcus promised that he would be watched and cared for but Teddy, the simple farmer, was all against it.

'He'll fall in with artists and scatter brained people,' he said to Kit and I. 'I want him to get his exams behind him and keep his feet on the ground. No good ever came of rushing down to London to paint bloody pictures.'

'He's obviously going to have a future of sorts in the art world, Ted,' Kit pointed out. 'If his heart's set on it then we better let him go. London isn't the other side of the world so if it doesn't work out then we'll have to go and fetch him back.'

For myself, I said very little. Actually, the thought of Peter being removed from the near vicinity struck me as something of a blessing. I can't quite explain quite why I thought so but I remember that I did and was pleased when the offer was finally accepted.

Apart from Teddy's insistence that Peter wait until the end of the Christmas term, plans for his departure were speedily put into action. In the mean time it was apparent that he was still very much involved with Rose Bonnington. No one understood such an unlikely friendship but we were all aware that, once she was fully recovered, it continued exactly as before. Kit himself saw them, arm in arm, walking down the High Street during a snow storm and came home full of apprehension as he thought the bitter Midland weather unsuitable for her delicate constitution.

'She's a grown woman,' I said, without realising my misuse of words.

'Bonnington hates the sight of him, you know.'

'Rose is twenty two or more,' I said. 'She may be -well-what she is but that apart she's every right to live her own life without her father dictating.'

But Kit was to have another disturbed night due to Rose

Bonnington. She had only been home a little under a month when she was struck down once again by the same stomach ailment which had forced her stay in hospital only a few weeks before. Kit said that Bonnington blamed the illness on Peter's enticing her out in the cold and Eleanor sided with him saying he had no right to be tempting their precious daughter out of the house in winter or at any other time.

'What did you say?' I asked Kit.

'I said it was nothing to do with me. Rose was an adult and must be allowed to do as she pleased.'

'Did you feel Bonnington blamed you just because you're his brother in law?'

'Of course not. I can hardly be blamed for being related to your peculiar brother.'

'I hope you thanked him for recommending Peter to Sir Marcus Delray?' I had often thought I should have written personally to Eleanor, expressing our gratitude for the introduction.

'No.' Kit, having had enough of asinine questions, left me to attend to John.

Poor Rose was again diagnosed with food poisoning and this time kept in hospital for over a week. She came home in a weakened state and flourished for little more than ten days before the illness struck again. This time Kit was not available to make the urgent house call as he was out on his rounds so Bonnington himself called an ambulance and Rose was hastened yet again to Stafford Infirmary.

Had she been a normal young woman possessed of average health I dare say she would have survived but inflicted as she was with frailty, poor Rose Bonnington did not recover from her third dose of food poisoning.

She died in our county town and I, for one, was distressed as I had grown fond of her. Also I grieved for Eleanor whom I knew must be devastated. Whether or not that was the case I never discovered as my letter of condolence went unanswered and the next time we met in the town, Eleanor Bonnington completely ignored me.

Chapter Seventeen

F ive years after the birth of John, Kit and I were blessed with a second child. Another son whom we named Philip. Philip was as fair skinned and blue eyed as John was dark with eyes that, in certain lights, shone as black as jet.

We were delighted with our second child chiefly because we had feared John would be bereft of brothers or sisters as five years is a long time to wait for another baby. By this time Isabel and Teddy's son, Michael was growing into a fine boy himself and John spent a great deal of time at the farm playing with him.

The year of Philip's birth was also the year of Pa's death. So long expected, it was still a sad occasion and we all mourned for the loss of a shadowy figure who had been part of our lives and yet apart from our lives. Pa was buried in St. Mary's churchyard alongside Ma. Dominic, Teddy, Peter and myself stood by that grave for some ten mintues contemplating our lives now that we were orphaned for although we were grown and far removed from parentel care there is always something evocative about the loss of both parents.

I wished Pa had lived to see Philip; not that he was over

interested in either of his grandsons but it seemed a pity that he was taken only weeks before my new baby appeared. Isabel, I always thought, was relieved to see the old man put into the ground and why shouldn't she be? Pa had seldom shown her any appreciation and never any affection but then his expressions of gratitude were scarce at the best of times. Towards me, she was friendly but distant. All my life I wished Isabel and I could have been closer but that was her nature and Teddy's coldness, although never discussed, did little to relax her. Once, and only once, I asked if they had ever considered having more children but I recall her reply was so offhand and brusque that I was unable to grasp her answer.

Dominic, whom we feared had suffered some disgrace or misfortune, suddenly proved us wrong by announcing that his plans to open a private hospital in Wolverhampton were complete. Over five months he had languished, moodily, at the farm, so what were we to think? No position in Stafford had been forthcoming but the new venture, together with a partner named Brian Thorn, quickly prospered making us proud once again.

Dominic and Brian, both highly qualified cardiologists, soon made a name for themselves and patients travelled many miles for consultations. At one time I thought Kit jealous of Dominic's sucess as he constantly poured scorn on the new enterprise, suggesting that the two surgeons lacked compassion for the poor and only interested themselves in the rich Since Dominic lost no time in buying a prestigious car and a fine house in Tettenhall, up to a point, I agreed with Kit.

Whatever was to happen later, I will always believe that my elder brother was a remarkable healer and due to his professionalism and care many lives were saved in the days before by-pass surgery became the widespread 'cure all' which it is today.

But the big news of the late sixties concerned Peter.

Sir Marcus Delray quickly took over the role of sponsor or

mentor. It was due to his patronage that Peter was able to enter the prestigious halls of The London Acadamy of Fine Arts where he was rapidly viewed as a painter of exceptional quality. Not that we had any correspondence directly from him. Peter was not given to writing letters, postcards or picking up an available phone to inform us of his progress. Our meagre knowledge of his success came from Sir Marcus himself and from news items which appeared in the national press.

At that time we were all under the impression that he gained commissions from word of mouth recommendations. Murals, still his speciality, had long since fallen from popularity until Mildred Tobias, a leading art critic of her day, spotted a sample of his work adorning the wall of a flat in Grosvenor Square. Apparently, an American gentleman had commissioned Peter to paint a mural in his home and Miss Tobias, a dinner guest one evening, had been enthralled with the result. Her influence and Peter's uncanny genius had immediately put him on the road to celebrity and vast wealth.

How we had scorned when he demanded a thousand pounds from Samuel Bonnington when now, we understood, that five and six figure payments were required if a Peter MacVee mural was to grace your wall. Naturally, I longed to see both him and his work but Kit said it was best to leave him alone as he would never fulfil the role of a loving brother or wish to share his life with any of us. Teddy and Isabel said much the same thing although, because of financial pressure, it was my belief that Teddy wrote asking him for funds to help maintain the farm which was at crisis point. It is also my belief that Peter sent him some much needed cash but failed to enclose as much as a formal note to accompany it.

We all talked of his sucess although, as a family, we remained far removed from it. Dominic, also basking in his own considerable achievements, sent us any snippets of information gleaned from newspapers, usually written and exaggerated by the gossip columnists. At one time it was rumoured that he was the escort of a royal personage but, despite our efforts, we discovered nothing more than the more sensational tabloids cared to infer.

But Peter reappeared two years later just after my precious daughter was born.

Anna surprised us by arriving at all. When Philip was born, Kit and I had thought our family quite complete. Two children, we told each other, constituted an ideal family and we were more than satisfied. Kit was approaching forty and working harder than ever whereas I, because of the lack of funds, was helping Teddy on the farm and also busy answering the phone at home so another baby had not been on our agenda. But when I found I was pregnant again the old thrill of the impending birth filled me with the usual emotions of joy and love for my unborn child. Kit beamed happily in spite of complaining that any more brats would bankrupt us. Anna came into the world on new year's eve nineteen sixty nine, the last day of the swinging sixties and she almost killed me.

Kit, John, Philip and myself had gone to the farm to celebrate the new decade which was to begin at midnight. Since the birth of my baby was not expected until mid January, the celebrations were not considered a risk to either myself or Anna. We had already bestowed the gender of female upon our unborn child as both of us longed for a daughter. My evening was cut short when Michael, mischievously, snatched a toy tank from Philip the result of which was a noisy tussle between the two small boys. Being almost deafened by their screams I leant down to grab Philip from the floor, where he lay, kicking and howling. As I bent to haul him to his feet I strained my back which, in turn, prompted labour. Kit, seeing my anguish, led me towards the sofa so that I might lie down and Teddy was most solicitous but Isabel, with all the good sense of a woman, rang for an ambulance and I was whisked away to dear old Stafford Infirmary where our beloved daughter was born on new year's day at one minute past midnight.

But, after the two relatively straightforward confinements, Anna's birth proved complicated. Delighted as Kit and I were with our precious little girl, my health was another matter. Almost fifty years ago medicine was no where near as advanced as it is today neither were people's expectations. Whether I contracted what would now be called a super bug or even whether such deadly virus's existed, I can not tell you but I certainly suffered a strange sickness which refused to surrender to, the then ubiquitous, penicillin. For a little over six weeks, I lay in that blasted hospital feeling too ill to take an interest in anything including my new born baby.

Kit visited almost every day and Isabel once each week. When work on the farm allowed it, so did Teddy. Dominic, when told of the seriousness of my condition, travelled to and fro from Wolverhampton to spend time at his sister's bedside. But whether my family were present or a hundred miles away mattered not a jot to me for I was deeply depressed and hardly able to speak to any of them. Post natal depression was not the topic on everyone's lips which it has now become. Like many subjects, it was considered either a private matter or, worse still, some nervous nonsense which existed only in the minds of hysterical women.

Looking back I certainly collected a full blown dose of it to accompany whatever else ailed me. Kit's counselling consisted of a combination of petting and verbal encouragement but when both lines of attack failed he took to administrating a mild form of nagging the content of which came under the heading of, 'pull yourself together.'

But I couldn't nor did I seriously try.

Until half way through Febuaray when an unexpected visitor appeared at the foot of my hospital bed.

'What's up?' asked a dispassionate Peter.

For reasons I have never been able to explain, I was overjoyed to see him. Over two years had passed since last we had met so perhaps the missing years fuelled my enthusiasum but, whatever it was that promoted such happiness is of no matter for it led to a speedy recovery.

We were all aware that he was doing well for himself. An hour long television program had featured his work just prior to Christmas and I, for one, had been overcome with pride but also filled with sadness that, because of his taciturn nature and odd behaviour, non of us had ever warmed to him. By rights we should have attended unveilings and exhibitions where we could have shown our delight a thousand times over. But Peter was, as they say, a law unto himself and we had kept our distance almost fearing rejection.

I told him how ill I felt, how listless and depressed. At one point I even found the energy to cry, such was my state of melancholia. Peter, dressed like a prince which is a strange comparison but the one which came readily to mind, extended a perfectly manicured hand and gestured that I should take it and follow him. Hardly having been out of bed for weeks on end, I felt strangely compelled to obey his silent command. I remember he led me to a dusty window where we both stared at the roofs of terraced houses and church towers. Peter told me I was looking at the whole world, staring at life and I must walk amongst it and take my part.

The damn fool thing was; I did exactly as he told me.

For some weeks, Kit had been pressing me to leave the hospital, as had the others. Dominic, who usually claimed my attention and bent my will, had also begged me to rally myself and go home but his pleas had swayed me not at all. One sentence from Peter and I was almost leaping into my outdoor clothes.

And that was the begining of my recoverey.

It was Peter who took me home. Driving an expensive Bristol, hand built motor car, he drove with concentrated precision through country lanes towards Borough Heath.

'You don't have to go home if you don't want to,' he said.

'Where else would I go?'

'Anywhere you want,' he said.

'I would be popular,' I smiled. 'Three small children and a doctor's surgery to run. I would be hunted down like an escaped convict.'

'You can do whatever you want, Vinnie,' he said. 'I do.'

And so it was that I resumed my normal life and soon became besotted with Anna. Much to our surprise Peter returned to the farm. He never asked Teddy if he may. No courtesy was extended to Isabel, whom presumably, was to cook and clean for him. Peter simply unlocked his old playroom and slept in what had once been my bedroom. Sometimes he would take his car and drive away, never saying where he was going or when he would return. We satisfied ourselves that these mysterious absences signified a new commission and we justified the days and nights he spent locked away in the upper rooms of the farm, as time devoted to painting masterpieces.

But he kept an eye on me.

When I least expected it, he would arrive by his old way of the kitchen door and watch me as I tended Anna or went about my domestic chores. If Kit was about he would usually give a curt nod of his head and disappear but when the two of us were alone, he would admire the baby and ask questions about her health and habits.

'You'll be married yourself one day and have babies of your own,' I told him.

'How do you know whether you'll like them or not?'

'What, like your own babies?'

'Suppose you didn't?'

'Why on earth wouldn't you?'

'Because they might not appeal to you.'

'What a strange thing to say.'

But Peter was strange. Whether, because he was possessed of genius or because he had suffered a lonely childhood, I can not say, but strange he was and I had to accept it.

Then Dominic and his partner Brian Thorn threw a party. It was to celebrate the opening of a small private hospital which they had funded and intended to run as a closed cardiac unit for the wealthy.

At first, Kit refused to go.

'I don't agree with it, Vinnie,' he told me. 'It's pandering to the chosen few. If Dom sees himself as a great heart specialist then he should administer to everyone. This lining his own pockets makes me sick not to mention his obscene affair with that partner of his.'

Of course I was not naïve; it had often occurred to me that Dominic and Brian were more than business or medical partners but the law had only just been changed and most people still regarded homosexuals in much the same way as they regarded lepers. I may say I wasn't amongst them but I shied away from expressing an opinion as, fifty years ago, such things were not open for discussion.

Kit took me to the party because, as the saying goes, I twisted his arm. Teddy was quite keen because he hadn't, at that time, seen the opulent house which Dominic and Brian Thorn shared in Tettenhall. Kit was lucky enough to have found a reliable locum for the evening and even luckier to discover that he had a grown daughter who agreed to watch the children so the evening of the party promised freedom from worry, good food and pleasant company.

On the way over, for we all piled into Teddy's old Ford Cortina, someone asked if Peter would be there. I said I thought it unlikely as he had been away for over a month so it was doubtful he knew anything about it.

'Dom would have invited him,' Isabel said.

'Of course he would,' I agreed, 'but how would he would he know where to send the invitiation?'

'That's true,' said Teddy, who added.' His kind of money's made a devil of a difference to the farm. Last month he gave me a cheque which I shall use to have the milking parlour revamped and the roof fixed.'

'He can afford it,' Kit said, moodily.

'Funny, isn't it?' Teddy continued. 'We were all brought up on the fat of the land thanks to poor old Ma's money but only Dom and Peter have done much good since. I'm always short and Kit works like a dog for bloody peanuts.'

Sitting in the back next to Kit, I felt his body tense as he prepared to critisize both my wealthy brothers. Dominic because he felt he made his fortune by pandering to the rich and Peter simply because he disliked him. I pushed two fingers into his side reminding him that we were supposed to be enjoying an evening free from tension or arguments.

Never having met Brian Thorn before I had no preconceived ideas about him. To be honest, (a silly expression for why would I be otherwise?) I had seldom thought about him at all; probably because I found his relationship with Dominic confusing.

Dominic met us in his long and lovely hallway. Naturally he made much of us, hugging and kissing me and shaking Teddy's and Kit's hand in welcome. Isabel he also kissed and escorted to an oak panelled cloakroom where she and I left our coats. I asked him if we could have a quick tour of the house and he said to "help ourselves," adding that he would like to be our guide but that guests were arriving and he needed to be on hand to do the honours.

Isabel and I, behaving like giggling schoolgirls, were excited at the prospect of being let loose in such a lavish house. Opening doors and viewing beautifully furnished rooms, we marvelled at Dominic's taste and obvious wealth for his home was indeed stunning.

The house of anyone's dreams!

Crossing a huge square landing we opened a bevelled glass door that led to what we considered to be the master bedroom and, still in our 'Alice in Wonderland' mode, we crept inside. Luckily our sense of awe imitated nervousness which, in turn, made us tip toe into the room. Sinking into a white Persian carpet we viewed ourselves in full length mirrors and admired a collection of original oil paintings which hung on what appeared to be an entrance lobby leading into the main body of the room. Again good fortune dogged our footsteps because, by virtue of the images reflected in the plentiful mirrors, we were able to halt further progress and depart in haste.

A huge overhead mirror reflected a tableux showing a four poster bed, draped in blue velvet covers, on which a naked Peter, entwined in the arms of an equally naked Laura Bonnington, were making love.

The situation requiring no comment from either of us so, although stunned, we turned tail and bid a hasty retreat. I don't think either Isabel or myself were prude enough to be shocked by the sight of two healthy young people engaged in what, not so very long ago, would have been considered a wicked act. My shock, for shock it certainly was, lay in the fact that Peter was using his brother's bedroom for such a purpose with a girl whom I thought he had rudely dismissed from his life a long time ago.

Some distance removed, on quite another landing, we paused to whisper comments concerning the scene we had just witnessed.

'So obviously he was invited,' said Isabel.

'He could have been staying with Dom for all we know.'

'How did she get here?'

'God knows.'

'Bet old Bonnington would have a stroke if he knew what she was up to.'

'I thought that affair was over and done with years ago,' said I.

'It was. Laura didn't speak to him after he dropped her.'

'Well, she's obviously speaking now.'

We were embarrassed and full of curiosity but we promised each other that we wouldn't mention anything to our respective husbands as it was none of our business. Peter was now considered mature and Laura over twenty one but the astonishment sustained by our discovery put an end to further sight seeing.

And so did the sudden presence of a strange man who appeared as if from nowhere.

'What the hell are you doing?' the man asked.

'I am Mrs. Barry, Dominic's sister,' I told him, 'and this is my sister in law, Isabel MacVee.'

'I didn't ask who you were. I asked what you were doing?' he thundered.

Isabel cowered at the outburst. The man, whom I took to be Brian Thorn, would have been disturbing at the best of times. A veritable giant of a man with a swarthy complexion, he stood well over six feet tall and possessed the physique of a prize fighter. His approach could only be described as menacing and I could see that our unexpected presence had filled him with rage.

'You must blame your partner.' I decided to offer apologies in an attempt to placate him. 'Dominic invited us to view your spendid home and we are admiring it with envy.'

At that point, I wasn't one hundred percent sure that the man was Thorn or that he shared the house but it was an educated guess and one that was to be proved correct.

'What's he think it is,' roared the man, 'a bloody side show to be trampled all over by common day trippers?'

With that unpleasant remark he departed.

'We better go downstairs,' I stated the obvious. 'Not the sort of chap I would want to upset twice.'

'How simply horrid.' Isabel was visibly upset. I could feel her trembling as her body touched mine.

'I shall tell Dom,' I took her hand. 'Beastly creature, I suppose we surprised him but that was unforgivable.'

It was at that point when we heard the noise.

Noise? It was the sound and fury of an uproar and it came

from the room where we had just seen Peter and Laura. A room we supposed to be the master bedroom and therefore Dominic's and the awful Brian's room.

To attempt a description of the subsequent scene is almost an impossibility. Men's voices raised to a roar and a woman's screams told their own story. Obviously Thorn had been bound for his bedroom when he bumped into us and, on reaching it, had discovered the naked lovers using his bed as a honeymoon suit.

Having already witnessed his mood and judged him to be a violent character, the cursing and commotion, which filled the whole house, was not unexpected. In the fleeting moments before further action took place I cursed Peter for behaving like a fool. Taking a girl to another man's room, knowing his stupid act stood every chance of exposure and yet seemingly not giving a damn, had wrought havoc.

"I do whatever I want, Vinnie."

How well I recalled the words he had used as we drove home from Stafford Infirmary! Well this time 'doing what he wanted' had literally brought the house down.

There are rows, disputes call them what you will, that are unpleasant, frightening even but something told me this one was dangerous. It had gone beyond the realms of a violent quarrel and, from our corner of the lower landing, I could hear the sounds of a full blown fight.

'I'm going to fetch Dom and Teddy,' I told Isabel.

'Don't leave me,' she quivered.

Poor Isabel was petrified but I knew I must fetch the men so that matters could be calmed before either Peter, Laura or the foul Brian Thorn got seriously hurt. As we hastened down the ornate staircase, we met Dominic, Teddy and Kit rushing towards us.

'What the hell's going on?' Teddy asked.

Briefly I explained.

'Bloody little fool,' Teddy exclaimed. 'Lead on Dom we've

got to put a stop to that shindig.'

'Brian's got a foul temper when he's upset.' Dominic told us what we already knew.

Once Isabel was in the hall, I more or less abandoned her. There was no one nearby that we knew but I felt she would be safer on the ground floor. For myself, all I wanted was to dash back to that bedroom to make sure the men weren't attempting to kill each other.

Which they were.

Or, at least, the brutish Brian was certainly giving a good impression of doing so as he had his hands around Peter's throat. Not being apt when it comes to estimating measurements, I cannot say what the dimensions of that room would be but they were vast. The distance from the door to the bed reminded me of a hotel corridor or the length of a coach on an express train. There were three doors leading from the room. One, I assumed led to a bathroom another to a dressing room and the third, a sliding door, opened onto a balcony. This balcony or parapet projected from the south wall of the house and overlooked a magnificent garden many feet below. It was through this door that Brian Thorn had dragged Peter and on this balcony that he was holding him in a vice like grip.

Heart racing I stood, rooted to a spot on the Persian carpet, wondering what Dominic could do to persuade his partner, lover or whatever he was, to release our brother and step back into the safety of the bedroom.

Teddy, white and shaking, shouted, 'Don't be a fool. Let the boy go.'

Dominic approached the balcony but it was Kit who really thew caution to the wind and actually went out onto the little parapet to seize Brian.

'Be careful,' I shouted in the way people say silly things such as 'Don't get wet' when they see someone venture out in a rainstorm.

'Leave the brat to me,' Brian raged.

'Brian, be reasonable.' This from Dominic, who strode closer to the sliding door but made no move to go through it.

'Randy swine,' Brian added to some other less than choice remarks.

There was nothing Peter could say. His throat was so constricted that words were denied but he must have been terrified. Idiot, he might have been but my heart went out to him for, surely, no one deserved such ferocious treatment for a transgression that was brainless and disgraceful but neither criminal nor destructive. Brian Thorn, I thought insane but there was nothing I could do except tentatively move towards Laura who was still huddled on the bed. She must have been grateful for my approach for she threw herself into my arms and sobbed. I felt more like smacking her than returning the hug but the situation was worrisome enough without a show of violence on my part.

Clearly I remember shutting my eyes in an effort to block visions of Peter either falling or being thrown from the balcony. Holding Laura, I told myself that such monstrous fears were absurd as no one would commit a murder for such a mild offence. Trying to take comfort from the fact that Dominic was also on the balcony, aiding Kit to gain Peter's freedom, did little to calm my fears. That balcony was too high for heroics and all I could do was shout meaningless phrases along the lines of, 'For God's sake, stop it.'

The actual second in which it happened I did not personally witness as my head was buried in Laura's hair and, I'm ashamed to say, we were both crying. Some few years earlier, when John was at the toddling stage, he had wandered some distance from my side in Borough Heath Park. On unsteady feet, I remembered him tottering headlong towards the boating lake and instead of rushing to rescue him I had shut my eyes and prayed. My prayer was answered in the guise of an elderly gentleman who grabbed him by his collar and plonked him down on the grass beside me. At that moment of equal terror I recalled holding John in my arms as the old man gave me a well deserved lecture on the proper care of small children!

Suddenly Peter too was in my arms. How he had managed to get free, I had no idea but I grabbed him much as I had grabbed my infant son all those years before. The three of us, Laura, Peter and myself held tightly to each other and our individual trembles merged into an almighty shake which racked our bodies.

And then there was a long piercing scream

Kit it was who had played the hero but it was Dominic who paid the price for, during the fury of the fight Kit had either lost his balance or been pushed from the safety of the balcony onto a ledge which ran some seven or eight feet beneath the iron railings that surrounded it. Our shrieks of terror were premature as Kit, very much alive, managed to cling on to the lead guttering which was secured to the underside of the parapet.

It was from there that Dominic, lying flat on his belly, attempted to rescue him. Brother and husband resembled circus acrobats as they hung, suspended high above ground level, clutching onto each other's hands. One trying to climb to safety and the other striving to lift him but, strong as he was, Dominic failed to lever Kit even as much as one inch. A combination of gravity, and Kit's substantial weight, threatened to pull him down. Teddy, Peter and I watched helplessly as the drama worsened, only Brian Thorn, with a look of something approaching satisfaction, walked calmly from the scene.

We all gripped Dominic. I rushed to hold onto his leg and Peter, the strongest of us all, grabbed him round the waist. Teddy took his other leg and we all tugged his body as he, in turn, tried to haul the weight of Kit's body upwards.

Dominic was successful. The effort was enormous but eventually, dripping in sweat, Kit successfully manoeuvred his body onto the edge of the parapet and hurled himself into the safety of the bedroom. But, in his final struggle to gain a foothold, the iron railings, which surrounded the perimeter of the balcony, snapped as though made of ice, leaving a six foot gap and a thirty foot drop to the flagstones below. And somewhere in the following dreadful seconds, Dominic, leaning too near the edge lost both his grip and his balance and fell over the then unprotected parapet.

Kit was rescued, Peter, Teddy and I unscathed but Dominic lay all those feet below and none of us knew whether he was alive or dead.

Chapter Eighteen

P an has been with me for exactly forty seven years.
I had no idea it was so long but obviously she would know
for such anniversaries mark the progress of our lives. She came
to this house when Dominic returned from Germany. At the
time we thought it necessary to employ someone who could
help us look after him but that was in nineteen sixty three and,
during the last five years, she has had only me to serve.

Where else would she go?

Her work here is far from demanding as I have a cleaning
woman called Mrs. Grafton who competes with what Pan calls,
'the heavy work.' I have the latest washing machine, dishwasher
and vaccum cleaner infact I have the latest everything in the
way of labour saving devices. Never having used modern
technology myself I can not say how such things are of benefit
but Pan offers few complaints. She misses Dom as do we all
and, although she hardly ever mentions him, I know she
grieves for the loss of Kit.

The fall, as you will have gathered, did not kill Dominic but
there were times when he must have wished it had. If I shut my
eyes, even lightly, the terrors of that evening in Tettenhall

come vividly to my mind and I relive each appalling moment as if I were watching a slow motion video tape.

The sound of his body crashing onto those falgstones can never be forgotten. Had a mighty tree fallen the noise could not have been more thunderous. Guests enjoying the party, three stories below, rushed in horror to see what had happened but few could bring themselves to stand and look and I recall more than half a dozen people fainting.

Peter, Teddy, Kit and I, hardly able to breath, raced down to the garden expecting to discover not our beloved Dominic but only his broken body. Laura Bonnington, to terrified to move, was left behind in that eerie room. It was Isabel, we discovered later, who finally managed to persuade her to leave her hiding place beneath the velvet quilt and go downstairs.

Dominic survived but at a terrible price. His face was smashed beyond recognition, several teeth were scattered yards from where he lay. His right arm was twisted beneath his body and both legs were broken. Injuries, almost beyond the capacity of the human body to sustain, refused to let him die. Of course Kit braced himself in an effort to alleviate his sufferings but he was a family doctor not a magician so there was next to nothing he could do. Finally the ambulance, which Teddy had summoned, arrived. The paramedics, although deeply distressed themselves, were marvellous for such an appalling accident could hardly be described as an every day occurrence. Tenderly placing him on a stretcher, they told us they would take him to the Queen Elizabeth Hospital in Edgbaston, Birmingham.

Teddy, when he had finally ushered the last of the stunned guests from the house, joined the rest of us to watch the ambulance drive away. Taking advantage of someone's kind offer to lend them a car, Kit and he then elected to follow it. Isabel, Laura, and I were driven back to Borough Heath by Peter.

Conversation, on that dreadful journey home, was limited

but our thoughts were centred on one man who, strangely enough, was not Dominic but Brian Thorn. Where he had gone and what he had done were the sole topics for what remained of the evening. Isabel was emphatic that the police should be called but Peter disagreed and I too was doubtful.

'How can we prove it?' I asked the others.

'You were all witnesses,' Isabel reminded me. 'You can tell the police how he attacked Peter; how Dom and Kit intervened and how that monster caused him to fall over the parapet.'

'And he will say it was just an accident,' Peter added.

At one point blame was hurled at Peter and Laura for their part in causing the tragedy but I think we all knew it was to late for recriminations. No amount of fury could undo what had happened and, just for once, Peter showed a modicum of contrition and Laura cried copiously. When we reached home, I phoned Samuel Bonnington and gave him a brief account of the disastrous events after which, thankfully, he came and collected Laura. When she left we all kissed her as, that night, she had suffered almost as much as the rest of us.

Brian Thorn was never publically punished or brought to justice. Peter was probably right in persuading us that he would claim it was an accident and I, for one, thought the less scandal brought to our family the better for all of us, especially the children.

Dominic remained in the QE 2 hospital for eight agonising months. One thing in his favour, and it was but a single blessing, was the fact that his proffessional standing inspired the medical team to extra dilligence when it came to his treatment and care.

The fall blinded him.

Medical details, describing his injuries, filled bulging files for that was at a time before computers stored such information. Almost every bone in his body was either broken or wrecked by hairline fractures. His right leg had to be amputated and so did three fingers from his right hand.

Operations were done one by one. A recoverey from one would mean he was strong enough to sustain another and so it went on. Speech was impossible as his jaw and upper palette were both shattered so odd grunts and incoherent mutterings were all that he could muster. Those once handsome features existed no longer and it was with intense pain that I stared at my darling brother. Since his head had taken the brunt of the fall, I avoided looking into his poor ruined face. His nose was almost obliterated, his top lip peeled away and his cheek bones smashed to ribbons but, worst of all, was the milky hue of those unseeing eyes.

We all feared the doctors were working to restore a cabbage. Twice Teddy told the medical team, who were doing all in their power to save him, that none of us wanted him to live merely for the sake of it. Kit predicted that Dominic would never speak again which echoed my own opinion that, even should a miracle occur and he managed to do so, the outcome would only amount to gibberish as we feared he had suffered massive brain damage.

Innumerable x-rays we taken and eminent men gave their various opinions as to his condition. Prognosis seemed in favour of survival but quality of life remained doubtful. Some of the doctors were optimistic, telling us he would eventually be able to communicate but others sighed and explained that even if a partial recovery took place he would never be able to leave either a hospital or a nursing home which provided round the clock care.

Kit was my support as I was Teddy's. Peter lingered moodily in Borough Heath for the first six weeks after the accident and then drove away without leaving a forwarding address or even a phone number. Gradually the daily visits had to cease because with three young children and Kit's practise, I just couldn't spare the time to travel to Birmingham every day to sit by a bedside where nothing could be achieved. Teddy, as usual, frantic with the farm and Isabel busy looking after

Michael and the now, far too large farm house, also gave up on frequent visits.

The seventies brought a new style of living to England. Old values went out of the window. Decimalisation changed the value of money over night, formal religion declined and immigrants from the commonwealth poured into the Midlands. Pop stars became more familier than the royal family and the celebrity culture, not as overwhelming as it is today but startling even in its infancy, began to excite the minds of the young. Everyone expected great things for themselves. Their rights became their needs and those needs required instant gratification.

One Sunday afternoon in the beginning of June, Kit and I made one of our all too rare visits to the hospital to see Dominic. I recall it being one of those early days of summer when a heat wave seems just around the corner and all thoughts of rain and cold disappear as if forever. We took John because he missed his Uncle Dom more than the younger ones and we thought, at eight years old, it might be a good idea to let him see for himself why his uncle could no longer take him for walks or play with him in the park. We were wrong of course but the visit had a reward of sorts in so much as John's screams on seeing Dominic, disfigured, immobile and snorting like one of the animals on Uncle Teddy's farm, produced an unexpected result.

Seeing his distress, Kit seized him and hurried him away before both he and Dominic became even more distraught. Sitting alone by his bed, I took Dom's good hand and wondered if his reaction signified more than the demented cries of a damaged mind. Dom, I thought was responding. He was trying to tell us to take the little boy away; under all those bandages and grafted skin, a sharp brain was trying to communicate. Dominic was plainly telling us that John must not be subjected to such a sight.

Kit thought the idea absurd.

'He doesn't know any of us,' he told me. 'Poor Dom, he can't see, he can't move, he can't even feed himself. What's the point of him carrying on?'

'I'm sure he recognised John's voice,' I said. 'He knows it's us. He's known all along but how can we prove it?'

Over the summer months, I visited regularly for I was convinced his mind was undamaged and it would be possible to get through to him if only I persevered. The doctors were adamant that my assumption was wrong and, apart from very basic care, I began to understand that the medical staff had written him off. He was alive, saved from certain death but brought back to a twilight world where he knew nothing of his past and had no expectations of a future.

During each visit I spent an hour, or sometimes longer, holding his, more or less, intact left hand at the same time uttering that old cliché along the lines of, 'Press my hand once for yes and twice for no.' You will have seen it portrayed in films or know of similar cases where people have responded. Nothing of note occurred for over a month but because I was so certain that the old Dom existed somewhere beneath the bandages I had persuaded Kit to buy a second car so that I could make the twenty nine mile round trip whenever a free afternoon presented itself.

It was mid August before I gained my reward.

'Are you in any pain?' I asked. It was a question that haunted my mind. Dom, even given that his injuries had altered and twisted every feature, had the look of someone who suffered constant pain.

No single or double pressure on my hand confirmed or negated my question. Now and again he twitched and sighed which confirmed my fears so I persisted with that same query for some five minutes.

Only to feel one sharp stab in the palm of my hand.

My hand which held his left good hand.

Dom had agreed. He had communicated. He had said, 'Yes'

he did have pain so I asked if he wanted medication. The long finger nails dug once more into my palm so I marched to the nurse's station, in the main ward, and asked for two paracetamol. A plain extremely thin nurse looked at me as though I belonged in the psychiatric unit.

'Your brother's Dominic MacVee, isn't he?' she asked, tartly.

'In the side ward, yes,' I said, adding, 'and he's in great pain. Will you give him some pain killers right away?'

'I'm afraid we have no idea if he's still in pain or not,' she shrugged. 'At first we knew he must be but now, although it's difficult to keep him comfortable, we think it unlikely that he suffers severe pain. I dare say he's sore but we really can't keep dosing him, it will affect his digestive system.'

Even that stupid nurse must have realised her opinion was banal for what if he was further affected by a handful of paracetamol? Surely nothing so trivial could possibly disturb his broken body and if it did, what would it matter? But I was lucky in so much as a doctor happened to wander onto the ward. He was known to me and a friend of Kit's so I told him that Dominic was in pain and naturally he was interested to discover how I had reached such a conclusion.

'He could hardly have told you, Vinnie,' he said. 'Is it just your opinion?'

'No, Dom told me.'

'But he can't speak and often he looks distressed, which I expect he is, but he's not suffereing anymore, we're convinced of that,' he finished rather proudly.

But I persisted. I told him why I was sure and he came with me to Dominic's small side room. There I gave him a demonstration of my hand holding routine and because he was an intelligent man and open to believe the impossible he took Dom's hand himself and plied him with questions. Some were answered by one clench of the hand, some by two and many ignored.

'Let's give him some pain killers and see if he responds,' he said.

A nurse was summoned and she arrived carrying a glass of white cloudy water which I took to be a dose of crushed aspirin or paracetamol. Holding it to, what remained of my brother's lips, she gently enabled him to swallow the mixture. Ten minutes later Dom's hand relaxed in mine and I knew the pain had eased. My friendly doctor studied him and agreed that he must have been soothed by the medication and that was the start of many such medical men and women discovering for themselves that Dominic was in his right mind and able to communicate.

I was ecstatic.

Kit, when I told him, shook his head and looked gloomy. 'Poor Dom,' he said. 'My one comfort throughout this whole horrible nightmare has been in my belief that he knows nothing about it. Now you tell me he may be aware of everything that's happened and I feel bloody terrible.'

'Yes, but we can work from here, Kit,' I explained. 'Now that I'm sure he knows who he is, who we are and where he is perhaps he can help to plan his future instead of us and the doctors planning it for him.'

'Perhaps he wants to die.'

'Perhaps he does but he won't. Surely we can make some kind of life for him?'

'We can put him in the best nursing home money can buy, or at least, we could if we had that kind of money otherwise I can't think what we can do for him.'

'We can ask him.'

'And he can tell us by gripping our hands how much he hates us for allowing him to live.'

'No, Dom will still have spirit, I know he will. Perhaps something more can be done to help him.'

Kit, as usual, walked away. I knew neither he nor Teddy would be interested in trying to map out any kind of future for

Dominic; they both thought he would be better off dead and I think Isabel was of the same opinion.

Peter returned from his travels during the following week and thought differently. He listened as only Peter could listen. Possessed of few words himself he might have been, but his capacity to listen to mine were unequalled. Excitedly, I told him that Dom's mind was intact and that with all my heart I wanted to help him to find some sort of life away from the hospital. I rambled on about pretty cottages with peaceful gardens where he could sit with a nurse on summer days. Where he could listen to the new cassette players which were the latest 'must have' in home entertainment. Talking books and classical music, I suggested, could fill his empty hours and the children could visit when they were older and wheel his chair along country lanes. In almost one breath I converted my poor brother's life into some idyllic Hollywood film script or 'happy ever after' story where the sun shone all day and everything was perfection.

'We could get him over to Berlin,' said Peter, in his usual bored monotone. 'Chap over there does this cosmetic surgery. He could rebuild him, Vin.'

'Rebuild him?' My mind was still in 'picture book romance' mode. It was a wonder I wasn't planning a June wedding with Dom marrying his young and pretty nurse, so sentimental had the knowledge of his awareness made me.

'Same surgeon who worked on an airman I painted a mural for. Crash took half his face away but he's been seen to by this bloke and he looks almost normal now.'

'What bloke?'

'A German. You wouldn't object to a German fitting up old Dom would you, Vin?'

'Cause not.'

'I'll see about it then.'

'But it would cost a fortune and how would we get him there?'

'By plane and I'd pay,' said Peter who, for him, had chatted long enough.

Of course it wasn't as simple as that. Peter, by this time, was a very wealthy man but the idea of moving Dominic, especially to another country, presented a huge problem. At first the medical team, who had worked so hard to pull him through the worst of his ordeal, were against any movement. There were all sorts of arguments for leaving 'well alone.'

The leading surgeon, who had performed most of Dominic's operations, came to see us one wet afternoon in September when we all sitting round Dom's bed and said, 'Mr. MacVee, I think if you take your brother away from here serious consequences may arise.'

Since he addressed Teddy, I didn't butt in with the answer which instantly occurred to me. How could Dom be further affected; his life wasn't worth living as it was? Surely any alternative was worth a try in an attempt to make it more bearable if only slightly so?

Teddy nodded agreeing that the doctor was probably right.

I fumed, nudging Kit to intervene and tell the bloody doctor that we loved Dom and only sought to improve what was left of his life. Kit whispered back that he, too, tended to side with the surgeon and what was more it was obvious that neither Teddy, Isabel nor Kit wanted to take responsibility for the move. At least they could stay their consciences by making infrequent visits to his bedside but man handling Dominic in the outside world was obviously beyond the pail as far as any of them were concerned.

I was dejected that afternoon. Winter was looming and our visits, in the coming months, would be hampered by bad weather, then Christmas would begin to occupy our minds and poor Dom would literally rot in that hospital.

Undeterred, I continued with my weekly visits and 'spoke' to Dominic through the hand signals. Now that he had grown accustomed to the routine his answers were speedy. When I told him there was a possibility that further treatment could be carried out, he showed enthusiasum. Pressure digs into the palm of my hand were almost always of a positive nature and the one press for 'yes' dominated our conversations so, as the weeks went by, my determination increased.

Everything, it seemed to me, depended upon Peter. Kit refused to even discuss transferring Dom and Teddy hardly bothered to voice an opinion. Peter, by this time, had disappeared once again and none of us had any inkling as to where we might find him but, just when I had almost given up hope, the back door opened and all six feet two inches of him appeared in the kitchen, frightening the life out of me.

'Where have you been?' I shakily, asked.

'Working,' he said.

'But I've been trying to find you. Why don't you ever bother to contact us?'

'What do you want?' Was the sullen reply.

Criticising Peter never resulted in anything other than a glowering response so I contented myself that he was actually standing in front of me which meant that discussions as to how it might be possible to move Dominic from an English hospital to a German one could begin.

But Peter was ahead of me in more ways than one. No discussions were needed; no complicated plans had to be agreed as he had arranged every detail of our brother's transfer to his German surgeon and he had done it immaculately.

Even Kit, Teddy and Isabel, who had thought themselves immune to such an idea, fell into line and within a week the whole family were talking of little else. Peter, reluctant to speak to anyone other than myself, turned me into something approaching an interpreter. Being the doctor amongst us, Kit made dozens of phone calls to Germany to explain details of Dominic's needs and a firm liaison was established between his Birmingham doctors and a Mr. Schell in Berlin. What constituted Dom's needs were difficult to define for where did one start? A semi-paralised blind man minus his right leg plus three fingers from his right hand not to mention a severely damaged spine and horrendous facial injuries. What did we identify as his immediate requirements?

Mr. Schell, during these many phone calls, enthused about Peter and his amazing talent but when it came to discussing Dominic, he was less than optimistic.

'Ask him if he'll come to England and see Dom for himself?' I suggested to Kit.

Many such calls later, Mr. Schell agreed to assist in any way he felt appropriate provided Peter, in return, would paint a mural in his apartment in Berlin. However he added that it would be well into the new year before he could spare the time to fly to England and even then, he told Kit, he couldn't promise any miracles as the case sounded very bad.

'But not hopless?' Kit asked.

'Nothing in this life is hopless,' he said. 'All things are possible but some are are less possible than others.'

Christmas, that year, was overshadowed by our various hopes and fears for Dominic. During lunch at the farm, I had to leave the table when my mind replayed a picture of the festive table only one year previously. Dominic had headed the family then and now he lay, unvisited, in a dismal side ward fifteen miles away. My tears would have distressed the children but my heart was with my eldest brother and I felt wretched that on this, the most family orientated day of the whole year, we were separated.

'He won't know it's bloody Christmas,' Teddy said. 'Wish he could be here even if it involved a wheel chair and a stack of bloody pills but, Vinnie, he can't see and probably can't hear very well either, I mean he never moves his head when we speak or go into his room.'

'He knew John cried the day we took him over.'

'Probably sensed something was wrong. They do you know?'

'Who do?' His observation annoyed me intensely. Already Teddy and Kit, together with several of our friends, had started classing Dominic as a lunatic; many had ceased their enquiries concerning his welfare completely. I knew Dom was as sane as myself but what was the use of that if we sentenced him to a life confined to a hospital bed?

But towards the middle of January, nineteen seventy one, Mr. Schell arrived from Berlin. He didn't come alone, two other medical men accompanied him. One was an eye surgeon called Max Hueber, the other, a younger doctor with stooping shoulders called Kaufman; Doctor Lukas Kaufman, an expert on skin grafting and artificial limbs. All spoke impeccable English so we were spared the toil of translating our woes into some sort of pigeon German.

Mr. Schell was indeed charming and lavish in his praise of Peter whose absence from our welcoming party disappointed him no end. On our way back from Birmingham Airport, which was then called 'Elmdon,' Kit chatted to Lukas Kaufman, telling him of our own expertise in the field of prosthetic limbs. Kaufman was well aware of Kit's nationalistic enthusiasm as he had completed his own training at Queen Mary's Hospital, Roehampton. That fact alone cheered my husband whom, I might add, had many reservations concerning this foreign medical team.

We did not hasten to Dominic's bedside as, although their journey had not been arduous, Teddy thought etiquette demanded the provision of hospitality at the farm before Dom was either visited or assessed. Mr. Schell appeared delighted with this diversion and everybody entered into something approaching a party spirit once we were all seated round the dinner table.

Everyone but me.

I couldn't wait to move this collection of medical geniuses to Birmingham so that Dom might be given immediate hope. The delay was particularly frustrating as Kit, Teddy and Isabel seemed hell bent on plying our guests with home made wine which made me realise that, within the hour, no one would be in a fit state to drive let alone pass judgement on my brother.

It was not until the following morning that I was able to escort the three doctors to the Queen Elizabeth Hospital. Almost at the last minute, Kit, who was interested if not optimistic, had to remain at home as one of his patients suffered a touch and go heart attack in his surgery. The ensuing drama obviously delayed the rest of the morning's schedule so with Teddy, busy in the milking parlour, and Isabel never displaying any intention of accompanying us in the first place, I was left to cope with the rush hour traffic and the three doctors all on my own. As I made slow progress down the Hagley Road towards Edgbaston Mr. Schell and Lukas Kaufman both told me that they had visited the hospital before but Max Hueber, the eye man, looked in wonder at the new buildings which rose on either side of the Bristol and Hagley Roads. Apparently he had dreaded coming to England principally on account of the fact that his sister had told him Birmingham was the most depressing city she had ever visited in her entire life. Since she worked as a tour guide exclusively in the UK, he had every reason to believe she would know what she was talking about. The new buildings and the wide tree lined streets came as a pleasant surprise and he seemed overjoyed to be able to disprove her opinion.

It was the first time I had been to the hospital at such an early hour so I had no idea of the routine to which Dominic was subjected every morning. When the nursing staff learnt that the men standing by my side were doctors they said they would hurry their administrations but it would still be in the region of twenty minutes to half an hour before we could see him.

Two hospital doctors appeared, each carrying, what looked like, the manuscript of 'Gone with the Wind,' such was the thickness of the type-written pages enclosed in their orange folders. Mr. Schell, who by this time I was calling Nick, and his two colleagues were invited to accompany them to an empty cubicle where they could discuss the case. I was left in the bleak corridor listening to cries of distress coming from my brother's room, where obviously any pressure on his wrecked body caused intense pain.

After, what seemed like an age, the nurses who had inflicted such unintentional agony, re-appeared in the corridor, gave me a weak smile and said I could go into his room as their work was finished. The others, I knew would have much to discuss so I went in to see Dominic who, by this time was sitting, propped up by a green plastic cushion, and looking the picture of misery.

I kissed him and told him the reason for my early visit. It would be a flight of fancy on my part to say that he displayed any enthusiasm. For one thing he was unable to move his facial muscles so a smile would have been impossible, but when he gripped my hand he pressed it hard and held onto it in a manner which I interpreted as pleasure. Patiently I told him that we were planning further treatment but it would mean leaving the QE2 and travelling to Berlin. Dominic did not respond to my news but I had the feeling he was wondering how such a trip could be achieved. I explained that Peter was now a wealthy man and had the financial means to charter a plane and pay for medical staff to fly with him. On hearing that the journey would be trouble free, Dom appeared to relax. Since he also gave the impression of being mystified, I explained Peter's success in the art world and told him how much in demand he now was. No doubt, due to the trauma, Dominic had forgotten any previous history regarding our younger brother for, as I described his murals and his travelling, he took a keen interest and whether it was my imagination or not, I thought he looked happy.

When the doctors returned, I left them alone. For one thing there were five of them and Dom's ward was so tiny that had I attempted to remain I would not only have been in the way but probably crushed into the bargain. Taking myself further down the corridor I found a rest area where I could buy a cup of coffee and there I waited for news of further developments.

It was to be a long wait and several cups of coffee were bought, half drunk or just ignored as nerves played havoc with my reasoning. The 'what if' syndrome mounted in my mind. What if these German surgeons had travelled in vain? What if the hospital medics had shown them x-rays and notes which proved that further operations or treatments of any kind would be useless? What if they had already decided that Dom was beyond their help or that his case was hopeless?

The longer my stay in the coffee drinking area the more my imagination played mayhem with my hopes. Visualising the doctors' return, I prepared myself for their sympathetic regrets as they explained they were unable to aid him further. They would add that oft heard platitude along the lines of: "Medical science is advancing daily and new techniques plus wonder drugs are just around the corner, so you mustn't give up hope." That was something I was perpetually told but just what magicians were involved in these mystery discoveries and promised 'cure-alls', I never discovered.

So often in life, our worst fears are proved groundless. 'The valiant never taste of death but once', was a favourite saying of Kits' and, that morning, in Birmingham I thought it to be true. For over two hours I had worried myself sick that Dominic would be written off and consigned to some medical scrap heap when that was far from what was to happen.

Doctors Schell, Kaufman and Hueber together with his own doctors at the QE2 were optimistic that the journey to Berlin, far from constituting a waste of time, could be of enormous benefit. They were adamant that nothing more could be accomplished where he was but enthused at the idea of Mr. Schell and his team affecting an improvement. So it was that Dominic was transferred to a private clinic two miles north of Berlin and work began on, what I can only call, his restoration.

Ten months after the appalling tragedy when, although our hopes were high for his eventual recovery, we still harboured intense bitterness towards Brian Thorn. Hardly a day went by without one or the other of us mentioning his name and cursing his existence. What had happened to Dom, we still referred to as 'the accident' but, of course, we all knew the truth and longed to see justice done.

Quite late one Sunday evening, Teddy rang to ask if we had seen the News at Ten on television? Kit, who took the call, said we hadn't been watching so what had we missed?.

Teddy said he thought not or we would have rung the farm to tell him. Apparently Isabel, the only member of the family who had been watching, said that news of a fatal car crash had just been announced. The accident had apparently taken place on or near Finchley in north London and it had claimed the life of a heart specialist by the name of Brian Thorn. The news reader had appealed for anyone who had witnessed the accident to get in touch with the police as information was required to assist their investigation into the fatality.

'He's dead,' Teddy reported, almost gleefully. 'Brian Thorn's been killed outright near the bloody M1 motorway.'

'There is a God after all,' I said and who could blame me for my hatred of that man, even in death, was passionate.

Chapter Nineteen

D ominic was to remain in Germany for eighteen months, during which time Peter's daughter Venetia, was born. Being what I suppose you would call 'family minded' I was delighted. Peter had married Laura Bonnington only two months before the arrival and, we all knew, he had only done so because of the baby. Samuel Bonnington had publically threatened to shoot him if he didn't do the honourable thing although unmarried mothers were rapidly becoming acceptable and Bonnington could easily have afforded to care for his grandchild without incurring personal hardship. Since he also made a point of telling anyone who would listen how much he hated and loathed Peter MacVee, we could never grasp why he was so insistant on the marriage. Simple convention, I suppose.

I had no illusions regarding Peter's feelings towards Laura. I knew he didn't love her but then I also knew Peter would never love anyone. Perhaps it is true to say, that if he had an attachment to anybody, then it was to me but the special kind of love needed to make a marriage work was alien to him. Apart from his work, Peter was cold, devoid of sentiment and utterly self absorbed. None of which undesirable traits deterred me from crooning over my new born niece and offering my blessings for her blissful future.

Looking back I often wondered why Laura wanted to marry Peter. We all knew that, in spite of his appalling treatment, she had continued to pursue him. No doubt, never falling out of love, she remained full of determination to hunt him down despite her better instincts or her parent's wishes.

After the tragedy of Rose, Eleanor and Samuel Bonnington kept aloof from Borough Heath society. Clinging onto their remaining daughter they distanced themselves from the town's folk and the MacVee family in particular. But whenever Peter appeared either at my home or at the farm, Laura lost no time in presenting herself on his doorstep. If the pregnancy was, as we all believed, deliberately designed to trap him, then she must have congratulated herself on her success.

Anna was almost two years old when Venetia was born, Philip eight and John, almost thirteen. Teddy and Isabel's son Michael was eleven so, apart obviously from Dominic, we had all managed to produce children of our own. Sometimes I used to think of Ma and wish she could have lived to see her grandchildren; how surprised she would be to know that Peter had not only fathered a child but married someone who could be termed his childhood sweetheart.

But Peter had no intention of playing happy families, no sooner had he endured the wedding day and Laura's confinement, which he avoided as though she carried a latter day version of the plague, than he disappeared again. Laura cried for his absence and Bonnington cursed even louder. There was nothing any of us could say or do. When Peter packed his bags and drove his flashy car towards the skyline, we knew it could be months or even years before we set eyes on him again. As for a forwarding address or a contact number: forget it! Peter kept his private life, private and Laura had to accept it as did we all.

Then tragedy struck.

Samuel Bonnington, whom I had personally diagnosed as suffering high blood pressure, succumbed to a massive stroke and dropped dead at the Mid Borough Heath Colliery. Naturally, although non of us had cared for the man, we felt sorry for Laura and particularly for Eleanor. Samuel had been a mere fifty six and, even in the mid seventies, that was still considered a very young age at which to die. I wrote to Eleanor, expressing our condolences together with those of Teddy and Isabel but I never received a reply nor any notification as to when or where the funeral would take place. Laura, closeted with her mother, kept her distance as well.

My niece was only three months old and, after a few weeks, my need to see her was overwhelming. If only Peter had made a home for his family how much easier everything would have been. As it was, I felt completely cut off from both Laura and Venetia. To make matters worse Kit, Teddy nor even Isabel showed the slightest interest in the baby. In fact irritation was evident when I so much as mentioned her.

'I'm longing to see her,' I told them.

'Seen one sprog, you've seen the lot.' I recall Teddy saying.

'You better call at the house if you're so desperate.' Isabel had advised.

And so I did.

The Bonnington house belonged to The National Coal Board so I worried that both Eleanor and Laura would have to leave to make way for the newly appointed manager and his family. Kit said little on the subject except, as was to be expected, he criticised Peter for causing even more complications. Reluctantly, I had to agree that whenever he visited and then departed a myriad of problems always seemed to follow in his wake.

'Why he married the girl in the first place, I can't imagine,' Kit said.

'Because he had to,' I reminded him. 'The question is, why did he get her pregnant if he wanted to avoid married life?'

'With his kind of money he could have paid her off then disappeared just like he always does without involving us.'

'Venetia would still have been our flesh and blood.'

'But without the wedding ring, not so obviously,' he added.

I fretted over that child. One of those women who peers into prams, I adored babies and knowing my own brother had fathered one, I intended to play a part in her life. One Sunday afternoon, I put Anna in her buggy and wheeled her towards the Bonnington home. It was here that Peter had begun his career and here that his daughter lived. I was the aunt and hell bent on viewing my neice.

Laura answered my knock and I could see that she was less than pleased to see me. My cool reception extended only as far as the hall. The comfort of the sitting room, it seemed, was denied. Once again I extended my sympathies regarding her loss and asked how her mother was coping.

'Quite well thank you and not in need of sympathy from any member of the MacVee clan.' Came the reply from behind a semi-closed door.

'Eleanor,' I called to my unseen hostess. 'I only called to say how sorry we all were to hear about Samuel. Believe me, I don't want to intrude on your grief but I would love to see the baby.'

I might as well have spoken to the wall, which in a way I did since Eleanor Bonnington refused to greet me face to face. Her only remarks were shouted from behind that damned door and each one consisted of angry words deriding Peter for his desertion of her daughter and granddaughter.

'I couldn't agree with you more,' I called back. 'We're all annoyed with him but he's an artist and a very good one so we have to make allowances for his temperament and try to forgive him.'

Forgivness was not the order of the day where I was concerned as Laura was instructed to show me out on the instant. I remember pleading with Eleanor to allow me to stay and see my neice but she would have none of it so, reluctantly, I turned Anna's buggy round and walked back to the centre of the town and my own home.

But fate, for once, took a hand and this time fate was kind. Some two weeks after my futile visit, Eleanor Bonnington was taken ill. Whether she was affected by her husband's death or her own stubborness over the baby, I cannot say but some nervous problem suddenly struck and Laura was forced to send for Kit. Being Kit he didn't tell me where he was going and I never thought to enquire as, after morning surgery, I knew he always started his rounds. It was over lunch that he nonchalantly mentioned he had attended Eleanor and that he had sent her to hospital.

'She must be very ill,' I commented, 'for you to dispatch her. What's wrong?'

'No idea but she's in a hell of a state. I think, for her own safety, she'll have to be watched very carefully until some trick cyclist can sort her out.'

'She's having a breakdown?'

'A big one.'

The news, although I was saddened to hear it, meant that Laura and Venetia were alone in, the soon to be, repossessed house all on their own.

'How long will she be away?' I asked Kit.

'Who knows?' he said. 'Mental health problems aren't like physical ones, we never quite know what we're dealing with so it's down to expertise, pills and a large slice of luck.'

'Well, I'm not leaving that girl and the baby on their own in that great place,' I told Kit. 'I shall arrange to have them brought here.'

And so it was that Laura, now my sister in law, and little Venetia came to live in this house and were watched over by me. Already having reared two boys and busy with Anna who, by this time was walking and full of mischief, I was more than capable of looking after a new baby. Which, since Laura showed little interest in her daughter, was just as well! Her only topic of conversation and interest in life, apart from a slight concern for her mother, consisted of queries as to where Peter might be found? Often she would wander up to the farm to find out if Teddy or Isabel had received any news of her errant husband or she would take the train to Stafford to sit by Eleanor's sick bed and pester her with her own miseries.

Eleanor Bonnington was eventually moved to a psychiatric hospital in Birmingham and Laura spent the week in a guest house nearby so that she could visit every day. Only on Saturday afternoons did she return to see Venetia; always hell bent on rushing back immediately after lunch on Sunday. Kit was unhappy, in fact the following few months constituted the only period in our married life when I could say we were blessed with anything other than joy. Venetia, unlike our own children, was a discontented baby and one who believed in cursing her luck in the early hours of the morning. It was essential that Kit had a good night's sleep as his work was demanding and his days long. By this time we were paying a massive sum every month to an out of hours agency so there was no reason for his sleep to be interrupted. Venetia, however, thought otherwise and usually proceeded to scream at two o'clock in the morning.

For myself, I didn't mind, she was a pretty baby and I loved her dearly but I did worry for Kit.

'Laura will have to take her to Brum,' he told me. 'We can't have this every blasted night. Anna doesn't cry and didn't when she was tiny so I'm certainly not prepared to put up with this racket just for the sake of Peter's child?'

'I can't trust Laura to take care of her.'

'Nonsense, of course you can. You're just encouraging her to be lazy.'

'She's not bonded with Venetia. It would have been so different if Peter were here.'

'Well, he's not and we don't know when he will be so that

baby must go to her mother and leave us in peace.'

It was seldom Kit issued an ultimatum so I knew it wasn't an idle threat when he added that if I didn't dispatch her Birmingham, he would. In the end I was forced to ask Isabel if she would have Venetia for a few weeks whilst he calmed down and had some peaceful nights. Isabel, although hesitant, finally agreed and Teddy wasn't even consulted. I consoled myself that, with the farm house now almost empty and Teddy in the fields all day, she would be glad of an extra task to fill her days. In more frugal times, she had helped on the land and busied herself in the milking parlour but the input of Peter's money meant that she was redundant and, by that time, the farm itself was highly mechanised leaving her plenty of time to devote to a baby.

So it was, that before she was six months old, poor little Venetia had already twice moved home. Another problem presented itself in so much as it appeared that Eleanor Bonnington was failing to respond to treatment. Not being close, for obvious reasons, I did not visit or make frequent enquiries regarding her progress. Now and again I would ask Kit if he had news of her but even he knew very little except that she was still undergoing treatment and confined to the hospital which meant her case was ongoing.

'But she should be on the mend now,' I said.

'Didn't appreciate she was so dependent on that awful husband of hers,' Kit answered.

'You think she's just crumbled?'

'Apparently so but don't forget she lost a daughter too. Unfortunately people with Rose's condition often die young.'

I found it irksome that Eleanor Bonnington had made such a point of hating us but, putting myself in her shoes, I could understand how depressed she must feel. Had I lost Kit and a child I think I too would have needed psychiatric care but, turning against us as a family, was sad for we could have supported in her time of need. Unfortunately, her loathing of

Peter only added to her problems and, for that, we all got the blame.

One month later, the Bonnington house was taken over by a new area manager and I worried where she and Laura would live when she eventually recovered. Samuel, for whatever reason, and there was much speculation that he had been an inveterate gambler, had left her ill provided for and that additional fact played on mind.

Meanwhile Venetia was proving just as troublesome to Isabel as she had been to Kit and I and soon even Teddy had something to say on the subject of broken nights.

'It must be possible to track Peter down,' he said. 'He's a bloody famous artist so we should be able to dig the bugger out.'

'He's a very private person' I reminded him. 'Peter's hardly the sort of man to court the limelight.'

But someone was footing the bills for Dominic's treatment in Germany. As a family obviously we monitored his progress and Nick Schell, Lukas Kaufman and Max Hueber kept in constant touch with us. So far, only Kit and I had made the trip to Berlin. We visited just two moths after he had been admitted so no improvement vast or otherwise was evident and we were told that it might be months before any progress would be apparent. However, when we arrived at the exclusive clinic, Dom was sitting upright in a wheel chair and we had the pleasure of pushing him out into the autumn sunshine. Had he remained in Birmingham such a feat would have caused him to scream with pain so we were comforted to see that some advancement had been made.

Once back home, we had to content ourselves with updates in the shape of weekly phone calls. Good news was usually thin on the ground and misleading. Kit, cynical when it came to so called wonder cures, held the opinion that it was in the clinic's interest to throw a favourable light on Dom's case as he was a valuable money spinner. I thought his words disparaging but worried that they might be true.

The fact remained that someone at the clinic must have had a contact number or address for Peter. Phoning Nick Schell one evening, I made it my business to enquire if such information was filed in his records but was told that since," Peter MacVee paid for Dominic's care by direct debit drawn on a Swiss bank account, no such data was required."

So that appeared to be that.

Until one day I strolled into my kitchen to find Peter presenting Anna with quite the most beautiful doll I had ever seen. My impulse was to rush into his arms and plant a kiss of relief on both his cheeks. This being Peter the deed was left in the wishful thinking stage which was a pity as I was overjoyed to see him.

'How lovely to see you,' I said.

'She likes the doll.'

'I should think she does, it's wonderful. Where did you get it?'

'New York.'

'I wish we'd known where you were, Peter. We've had a nightmare of a time with Laura and Venetia. I'm afraid I've farmed her out with Teddy and Isabel. We just couldn't cope with Kit's work and everything,' I added, lamely.

'Who's Venetia?'

'Only your daughter.'

'Oh, yes.'

'Now you're back you'll have to make arrangements to care for her properly and you must provide a proper home for your wife whilst you're at it.'

'Can't her mother see to her?'

'Eleanor Bonnington's very ill and, since you don't bother to keep in touch, you won't have heard that old man Bonnington died some months agao.'

'Something painful, I hope?'

'A stroke.' I ignored his cynical observation. 'Venetia's

absolutely lovely but she needs a stable life and she's not getting one with you God knows where and Laura spending every spare minute with her sick mother.'

'I got the message first time round.'

Peter obviously found both me and my preaching trying, so he simply marched through the kitchen door and disappeared by way of the garden gate. I rang Isabel and told her he was back and that I'd explained the problems concerning the Bonnington clan. She was delighted because we both assumed that it signalled the end of our baby sitting stint with Venetia.

Or so we thought.

Peter took up his usual residence at the farm, basically ignoring his daughter and only once taking the trouble to visit his wife. We all nagged and Teddy, after drinking too much elderberry wine, seized him by the scruff of his neck and ordered him to behave like a married man. I remember Peter, thinking the remark funny, laughed in his face and flung him half way across the room. But somewhere along the line, he must have taken note of our acid comments because, not long afterwards, he commissioned a house to be built at the foot of Borough Heath Forest; designing it himself.

Week by week we all took an avid interest in the house that Peter was building. My sons literally spent all their free time marvelling at the imposing structure that seemed to grow in size and capacity before their eyes. It was a mansion. Even today, when I turn the pages of modern magazines and see glossy photographs of houses in which the so called rich and famous spend their lives, I think them shabby hovels compared with Peter's house.

It stood three stories high, possessed six bedrooms, each with its own bathroom and dressing room. Downstairs was luxury personified. The entrance hall would have encompassed our entire ground floor and this house is no mean residence when it comes to size. Each room led off from a huge blue and gold carpeted hallway that extended from the bow windowed front to the palatial glass doors at the rear. Kit always said we could hold the Staffordshire Hunt Ball in the kitchen alone and Teddy suggested we hire the whole thing out as a hospitality facility for every soldier in the British Army.

It took exactly seven months and two days to complete and that was simply because Peter hired a contingent of fifty five builders, carpenters, glaziers and gardeners. Anyone else, even a millionaire as he surely was, would have made some econimies however slight.

Peter made none at all.

To complete his masterpiece, four Romanesque pillars were built to support a colonial style balcony which projected, majestically, above the front porch. On completion, it reminded me of 'Tara' the home of Scarlet O'Hara in 'Gone With the Wind.' The extensive grounds, which ran southwards towards the heart of the forest, were copies of those created by Sir Edmund Loder for Leonardslee House in Sussex and, by the time of completion, the gardens were in bloom and looking for all the world as though years of cultivation had accomplished their glory.

To the best of my knowledge Laura never set eyes on that house whilst it was in the building stage. Had the poor girl possessed even a modicum of desire to suggest what would go where or argue a preference in décor, her opinion was not invited.

Isabel and I although excited and to some extent overawed by the project whispered, behind our hands, that it was wicked of Peter to deny her the thrill of taking an active part in the venture.

Strange to say, although he took a fervent interest in Anna, his own daughter, Venetia, was more or less ignored. Teddy and Kit paid little attention to the house but when it came to the subject of his attitude towards his wife and child, both men had plenty to say.

'Bloody great mansion like that,' Teddy sneered. 'What's he

want to do, impress the neighbours with his wealth and fame? Ostentatious bugger!'

'P'raps he intends to breed a dozen children,' Kit observed.

'Bloody well hope not, he'll only desert them like he deserts the rest of us.'

'He must be worth a fortune,' I told Kit.

'Well, he managed to inveigle a thousand quid out of old man Bonnington before anyone was aware that he we had an international genius on our hands so he must be demanding a hell of a screw now he's daubing on the walls of celebrities.'

The men were jealous. I could plainly see that Kit certainly was and Teddy, forever the farmer and proud of it, had little time for the outward show displayed by our younger brother.

'It's horrible having to be dependent on him,' Teddy once told me. 'Trouble is this house takes a hell of a lot to keep it going and so does the farm. Without Pete's cash I'd be in queer street.'

'But we could manage,' Isabel reminded him.

'After a fashion but not half as well as we do now.'

I knew Peter had offered Kit a loan when he once mentioned how much we would like to build a separate surgery onto the side of our house. As it was, we had to turn the hall into a waiting area and what should have been our dining room, into Kit's surgery. Now that the children were growing up it would have been wonderful to have had the whole house at our disposal, but Kit wouldn't hear of it. Left to me, I would have accepted gratefully for we had recently heard that Peter had been commissioned to paint a mural in The White House, no less. A few thousand pounds for our extension would hardly have troubled his pocket or disturbed his bank manager, so I tried persuasion.

'He'll be paid by the United States Government,' I pointed out. 'It will be a vast amount.'

'I don't care if it's millions,' Kit replied. 'I wouldn't touch his money.'

My observation brought forth a tirade of abuse concerning Peter's lack of humanity towards his family hotly followed by an emotional argument concerning vast riches being a poor compensation for loyalty and love.

'It's just his way,' I was defensive, 'and look what he's doing for Dom.'

'He's paying the bills but he's not visiting or caring one way or the other about Dominic himself. It's another of his flashy gestures but there's no heart in it.'

To me it didn't matter a damn whether Peter had his heart set on Dominic's recovery or not. Due to his vast wealth we had hope for his future whereas without serious cash, we had none at all.

During the final stages of the building, Peter went away. Whether the lure of painting a mural in The White House proved a bigger draw than watching the completion of his mansion or old fashioned boredom, at remaining in one place for so long drove him away, I have no idea but up until the time of his departure neither Laura nor her mother had even seen the house. I had kept them informed by phone and letter and once I had travelled to Birmingham with a portfolio of photographs in an effort to fire a glimmer of enthusiasm in both mother and daughter.

Eleanor Bonnington, by this time, was greatly improved, not completely over her breakdown but pronounced fit enough to leave hospital and live a normal life. When the last brick was laid and the water and electricity in full working order, I drove to the guest house where Laura was staying and helped her pack her few belongings so that she could return to Borough Heath and see the house for herself.

'No husband to carry me over the threshold,' she remarked, 'just his sister to cart me there and dump me on the doorstep.'

'Wait until you see what Peter's done for you.'

'You don't seriously expect me to belive he's done it for me, do you?'

'It's to be your home and Venetia's.'

'And my mothers"

'Until she's better, yes I suppose so.'

'Mother will never be well enough to live on her own.'

'Yes, she will. Kit has many patients who suffer breakdowns.' I was secretly horrified to learn that Laura seemed set on her mother becoming a permanent resident in my brother's house because I knew he would hate the idea and hate her into the bargain. 'They eventually get completely over them and live perfectly normal lives' I added, lamely.

'Mother won't be like that.'

'Of course she will, it was just the shock of your father dying as suddenly as he did that caused the problem. Once she feels more herself she'll want her independence more than anything.'

'How do you know?'

'Because everyone does. No one wants to be a burden to their children for the rest of their lives.'

'In any case,' Laura, I could see, had her own ideas which had no bearing on my half baked medical platitudes, 'I want mother to live with me. Peter's never at home for five minutes and I can't cope on my own.'

'You won't have to. Isabel and Teddy are just half a mile down the road and we're only in the town. Anyway you have a daughter, you'll never be alone.'

But Laura showed little interest in her maternal status and I could seen that her mother was her chief requisite. Peter, I was sure, would never agree to Eleanor living in his palace of a home and so I began to worry.

It fell to Teddy, Isabel, Kit and myself to install Peter's wife and mother in law in the mansion at the foot of the forest. We sold it to them. Neither showed any delight in the palatial building, both agreed with Kit, that it was ostentatious and slightly absurd. When the moment came to hand Venetia over to Laura, a look approaching disgust appeared in her eyes and she frowned as she took the screaming baby from Isabel's arms.

'Does she always howl like this?'

'Of course not,' Isabel said, somewhat unconvincingly. 'She's disturbed by the new surroundings. She'll soon settle down.'

Eleanor, hardly bothering to favour her granddaughter with so much as a glance, shielded her eyes from a sudden shaft of sunlight that lit up the colonial façade. Turning to us, she asked, 'Did he have to build something as vulgar and preposterous as this?'

'Apparently so,' Kit answered dryly.

We left them. We abandoned them is a truer statement. Even after we had marched them from room to room, in the manner of estate agents eager for a sale, we received no hint of enthusiasm from either woman and Kit, I could see, was fast losing his temper.

'I agree it's a bloody monstrosity but surely it has some merit,' he exclaimed. 'It's worth a million and she's to be it's mistress. Anyone would think we'd just installed them in a council flat on an inner city sink estate.'

But the rest of us couldn't reply. The whole picture was gloomy and none of us could, in all honesty, defend Peter's house. It was ridiculous, it was pretentious and, for a woman just recovering from a mental breakdown, it must have been terrifying.

'They'll get lost before nightfall,' Kit observed.

'Or lose the bloody baby,' Teddy laughed.

'Don't you dare say that.' Isabel turned on him and for the first time in our long acquaintance, I saw a look of hatred in her eyes. 'Babies mean nothing to you but to most normal people they are a priceless gift from God.'

'Let's hope God's not feeling over generous in the near future then.' He also looked venomous. 'I can do without gifts like Venetia.'

We trooped back to the farm where Isabel provided a cold lunch. I thought the place looked run down and the atmosphere was decidedly oppressive. We spoke of the house and naturally the topic over the ham salad centred on Laura and Eleanor. We all thought they would settle and, in time, find the place fascinating but decided it had come as something of a shock on first sight.

Michael wandered in and asked where our boys were. Kit explained that we had been "Seeing Aunt Laura into her new home and John and Phil were left at home."

'Why?' asked Michael.

'Because we wanted to have plenty of time to help your aunt and her mother to settle in.'

'My friends say it's a white elephant,' the small boy told us.

'No it's not,' Teddy shouted at him. 'Not my taste, not any one's taste but it will always be worth a fortune specially when people know who built it and who lives there.'

'Famous Uncle Peter,' said Michael.

'A white elephant,' his mother explained, 'is something you think will be valuable but turns out to be worthless. Have I said that right, Kit?'

'I think so.'

But Kit wasn't interested, neither was Teddy; his heart, as usual, was outside on the land and as soon as we had finished the meal, we decided to head for home leaving him free to dash out into the cow yard. I kissed Isabel as was my custom and tweeked Michael's cheek. After that we left.

'I don't want to to spend the evening discussing whether or not we ought to go back to that ghastly house and see if the Bonnington ladies have settled in,' Kit warned, 'so let's have dinner straight after surgery and then watch the box.'

I agreed that was my preference too although my thoughts remained focused on Laura and Eleanor and especially on baby Venetia. Three weeks later Peter re-appeared and took up residence in his mansion with his wife, his daughter and his mother in law.

As a family, we all felt our responsibilities had come to an end.

The master was back and he must care for his family.

We were absolved.

Chapter Twenty

Anna's coming to visit on Saturday.

I must remind Pan to make her bedroom habitable but Pan will only shrug because Anna's already written to say that she's bringing her new friend with her. His name is Bryn and whoever this Bryn may be, he's black. Pan wouldn't admit it for the world, but she isn't keen on black men or Italians or Americans or anyone who hasn't been born and bred in the Borough Heath.

Anna's friends seldom appeal to me but that's not because they are invariably black or foreign or possessed of extreme left wing tendencies; it's because I want her to find a steady, and hopefully, professional man of her own age and marry him.

I am the perfect product of my generation. Snobbish and conservative and, what's more, I have the white linen gloves to prove it!

Anna was deeply upset when Dominic died last year. John and Phil were equally saddened although John, following in his father's footsteps as a doctor, observed that Dom had proved himself something of a phenomenon in surviving as long as he had. Towards the end of his life, he lost his sight once more and became deeply depressed. Thanks to the tireless efforts of Max Hueber and later to the administrations of Moorfileds Hospital in London, his eyesight had been almost perfectly restored. His first retina transplants were hardly the commonplace procedure which they now are so, thanks to Hueber's expertise, he had many years of almost normal vision.

It was Peter who brought him home from Germany. One year and nine months he spent at Nick Schell's clinic and in that time no less that eleven operations were performed. Personally, my special gratitude was directed towards Lukas Kaufman whose brilliance in constructing and fitting artificial limbs enabled him to walk almost naturally. During the first few months, Dominic had shown little interest in his recovery which was understandable. My poor brother was only in his late twenties when everything, it seemed, had been taken from him. Unable to speak, see, move or even feed himself, I doubt the prospect of a long and continued existence appealed. It wasn't just the expertise of the doctors we had to prasie, it was the enduring care of the nursing staff and the speech therapists who taught him how to speak with a broken pallette and a torn tongue. It was the persistence of the psychotherapists who encouraged him to walk and use limbs he thought useless. A team of twenty or more caring people devoted their time and patience to restoring not just his body but his will to survive. Even after all these years I still pray and give thanks for their perseverance although I expect that, by now, the majority of them are dead.

That is perhaps the greatest tragedy of old age. Those we love and value are taken from us and live only in our memory as do Shakespeare's, 'Roses in December.' But my memory serves me well when I think back to Dominic's home coming. Of course we knew weeks in advance that he would be back in good time for Christmas and the new year and we dashed around like headless chickens making excited preperations. It was agreed that he would go straight to Peter's house which Kit had taken to calling, The Taj Mahal. Personally, I would have preferred him to have gone to the farm because, after all, it had been his home for so long that I thought he would find comfort in its old familiarity. I was over ruled by Teddy. Looking back I believe he and Isabel were terrified at the prospect of coping with anyone who had been as damaged as Dom and probably felt they wouldn't be up to the task of caring for him. In any case even I had to admit that things at the farm were far from happy so it was not an ideal place to house a semi-invalid.

Our own visits to the farm were devoid of any joy on account of Teddy and Isabel's constant bickering. A row would start out of absolutely nothing and Isabel, in particular, would lose her temper, curse poor Teddy and cause embarrassment all round. Even our children began to comment on the shouting matches which broke out between Uncle Teddy and Aunty Isabel so the thought of Dominic having to endure such an atmosphere just when he was trying to convalesce, was something none of us wanted.

Acutely aware, as we were, of Teddy's personal circumstances, Peter's domestic arrangements remained a mystery. We had all anticipated mutinous objections regarding Eleanor's presence but either he didn't mind or, if he did, he kept his opinions to himself. Laura never invited any of us to visit so I was as bereft of sightings of my niece just as I was when first she was born. However I made it plain to Peter that once Dominic had settled in we should all require frequent access. The thought of being faced with a situation where we had to beg to see our long absent brother was unthinkable but, thankfully, Peter readily agreed that whenever any of us wished to visit Dom we were more than welcome to do so.

'He'll be on show twenty four hours a day,' he told me.

'Don't put it like that,' I admonished.

'Well, he'll soon feel like a freak with you lot queuing up to gawp at him day and night.'

'You know very well we shall do no such thing but since

neither you nor Laura and certainly not Eleanor ever dream of inviting us, we have to invite ourselves.'

'Do whatever you want.'

Peter shrugged, leaving me with a host of unspoken questions regarding the care of my eldest brother but that was his way and I had to accept it. We were all indebted to him and, odd as he might have been, we knew it was due to his phenomenal success that Dom was in a position to come home at all. What was more, when he collected him from Birmingham Airport, he hired a specially equipped vehicle complete with a nurse so that Dominic could be brought home in the height of comfort.

Even Kit remarked that he had some human feelings after all!

We left Dominic strictly alone for three days after his home coming. Desperate, as I was to rush to Peter's house, I kept my distance thinking it best to give him time to acclimatise. But it was Dom who contacted me.

'Hello, Vin.' That familiar voice brought instant tears to my eyes although, during his stay in Germany, we had spoken, when speech was available to him, twice and, sometimes, three times each week. This was Dom only a mile away, ringing to say he wanted to see me.

What joy!

All of us, even bluff old Teddy, had to hide our tears when first we saw him. I know I was quite overcome and had to be chastised by Dom himself.

'Oh Vin,' he said. 'If this is how you react, I shall have to ban you.' But his own eyes were not exactly dry.

'You can see and you can walk.' I stated the obvious since he had stood, unaided, and slowly walked across a luxurious carpet to hug me.

'I can do a hundred things,' said Dominic, 'mostly pinch myself to make sure I'm really here.'

As was to be expected, much of what we had to say involved

details of his treatment in Berlin and we never failed to applaud the people who had affected the miracle. After that, and when I had treated him to a detailed account of my own family life, Dom usually turned the subject to The Taj Mahal. Seemingly both amused and in awe of his surroundings, I noticed that Peter's attention always came in for special praise as apparently it was he who cooked his meals, helped him dress and sat with him during the evenings. Of Laura or her mother, he saw very little but our, oft criticised, younger brother was undoubtedly excelling in the personal care department.

'I worry that I deprive Laura of his company,' he once said.

'I have a feeling the deprivation would be hardly noticeable,' I told him.

'Sadly I have to agree.' Dominic shook his head and changed the subject.

Although he could walk reasonably well, he couldn't walk far but I found wheeling his chair an easy task so, together, we once again explored the countryside which had been the playground of our childhood.

'I'm always afraid I'll tire you.' He used to worry.

'I'd wheel you to Timbuktu if you asked me,' I laughed.

And, figuratively speaking, I did. Almost every fine day, and we had many that particular summer, I drove to the Taj Mahal and struggled to push my beloved brother through Borough Heath Forest and often all way to the little village where we used to cycle as children to buy our weekend sweets.

'Such a lot has happened since those days,' he said.

'Not all good either.'

'But good for you, Vin. You and Kit are happy and the kids are wonderful.'

'We're very lucky,' I said and meant it.

'But neither Teddy nor Peter have much to write home about in their marriages.'

'Certainly not Peter,' I agreed, 'but he should never have married. I don't mean he shouldn't have married Laura, I mean he shouldn't have married anyone. He's no more suited to married life than you would have been.'

I think that was the first time we ever touched on Dominic's sexual orientation. Sorry to use that modern cliché but it seems appropiate. Dom spoke of Brian Thorn, their relationship and the resulting tragedy.

'You'll hardly belive it Vin but when I heard Brian had been killed I was upset.'

'I wasn't,' I said with feeling. 'I almost jumped for joy.'

'That night,' he stuttered, 'the one when the accident happened, he was drunk. If he hadn't been I really believe he would have seen the funny side of Peter's audacity in shagging a girl in our room.'

'There was no funny side to it, Dom. Only Peter would have done such a foolhardy thing but the way Brian treated him and you was inhuman.'

'I expect he got a kick out of it.'

'What out of knowing what he did almost killed you?' I was horrified.

'Of course not, I meant Peter. He would have thought it hilarious to have sex with a woman in a queer's bed.'

I can't think I answered because I don't like the word queer and I'd never used it as a label to describe Dominic. Strangely enough, I still think about both of them, but it is with sadness because although they were highly gifted men their way of life was unnatural. In my opinion, life is quite hard enough without the complication of being different or being thought to be different.

Poor Dominic was hardly likely to have any kind of love life after what happened. Even with all the treatments and subsequent improvements romance, in any form, seemed unlikely and I even grieved for that. For what good is a life lived without love; without someone of your own to whom you can turn in times of trouble and trust no matter what problems or pains you have to bear?

But, as time went by, it was the children who filled the void and provided love in abundance. John and Phil he adored, and little Anna became his special friend along with Michael who, only living a stone's throw away at the farm, was usually to be found at his side whenever time and circumstances permitted. Should either of our two sons receive a new toy or an exciting piece of news they would immediately rush for their bikes and peddle up to Uncle Dom's as though their lives depended on his sharing their excitement. Anna, still too young to go anywhere unattended, would cry on discovering she had been abandoned and left with only poor old me for company.

It was through Michael that we learnt the true extent of Teddy and Isabel's domestic problems. Daily, he would pour out his troubles to his newly discovered uncle for, at not yet thirteen years old, the rows and unhappiness that constituted life at the farm were becoming too much for him to bear.

Due to Michael's tales of woe we learnt that Teddy and Isabel were sleeping in separate bedrooms and hardly speaking. I suppose under normal circumstances we would have remained ignorant of such intimate details but, due to Michael's outpourings, we worried for their unhappiness.

'What's at the bottom of it, Vin?' Dom asked me one afternoon when we were on our way to the town.

'No idea,' I said, adding 'Although it's a long time since it happened, I don't think Teddy has ever got over the disappearance of Dorothea. Perhaps, to some extent, none of us have but, as they say today, we've moved on.'

'What do you think really did happen?'

'To Dorothea?'

'Yes, I mean she literally vanished. We might just as well believe she was kidnapped by men from Mars and whisked away in their spaceship since no one's ever come up with a better theory.'

'I suppose she was either murdered or she met with an accident. Either way no body ever showed up.'

'Gruesome thoughts, Vin.'

'Well, unless she'd made secret plans to run out on us all, which would have included her parents whom she genuinely appeared to love, there was no reason for her to go into hiding. Anyway, how could someone remain hidden all these years? The police were very thorough and so were we but nothing has ever come to light.'

'And you think Teddy still dwells on it?'

'Oh, I can't say, Dom. I mean it's not something we ever discuss but there must be a reason why they're always arguing. You'll probably find out more from Michael since he keeps you informed. Poor Michael,' I added.

Deciding there was nothing either of could do to rescue Teddy and Isabel's fraught marriage we spent the rest of the afternoon happily buying new clothes for Dominic. His eyesight, although wonderfully restored was nowhere near perfect, so I wheeled him into the one gent's outfitters Borough Heath boasted and helped him choose at least half a dozen shirts, three pairs of trousers, a very smart blazer and two pairs of shoes.

Later, after he had insisted on buying sweets and playthings for the children, we went back to my home where, after a hearty dinner, he and Kit began a game of chess. Somewhere in the region of nine o'clock the door bell rang and I sighed thinking it might be an urgent call for Kit. Instead, my bell ringers turned out to be Teddy and Isabel which, in itself was a shock as I believed they no longer went out together and had certainly abandoned any outward show of affection. Ushering them into the sitting room they appeared delighted to be seated next to each other on the sofa and, whilst taking a drink with Kit, Dom and myself, Teddy, much to our amazement, put his arm round Isabel's shoulder and she placed her hand on his.

'We came to let you know we're going to be parents again,' beamed an elated Teddy. 'Isabel wanted to tell you when we were altogether as family.'

'Congratulations,' I said.

Kit shook Teddy's hand, adding his own declarations of joy.

But in view of our earlier discussion, Dominic simply stared at them with an expression which could only be described as one of utter disbelief.

Chapter Twenty One

'Were you shocked or relieved, Mummy?' Anna has just asked me.

'Oh, I think a bit of both, darling, but your friend doesn't want a run down on our lurid history.'

A very dark gentleman is lying stretched out on my sofa. I wish he wasn't. He can't be much more than forty one or two and he should be sitting properly not lolling about like an old man or a laconic youth.

'On the contrary, Mrs. Barry, I'm fascinated.' His name is Bryn and he originates from Zambia. He's years younger than my daughter so the relationship both puzzles and annoys me.

'I can assure you there's no fascination in death particualry when the dead person happens to be a mere girl.'

'I'm sorry Mrs. Barry, it's just that I've read an account of the case and I find it intriguing.'

Surely he realises he's making matters worse? I shall leave the room in a minute but I find it hard to tear myself away from Anna. It's five months since she last visited and I wish with all my heart she had come alone and not insisted on bringing this colonial person with her. The subject under discussion is also the last topic I wish to air so I must make a move and put a stop to further morbid enquiries.

'But it put an end to all the mystery.'

'Yes, darling, it did but it caused a host of new problems so, if you don't mind, I'll just go and see if Pan wants a hand with tea, she's over seventy herself you know, Anna.'

'She'd remember all about it, wouldn't she?' Anna looked hopeful.

'Of course, she's not senile.' I wanted the conversation to stop right there so I raised my voice and became the mother of old addressing my child. 'The whole subject is a closed book, Anna and I don't want to hear another word about it.'

'But you surely wouldn't mind if I showed Bryn the press cuttings especially those from around the time the body was found?'

'Of course I would mind, it would mean the rest of the day would be spent discussing it. Anyway,' I added, petulantly, 'the cuttings are in a box somewhere in the loft and I don't want the whole place turned upside down with you two searching for them.'

'I give you my word Anna and I will leave your loft just as we found it,' said Bryn.

Unbending, only because I had to, I inhaled a deep breath and proceeded to deliver a short explanation of the events of 2001.

'As you know, Bryn,' I disliked using his given name in the same way as I slightly disliked him but only because I saw him as an intruder on my precious time with Anna. 'The body of a young woman was unearthed on our farm land but, at the time of the discovery, no positive conclusion could be reached so, although we were all convinced we had discovered Dorothea, none of us could be absolutely certain and that's why I don't want to start speculating all over again.'

'I promise not to speculate,' he said.

I went into the kitchen to talk to Pan and take my heart

pills. Anna and Bryn, I knew were intent on making their way to the loft where they would search for the box containing the press cuttings. There was nothing I could do to stop them, so swallowing half a dozen assorted pills and helping Pan make tea seemed a better way of spending the next half hour than fretting over newspaper reports which were over half a century old.

Once we overcame our surprise concerning Teddy and Isabel's expected baby, the news made us happy. Unlikely as it was, the prospect of their becoming parents again after a gap of more than twelve years, was an event to celebrate. I thought it signalled the end of their matrimonial strife and prayed that the new arrival would bring renewed love into, what had become, a joyless union.

'Beats me how Teddy found the time to father another child,' Kit said.

'It's not the time it's the inclination,' I added. 'Isabel has always given me the impression that he wasn't interested in sex.'

'Not to mention the separate bedrooms.'

'A moment of passion after the harvest supper or do you think they've just been kidding us all along and their rows are no more than a silly habit?'

'Ask me another,' said Kit.

But whatever had prompted the second coming, as Kit referred to the pregnancy, Isabel did what expectant mothers are supposed to do, she bloomed. From being amiable but distant she became cheerful and affectionate. Dominic, who hadn't personally been privy to the quarrels between her and Teddy, began to believe that young Michael had either made them up, exaggerated or imagined them. I didn't contradict his belief as boys often get the wrong end of the stick and Michael had reached what was usually termed, 'the awkward age'. I was reminded of our own ages when Ma first told us she was expecting Peter. Over the years I have often worried that our indifference greatly contributed to his turning into the odd ball which he remains to this day; so I made it my business to coach Michael in the art of brotherly love.

Isabel wanted a daughter.

That was understandable. She had lost Rose all those years ago and already had a son so we all agreed that a girl would be wonderful adding the time honoured sentiment that just as long as the baby was healthy we would all be happy no matter what it's gender.

Having heaved a sigh of relief and decided all was now well with Teddy and Isabel we turned our attention to Laura and Peter. Eleanor Bonnington presented few problems as her depression, although more or less under control, narrowed her life to such an extent that she seldom left her room or suit of rooms since she occupied the entire third floor. During my visits to Dom, I always enquired after her health and was told by an indifferent Laura or a, seldom in residence Peter, that she was fine. Since this statement was unconfirmed due to the fact that I never actually ever set eyes on Eleanor, I can not tell you whether she was fine or ill and, to be honest, I wasn't particularly interested. The Bonningtons, with the exception of poor Rose, had not appealed and, clearly none of them were exactly over the moon about us. Granted Laura had fallen for Peter and succeeded in dragging him to the altar but more than that she had failed to do. If he displayed any affection for either her or his daughter I can only say that none of us were in the close vicinity when he did so. Ventetia, I saw quite often but she was a clinging miserable child who ran and hid whenever anyone so much as glanced in her direction. Naturally, whenever I had half a chance, I qizzed Peter regarding her unnatural shyness and advised how to deal with the problem but, as he displayed not a vestige of interest in the poor girl, he merely shrugged and walked away.

It was a very different story when Isabel's daughter was born. Black haired and possessed of Dominic's bright blue eyes, she arrived in the early hours of Boxing Day, nineteen seventy nine at a time when the road to the farm house was cut off by banks of soft snow. The ploughs had been out during Christmas evening but further storms had covered the highway and Teddy couldn't open the five barred gate which led to the front door. The phone lines went down shortly after he phoned us and the tractor failed to shift the snow so by the time Kit and, the somewhat unlikely figure of Peter, had shovelled their way to the door, Isabel, with a nervous Teddy in attendance, had already obliged by producing her daughter. When it came to bringing calves, lambs and piglets into the world he was a master but delivering his own wife turned him into a shivering wreck. However, we all agreed that, as Christmas presents went, Maria could not be bettered.

Kit joked about the fact that whereas he had found Isabel and the baby to be in perfect health he had had to administer medical aid to Teddy as the trauma of playing mid-wife at five o'clock on a snowy Boxing Day morning had laid him low.

Merriment all round!

Peter, who had spent the last five months roaming the world; even making television appearances devoted to the subject of long canvas painting, suddenly became a fixture in The Taj Mahal. Whether the rich and famous, who accounted for ninety percent of his clientele, had lost their fascination with twenty foot murals or whether, at thirty five, he had grown tired of weilding brushes in sultan's palaces and other assorted mansions, he never said. Not that any of us expected him to say anything. Peter was not given to idle conversation or interesting comments regarding his work, his feelings or the world in general.

Teddy, delighted with his newly born daughter, appeared happy and the farm turned into a real family home once again. Luckily he was not straining under financial pressures otherwise I doubt it would have continued as a viable business. More and more supermarkets were opening and their produce was bought cheaply from overseas. Teddy was what would now be termed as an organic farmer and the cost of his dairy goods and home killed meat could not compete with bulk buying and foreign imports. Peter's fortune subsidized any losses and Dom, Kit and I were enthusiastic about the farm's future.

Then, out of the blue, Teddy had to have an operation. Kit started the ball rolling, if that's the correct expression, when he told me that he was worried about Teddy's weight.

'You think he's overweight?' I asked.

'Just the opposite,' Kit replied. 'The flesh's hanging off him he must have lost over a stone since Maria was born.'

'That's fatherhood for you,' I laughed.

'No, it's more than that. I wish I were his doc, I'd like to have a word with him about it.'

'What's stopping you?' I began to worry as images of a thin and gaunt looking Teddy entered my mind. 'You don't have to be his doctor to ask him if he knows why he's losing weight.'

'No, but I feel it's not my place.'

We had one of out small splats over his last remark so, dressing Anna in a warm coat, I took hold of her little hand and marched her up to the farm where I intended to speak to Teddy myself. Since Kit had put the idea in my mind I couldn't let the matter rest. We all knew how hard he worked and, like the rest of us, middleage was telling its tale. Never the less, Kit was right in pointing out that he looked emaciated and, when I thought about it, I had to admit he had not looked well for some months.

Leaving Anna with Isabel and the baby, I went down to the cow yard to seek him out. Teddy, as usual, was working like a maniac mending fences just below the milking parlour. Immediately I quizzed him regarding his health and, in doing so, upset him profoundly.

'Don't bloody keep on,' he said, after I had asked how he felt for the sixth time. 'I'm fine, just overdone what with the baby and the work. I'll eat a bit more if that will make you happy.'

But I knew I had touched a nerve for Teddy was always sweetness itself to me and suddenly he was shouting as if in a rage. 'You're not fine, are you Ted?' I stated rather than asked.

'What you'd call a bit run down Vin, that's all.' He clamed down.

But that wasn't all. It took over a week of cajoling but at last I persuaded him to go and see his own doctor, a caring man called Simon Radcliff who, by virtue of being local and in the same profession as Kit, was a great friend of ours. Simon came to see us after his own surgery one evening in Febuary and told us that he had sent Teddy to hospital for tests and the results showed he had a malignant tumour in the sigmoid colon. In other words he had bowel cancer. Naturally we were beside ourselves with worry. After the trauma of rescuing Dominic from certain death and Maria not yet three months old, our reaction was magnified. Even the usually pragmatic Kit showed signs of strain and began to talk of the problems of long term illness and the unpredictability of chemotherapy.

Naturally, Teddy had to have an operation but it was deemed a great success and was followed by three months of radio therapy which involved twice weekly visits to Stafford Infirmary. During his absence the farm was ably run by the hands and most especially by Peter.

Always a close family, we all made it our business to care for Teddy. I was constantly dividing my time between he and Dominic only too aware that both my brothers were in need of their little sister in this new time of crisis. Dom insisted that I concentrate on Teddy and Isabel assuring me that he, himself, was thoroughly pampered by the boys and waited on hand and foot by Peter's staff. The fact remained that, since he had been through so much, I felt the need to be at his side as much as possible so when I discovered, to my great astonishment, that Peter was working on the farm the news came as an unexpected bonus.

'I can't believe it,' I said to Isabel as we watched him herding the cows. 'I fear for his hands, they're so beautiful.'

'He's family and he's strong,' she said. 'Why shouldn't he help out?'

I thought her callous. Peter had money enough to employ an army of men and his precious talent should have excluded him from rough work but there he was labouring day after day with hardly a word of thanks from his sister in law.

Teddy, up to a point, was grateful but at the same time exceedingly fretful. Single handed, he had worked that farm from boyhood and since he had never favoured Peter, he sulked and also failed to appreciate our brother's efforts.

'Idiot,' he said. 'He's no bloody idea what he's up to. Isabel has to abandon me and the baby to go and give him instructions. Yesterday, she spent the whole afternoon showing him how the bloody irrigator works.'

'For God's sake be thankful,' I told him. 'Peter's trying to be nice, which is something we've all longed for, and he's working long hours. The men need a MacVee on the land to keep them in order and he's doing just that.'

So Teddy shut up and continued with his treament which, thank God, cured the cancer. As he regained his health, I was able to spend more time with Dom and my own family. Another crisis averted and life seemed settled once again. Dominic started to write his medical books which, as you may know, became standard works in universities all over the world. I am told they are translated into seventy five different languages and even today many heart specialists reach for their leather bound, 'Dominic MacVees' in the great consulting rooms around the world.

Laura and Eleanor remained shadowy fingers, melting into the background of their sumptuous home. Peter ignored them both and, up to a point, side stepped Venetia as well but, naturally, I saw all three during my constant visits to the Taj Mahal and thought them lucky to live in such style.

Peter, at this time, was exceedingly hansome. He had grown a beard which suited an artist and suited him. His hair, long, still flaxen and his eyes the colour of a summer sky presented him as something of a heart throb. Sometimes I wondered if he indulged in affairs with other women since, as far as any of us could see, Laura held no appeal.

In nineteen eighty two, Kit bought a partnership in a group practice still in the Borough Heath area but two miles south of the town. Four other doctors were involved but it meant that our house was free of patients and extra space was available everywhere. How wonderful it was to have the square hall newly carpeted and turned back into what it was meant to be; a welcoming area to all the ground floor rooms. Kit's surgery, which should have reverted to a dining room, we made into a television lounge which was mainly frequented by John and Phil but sometimes by Anna as well. As the boys approached their mid teens, it housed something horrible called a boom box, later replaced by stereo equipment so that unbearably loud pop music was played at all hours. But we were happy and Kit had more free time than ever before.

With the extra income, derived from his newly acquired status as a partner in a progressive practice, we bought a small flat in central London. It was situated in Bourne Street very close to the Embankment and Sloane Square. I think we paid ninety thousand pounds for it and considered ourselves extravagant. I might add that when I sold it just two years ago it fetched almost half a million so I'm glad we were extravagant! As the children grew older and less dependent we started to take short breaks in London and, later still, whole weeks and even longer when the weather was fine. But at the time of Teddy's illness they were still very young and Maria was only three and a half months old. Dom seemed settled at the Taj Mahal and we were still in the thick of the town centre where Kit, as usual, was rushed off his feet.

Sometimes, after I'd spent an hour or so with Teddy, I

would wander round the farm and seek out Peter. If neither Teddy nor Isabel saw fit to thank him I certainly felt the need as I worried that he would fancy himself taken for granted and rebel.

'Enjoying yourself?' I joked one day on discovering him up to his eyes in mud.

'No.'

'I know you're not.' I reached out to caress his blonde hair in a show affection but he ducked as if I held a loaded gun to his head. 'But, Peter, you're doing a great job and Teddy is so grateful.'

'I'll take your word for it.'

'You should know him by now, he's a bluff old farmer, not given to pretty speeches.'

'This place is mostly mine anyway,' he said and I knew he was referring to the vast amount of money he had invested just to keep it afloat.

'We all owe you a great deal, Peter.' I stood beside him and for a moment was transported to the days of our childhood as my eyes scanned the fields. A host of memories flooded back reminding me of the thousands of times was had played and raced across the land that was now becoming something of a liability. I was also reminded of our callous disregard of Peter and wished our attitude had been otherwise. 'And what you've done for Dominic is fantastic,' I added.

'Better get on,' said my reticent brother as he marched away; three pronged fork slung like a rifle over his right shoulder.

As I watched him stride across the slopes of the meadow towards the hills where the sheep grazed, I wondered what had persuaded him to turn his hand to farming. Peter, who always appeared devoid of affection let alone love, had saved Dominic and was now, selflessly, coping with the farm. At home, in his million pound mansion, his wife, child and mother in law were waited on like royalty but to him it was all meaningless.

Walking home I decided to make him the topic of the evening's conversation and hear what views Kit held. As a doctor, I knew, he held educated opinions regarding human quirks and Peter's present actions were intriguing.

Kit was too late home that particular evening to enter into any deep psychological discussion as to why an introverted artist should exchange his brushes for a muck spreader, so the mystery of Peter the farmer was delayed.

But not for long.

A long period of bad weather had coincided with Peter's farming exploits which, in turn, had prevented Dominic from venturing out of doors. Persistent rain and gales had quite suddenly given way to warmer dryer weather so I was finally able to wheel him down to see Teddy and Isabel. I knew he was partuculary anxious to see Maria of whom he was inordinately fond.

'You'd think she'd bring her to see me,' he complained. 'I'm not exactly in a position to jump on a bike and ride over to see her.'

'Oh, Dom,' I explained, 'what with Teddy's illness, a new baby and the farm, I think Isabel can be forgiven.'

'Sorry, Vin, you're right. Sitting peering out of a window all day I forget people have lives to lead.'

'But you're writing?'

'Jotting down ideas. Holding the pen is still difficult and the typewriter is a pain.'

'It will get better, Dom.'

If I said that five word sentence once I must have said it a hundred times but I was right, it took forever but, in the years to come, Dominic did improve wonderfully well.

When we reached the farm, instead of making for the kitchen door, I wheeled his chair round the old rose garden and along the concrete paths beside the long lawn and the cloudy fish ponds that Pa had built over thirty years ago.

'Wheel me to the sheep pens, will you Vinnie?'

'If it's not too muddy I will.'

And so we went this way and that, all the time commenting on things and people long gone. We talked of Ma and Pa and tree houses we had built. We were children again seeing the farm and the animals through childish eyes. At one point we mentioned Dorothea, wondering once again what mysterious happening had caused her to vanish. Mostly we laughed and our recollections made us happy.

'Do you remember when that old sow had fifteen piglets and you, Teddy and I used to dress them up?' Dom asked.

'I do. Pa was furious when he saw one of them wearing his red scarf.'

We laughed as we stared into the then empty sty for Teddy had recently given up pig farming as cheap imports of pork had rendered it worthless. The brick sty was built in a time when men knew how to perfect their labour and the years had hardly blemished its flint walls. The little gates that kept the pigs enclosed were still intact but one swung open in the light easterly breeze. Inside the sty itself we heard a noise. A human noise, almost a moan.

'There's someone in there,' Dominic stated the obvious.

'Michael and his playmates probably.'

'We used to go in the stys, remember Vin?'

'Course I do.'

'Can you wheel this thing any closer, I want to take a peep inside.'

'If you must.'

I wish we hadn't.

I really do although some might say it's better to know than live in ignorance! The whispered sounds ceased as I wheeled Dom's chair closer to the open arch that led to the interior of the sty. The chair proved too wide to wheel through the gap so we stood in the breeze listening for further sounds. None came but we knew people or children were within and the atmosphere, imitating the recent bad weather, felt chill. If

Michael and his play-fellows were inside then we would have expected them to come rushing out, possibly to frighten us or hold us up at gun point with nothing more harmful than water pistols. I remember feeling slightly uneasy in case tramps or gypsies had converted the disused stys into living quarters but Dominic, I could see, was determined to discover who or what lurked behind the flint archway.

If you have never seen a pigsty it will be difficult to visualize quite how big they are. Ours were semi-detached providing in the region of twenty square feet of open pen and twelve square feet of interior space where the pigs could escape from bad weather. Having been recently abandoned they provided endless possibilities for people of Michael's age. A sty could be transformed into a fortress, a castle oh, absolutely anything for a child's imagination possesses wonderful powers of invention.

But no child would have been welcome in that sty on that particular afternoon for it was already fully occupied and neither infant nor animal was in residence. On the floor, lying on a faded blue mattress covered by a tartan blanket, lay Isabel and Peter. With hindsight it seemed I was destined to intrude on my little brother's sexual pleasures for hadn't I found him with Laura in Dominic and Brian Thorn's bedroom doing exactly the same thing?

A pigsty does not provide a convenient turning space for a wheel chair so, although I desperately wanted to retreat, I lacked the room to make a hasty manoeuvre. In the manner of someone viewing a repeat of a familiar film I stood, seemingly spying, on my brother and sister in law. Since the scene could hardly be termed, social, the notion of shouting a greeting seemed absurd. Sooner or later I knew Dominic and I would have to face confrontation for we could hardly conceal our presence. Even, had we been able to steal away, that wheel chair, I recall, had an audible squeak which would have immediately drawn their attention.

'Well, well,' said Peter, when he did look up and deign to

speak, 'you seem to make a habit of ruining my love life.'

'It's not intentional, I assure you,' I replied, with all the menace I could muster.

'Oh, Vinnie,' Isabel whimpered, 'don't tell Teddy.'

'He's recovering from cancer,' I reminded her. 'The last thing he wants to hear is a blow by blow account of his wife's adultery with his brother.'

'God, you're stuffy. You should listen to yourself,' Peter dared to say.

'What do you expect, an apology for the intrusion?'

'You could have said 'whoops' and walked away,' he laughed.

'We should have done that when you took Laura to our room in Tettenhall,' Dominic said quietly. 'It would have saved my life.'

Isabel, I was pleased to see, looked the picture of guilt but Peter, not noted for his gallentry at the best of times, jumped up, donned his clothes and pushed us wheel chair and all, out of his way as he leapt over the wall of the sty and ran towards the fields. Strangley enough even after all these years, I remember he was whistling 'The Sky Boat Song,' and it haunts me to this day whenever I hear it.

My one desire was to hurry away, leave Isabel to her tears and wheel Dominic from the whole sickening scene. He, always the gentleman, begged me to stay and calm her. Whispering in my ear, he said to remember she'd been under a hell of a lot of strain. New baby, husband diagnosed with cancer and the farm losing money by the day. I think he even mentioned post natal depression in his defence of our sister in law. So I helped Isabel to her feet and promised I wouldn't tell Teddy. I even managed to stop myself upbraiding her, which was an effort as I was infuriated at her betrayal of Teddy with, of all people, Peter.

I wonder if I would be so shocked in this day and age? Probably not, we've all become so immune to loose morals and people doing whatever they fancy that I may have shrugged and said, 'that's life,' or uttered some other silly expression. When Anna sleeps with her current lover, I'm no longer outraged so maybe Isabel and Peter would have been forgiven or, at least, understood.

But not then.

I grieved for Teddy. Acknowledging he was not the best of husbands and knowing full well that Isabel considered him cold and unloving, still I condemned her. I thought of the acid remarks they exchanged before Maria was conceived and the tales Michael told Dominic about rows at the farm. But the image of her and Peter, locked in each other's arms, obsessed me. I didn't tell Kit simply because I knew he would have told me to forget it. He would have said no good would come of bringing it into the open and it was none of our business anyway.

Maybe he would have been right.

By the Christmas of that year, Teddy was back to almost perfect health. It really was a bonus for all of us considering he had ignored his cancer for over eight months. A total cure had been affected and even Dominic and Kit, the professionals amongst us, praised the doctors and the new technology that had saved his life. Dominic himself was also much improved. The wheel chair had been abandoned and, although taking his arm and walking with him was a slow procedure, I was delighted that he could do so much unaided. Venetia was certainly beautiful if not communicative and Maria, an attractive little chatterbox, was everyone's sweetheart. My sons were almost as tall as Kit and John had already set his heart upon becoming a doctor. Anna, Phil and Michael were less academic but happy and healthy children so we felt, just for once, that our blessings outnumbered our trials.

In the latter part of the year, Dominic announced that he intended to buy a bungalow which was situated half way between the farm and the Taj Mahal. I was wary. He would, I knew full well, never be better than he was at that time but there were still quite a number of things which he found difficult. Living in Peter's palatial home, staff were always on hand to help out but once on his own, he would not be able to afford such extravagances. My worries were short lived as, within the month, his first book on the science of cardiology was published and it became an overnight success.

So it was that the bunglow was bought and transformed into an 'invalid friendly' home. We all helped. Kit spent what spare time he could grab putting the garden into some sort of order. It was a large garden and we laid a lawn and employed two men to make concrete recesses where pretty seats could be permanently fixed so Dom had somewhere to sit during the summer months. Peter, as usual, was generous with his money so every room was newly decorated and carpeted. A room, which the previous owners had used as a dinning room, was converted into a study and it was there that Dominic wrote his twelve medical books which eventually made him a wealthy man. Our boys loved the place and spent a great deal of their school holidays helping Uncle Dom; gardening and even cooking for him. I flapped around making sure he had everything he needed and tended to annoy him with daily phone calls to enquire if he was, ' all right.' He and I never spoke of our knowledge concerning Peter and Isabel but I always thought we were somewhat stilted when Teddy was in the vicinity. Poor old Teddy what with all his hard work, his early loss of Dorothea and then his beastly illness, I thought his life had been far from easy. To be told his wife was unfaithful would have been an added heartbreak so we talked of other things and concentrated on helping Dominic when and if he allowed it.

Then Eleanor Bonnington died.

She wasn't exactly in the grip of old age, I think she was in her very early sixties and, apart from sporadic depressive episodes, she was free from the severe nervous problems which had beset her after Samuel died. She and Laura were inseparable which, in view of Peter's neglect, was a boon. Whenever I visited mother, daughter and granddaughter were generally to be found closeted together and all three assumed an air of disapproval at my intrusion. Family gatherings at the farm they shunned and invitations to our house they refused. It was no good discussing the situation with Peter since he gave the impression of hardly caring whether they lived or died. Never the less they were pampered and, I always thought, extremely lucky to have such a grandiose home and a plentiful supply of money to enable them to live as they pleased. Eleanor's death came as shock to us but, to Laura, it was a devastation.

Peter, arriving as usual through my kitchen door, gave us the news early one Sunday morning.

'What happened?' Kit asked.

'Don't know.'

'We didn't know she was ill, did we Vin?'

'No,' I said, for I could see Peter was totally unmoved by the passing of his less than loved mother in law.

'She was pretty old,' he said.

'Pretty young I would have said,' Kit argued.

'Anyway, thought I'd let you know.'

That was all he came to say and, being Peter, once his mission was accomplished, he went.

'I must ask Simon Radcliff what saw her off,' Kit said once the kitchen door had slammed. 'Unlike old Simon not to let me know a member of the family was on the way out.'

'Would you call her a member of the family?' I asked.

'Sister in law's mother?' Kit contemplated. 'Vaguely, I suppose.'

But Doctor Radcliff couldn't tell us. He said Peter had called him to the house but Eleanor was already dead when he arrived. We gave him a drink and he sat with us for over an hour.

'What do you reckon killed her then?' Kit asked.

'M I,' he said, which I knew meant a heart attack. Myacardal Infarction if you are wondering what the letters stand for.

'Did you know she had a heart problem?'

'No, news to me but probably news to her too. Nice way to go specially when you're not expecting it. S'pose I should have asked for a post mortem but there's no reason to think it was anything other than natural causes.'

So that was that. Eleanor Bonnington followed her husband to a relatively early grave. Peter left all the funeral arrangements to Laura who, it goes without saying, hadn't a clue what to do. In the end it was Kit and I who organized the cremation but it was at The Taj Mahal that the wake took place. In view of the fact that Peter had all the money in the world to give poor Eleanor a good send off we employed a firm of caterers from Birmingham and invited as many people as we could think off to join us in bidding her farewell.

Many town's people had 'rubber necked' outside Peter's mansion but, of course, never set foot in it so, out of nothing more than idle curiosity, they eagerly accepted our invitations. Once condolences had been offered it seemed everyone expected a grand tour of the house and I obliged. Glad to have something to do, for Laura had hardly anything to say and Peter was nowhere to be seen, I showed the so called mourners each and every room and quite enjoyed their gasps of admiration and awe at discovering that anyone from poor old Borough Heath could afford such luxury. The lady who cleaned the church was overheard whispering to the verger that the place put her in mind of a Hollywood Mansion!

Venetia hovered for not more than ten minutes and then disappeared upstairs. If she was upset by her grandmother's departure, she showed no sign of it. Laura, taking neither food nor drink, refused all attempts at conversation which I found both trying and discourteous. Thankfully, at some point, she remembered her manners just enough to thank everyone for coming after which, pleading a bad headache, she retired to her room.

'She's going to be lonely with only the child for company,' Kit whispered.

'Hardly going to be consoled by a loving husband,' I whispered back.

'I wish she'd get out more and join in with the rest of us,' he added.

But Laura never attempted to join in anything. After Eleanor died she became a recluse. Matters were made even worse when Peter, apparently taking a rare interest in his wife and daughter, insisted that Ventetia was sent to boarding school. Of course he never bothered to tell any of us of his intentions that was left to Simon Radcliff who, for some reason, seemed privy to his plans.

'Good God,' Kit exclaimed. 'Poor Laura will be all alone in that monstrosity and with her withdrawn temperament, she'll go mad just as her mother did.'

'But Eleanor got better,' I reminded him.

'Never quite better, Vinnie,' Simon reminded me. 'She was a chronic depressive all the while she was my patient. How was she when you were her doc, Kit?'

'Okay until she lost her daughter and then her husband so, when she had the breakdown, I blamed her circumstances rather than any inherited mental problems.'

'Do you think losing Rose and then Samuel caused the trouble?' I asked.

'Oh, I should think there was a family history of instability, wouldn't you, Kit?'

'More than likely.'

That sparked off a long and tedious conversation on the subject of clinical depression between the two medical men so I left the room to see to Anna. Maybe I should have stayed to listen and learn for within two months of her mother's death, Laura suffered a similar breakdown to the one which Eleanor

Bonnington had undergone after Samuel died.

Peter, with money to burn, took no time in installing her in a plush nursing home the name and address of which he was loathed to impart, thus none of us were quite sure where the poor girl had gone. Venetia, he dispatched to an equally posh school in Paris so, as you can gather, within a matter of days we were bereft of both our sister in law and our neice.

The Taj Mahal, in all its glory, was not, however, to stand empty for any length of time. Only half a mile from the farm and Isabel but apparently too far when it came to matters of the heart, for within one month of Laura and Venetia's departure, Isabel moved from Teddy's home to Peter's taking Maria with her.

Teddy and Michael were abandoned without, apparently, a second thought but the rest of us were stunned. Of course Dominic and I were aware of their relationship if only because of what we had seen in the deserted pigsty but neither of us had feared the episode would lead to a major drama. A stolen hour on a makeshift mattress hardly led us to anticipate the break up of a marriage and the transference of a wife and child to her husband's brother!

But that's what happened and Isabel's only comment on the whole wretched affair was a half hearted remark degrading Teddy whom she said was more interested in his cows than in either her or Maria.

'Anyway,' she added, 'a child needs to be with her father and Maria is no exception.'

'But you're taking her away from Teddy.' I was perplexed.

'Her real father, Peter, I meant' she said.

Chapter Twenty Two

For two years, even a little more, we cold shouldered both Isabel and Peter. To Teddy, hardly inconsolable I have to admit but still an object of pity, I gave my full attention.

'Your brothers are a bloody nuisance ,' Kit told me. 'You're either fussing over Dom or feeling sorry for Teddy and very busy despising Peter so I hardly get a look in.'

'True,' I had to agree. 'I wonder if other sisters would be so caring?'

'Course not you should concentrate on the boys, they're running wild and poor little Anna's always conveniently stowed away with Dom in his blasted bungalow.'

But Kit really didn't mind. He loved Dominic and felt sorry for Teddy so he too gave up a great deal of his precious time to visit both of them. At some point it became quite obvious that Teddy could no longer manage the farm particularly as the need to do so was non existant. Since Peter had stolen his wife and left him with a adolescent son it was hardly surprising that he turned his back on future handouts just to keep the place ticking over so consequently, he was running into debt. In any case who needed a huge farm and an even bigger house when they lived alone and had to struggle to keep it going? Teddy was cured of his cancer but he wasn't as strong as before and Michael was at a vital stage in his schooling. So it was that we decided to sell up, land, animals, house, equipment, the lot.

It was a bitter decision. Not only had it been our childhood home but Ma's family had worked the land for two centuries before any of us were born. Memories packed it's every corner and the house was a beautiful building into the bargain. Dominic, Teddy and I walked the acres and discussed the possiblities of a sale.

'Where will you live, Teddy?' I had asked.

'Who cares?'

'I do.' I told him, for Teddy had been making fatuous statements of that ilk for some time. Regrettable but also understandable. The debacle of Isabel had left him feeling worthless and something of a fool. One small mystery, which I personally found perplexing, remained and that was the question of why he had assumed Maria was his daughter in the first place? Considering Michael's version of his parent's marriage plus everything we had seen and heard for ourselves it seemed unlikely that further children would have been conceived. Teddy should have known Maria couldn't possibly have been his daughter unless, after drinking too much of his own home made wine, Isabel had persuaded him otherwise.

'You could share my place,' Dominic offered.

'I'd get on your nerves.'

'I'd probably get on yours, but it's a big bungalow and there's ample room.'

'No, ta.'

'Oh don't be silly,' I said. 'If we sell the farm Teddy will have plenty of money. He can live wherever he likes.'

'It's got to be shared,' Teddy reminded me.

'Between the children,' I replied. 'Kit and I don't need it. Dom's fine now he's a successful author but, if you ever decide to snuff it Teddy, you can leave the money to Michael and our brood.'

'Are you sure, Vinnie?'

'Positive.'

And that's how the farm and our connection with it ended. It was eventually sold by a London agent for almost half a mllion. In the early eighties that was a fortune but it was a fine building and the land alone would be worth six times as much today. Teddy bought a cottage in the Derbyshire Dales and stayed with us whilst it was being renovated. One ugly scene ensued in the form of Peter and Isabel making a claim against the estate which incensed the rest of us. Peter insisted that, as he had invested money in the farm to keep it viable, he was due more than a mere quarter of the proceeds. Dominic argued that, annoying as it was in view of his abominable behaviour, he was within his rights and since none of us wanted an affray with him, Teddy handed over his share plus thousands more to cover his various loans and handouts. After that, he and Isabel kept their distance and any interest the rest of us felt towards either one of them lapsed and we left them strictly alone.

Before Teddy left the farm there was a multiude of things that needed to be done. We understood that the buyers intended to turn the house into a hotel or a motel so they had no interest in the farm as such. In view of this, Teddy was able to make even more money by selling the stock and equipment. Sale after sale he attended and the local auction houses were kept busy selling his tools and later the heavy goods such as the tractors and the combine harvester. Farmers from all over The Midlands came to Borough Heath to buy at the various sales he held on site. Today they might have qualified as car boot sales for often he had open days where he successfully pocketed extra cash from the sale of rakes, sheep shears, rat traps, yard brooms and odd and sods of all descriptions. In the end I think he saw it as something of a hobby as he began to spend his days searching for items that the rest of us would have condemned to the local tip.

It was whilst he was dismantling a dilapidated shed at the end of the kitchen garden where once, many years ago Ma had kept two goats, that he found the body. He told us he believed the shed contained an old wine press and a load of Kilner Jars, which had been popular during the war, and which he thought might rate as collectables. The shed had fallen into complete disrepair so Teddy decided to demolish it.

Beneath it's rotting base and some eight inches under the top soil lay the remains of a human body. Whether the remains were male or a female it was impossible to say for decomposition was all but complete. Only the forensic people, we assumed, would have the answer but, naturally, we all believed that the mystery of Dorothea's disappearance was solved. Teddy, deeply shocked by his gruesome find, reacted with both sorrow and relief.

Further sales of equipment and clearing up in general was, of course, put on hold. Once the police and forensic teams were alerted an army of technicians moved in and stayed put for over a week. Teddy found himself surrounded by men in white suits who ordered him to keep out of their way so much so that he felt forced to leave the farm altogether. Feelings of shock and grief were quickly overtaken by extreme irritation and increasing frustration as, naturally, all his personal belongings were left in the house. Even collecting a few clothes for Michael and himself proved trying as the police questioned our every move. In the end Kit and Dominic contacted the chief constable of Staffordshire and made a formal complaint to the effect that Teddy was being denied access to his own property.

Thankfully their complaint was treated sympathetically and he was allowed in and out of the farm house without further harassment. We all helped to pack his clothes and essentials at the same time grabbing anything of value plus the many items which qualified as heirlooms. After that he and Michael came to stay with us whilst the scientists carried out their gruesome task and the police reopened the case.

Although Dorothea's father had died, her mother was still living as were her two brothers and they were summoned from Derbyshire for further questioning. All three moved in with Dom whilst we waited to discover if the solution to our mystery was about to be revealed .

Those were the days before DNA testing had come to the fore and although forensic science had dramatically advanced it was still far removed from the sophistication of today's technology. The remains were dispatched to a laboratory in Berkshire where a detailed examination was performed but, I have to tell you, no conclusion was ever reached.

As a family each one of us was convinced that the decomposed body was that of Dorothea but since it was reduced to a mere skeleton, unclothed and fragmented, the pathologists and medical examiners could not confirm our belief. We were all questioned once again and shadows of the night when the storm raged over the forest and the farm came back to haunt us.

The publicity surrounding the discovery delayed the hotel company from completing the sale as, obviously, Teddy's find resulted in a murder enquiry. Our common sense told us that, regardless as to whether or not the body could be identified, no one suffering a natural death would be buried under the floorboards of a goat shed! To that end the investigation into Dorothea's disappearance started all over again and we had to endure further gruelling interviews as did surviving farm hands, town's folk and anyone, however vaguely, connected with the family.

And that all came to nothing.

The only person who seemed unperturbed by, what amounted to police harassment, was Isabel. I used to watch her, hand in hand with Maria, shopping in Borough Heath High Street and wonder how she lived with herself after her wretched treatment of poor Teddy. I, for one, had taken to

ignoring her and, on the very rare occasions when Peter
appeared on the streets, I made a point of looking the other
way. Secretly, I used to wish it were otherwise for life is short
and I had been fond of Isabel and Peter, whatever his
transgressions, was still our brother and the father of my niece.
Also, I was intrigued by a centre page spread, in a recent edition
of the Daily Mail, which carried a photograph of Peter, and a
lengthy article, erroneously headed; 'Peter MacVee, who is
currently assisting Staffordshire CID with enquiries into a
twenty year old unsolved mystery, has been commissioned to
paint a mural in the throne room at Windsor castle.'

'Your errant brother's reached the very top of the tree,' Kit
told me after I'd pushed the article under his nose. 'The Queen
herself wants him to daub her walls at Windsor. Little bugger
will be knighted before he's forty five.'

'I expect he will.' I grabbed the paper from Kit. 'I could cry.'

'Whatever for, the Queen's bad taste or Peter's mounting
fame and fortune?'

'For the fact that he's one of the most famous painters in
the world and we don't even speak to him.'

'Cry away, Vinnie, the boy's no good except as a pavement
artist. Look what he did to Teddy?'

'He stole a wife Teddy didn't want,' I stormed. 'She was
miserable at the farm and she fell for Peter. It wasn't as though
he ruined a happy marriage; they'd been fighting like cats and
dogs for years.'

'But his own brother.'

'That's just sentiment,' I answered. 'I want this childish
nonsense to stop. I want us to be a family again.'

'Then see what your brothers have to say. I'm just the in
law.'

So that's what I did. I spoke to both Dominic and Teddy
and told them that I wanted to patch things up and intended to
talk to Isabel and Peter.

'What's done is done,' I said, using an old cliché but it

summed up my feelings. 'I want to be friends with them again and Michael ought to be able to see his mother.'

'As you will, Vinnie,' Teddy said. 'I've done with either loving or hating Isabel and Peter's not worthy of any emotion so if you want to ask them to tea I'll come and do the washing up.'

'You're sure it's not just because your curiosity's got the better of you now that Peter's hobnobbing with our soveriegn lady?' Dominic asked.

'Of course not. That's a horrid thing to say and not like me at all. You should know that Dom.'

'Sorry Vin, I do know you and I should have known better.'

So it was that the next time I spotted Isabel shopping in the town centre, I hurriedly put on my raincoat, rushed down the High Street and followed her into the chemist's shop.

'Isabel,' I said, catching up with her just inside Boots. 'May I speak to you?'

It was a formal request. The question of a stranger to a celebrity or a secretary to her boss. She turned at the sound of my voice and looked at the ground but little Maria rushed towards me and I picked her up giving her a hug. 'It's Aunty Vinnnie,' I said, thinking that she may need reminding.

'I remember,' she said, which considering she was only three years old and hadn't seen me for almost two years, I thought pretty astute.

'We need loo paper,' she informed me.

I laughed. It was just the sort of thing a child would roar out and a grown woman whisper. Silly things can break granite and Maria achieved just that. Isabel smiled and I laughed.

'What's wrong with the supermarket?' I asked.

'We like to support our local shops, don't we pet?' said Isabel

And that was that. We went into the chemists together, bought the Andrex and some other items and then wandered out into a rain soaked High Street.

'Why don't we pop into the house and have a coffee?' I suggested. 'We're standing here getting soaked when the percolator will still be hot because Kit's only just left.'

I remember she hesitated offering a lame excuse about having to get home to receive a phone call but, in no time at all, I persuaded her to change her mind and we sat together in my kitchen drinking ground coffee whilst Anna and Maria happily played with a collection of dolls: for what did they know of betrayals and family feuds?

I can not say that I ever loved Isabel but, because she was a member of my family, I did my best to conjure up feelings of fondness towards her. Perhaps I succeeded for when she died just two years ago, I cried for a week.

I should not have cried at all.

I should have prayed that her soul would find peace and that our good Lord would grant forgivness.

Sheila M Barnes

Chapter Twenty Three

As no positive identification of Teddy's macabre find under the rotting boards of the goat shed was established, gradually the police and the forensic teams drifted away. We were in exactly the same boat as we were all those years ago when Dorothea came into our lives and vanished just as quickly. It had been almost two decades since her mysterious disappearance and the people of Borough Heath had moved on to such an extent that, a once enthralling mystery, proved less absorbing than a television soap opera or their newly acquired music centres which had overtaken conversation and popular interest. Where once the MacVee family and events at the farm had been noteworthy and of importance in the small community, now there were better things to do and entertainment was the order of the day. So, as the police departed and the hotel company moved in, our once prominent stance in the community faded to something approaching boredom.

Towards the end of the eighties people were no longer categorised by class or breeding and any lingering respect for the old established families vanished over night. Everyone believed that they had a right to aspire to anything they desired and the growing cult of celebrity claimed mass attention. Squires and elders of the community began to take a back seat as did professional people, politicians and even, to some extent, royalty itself.

The years of our lives started to rush away; the children grew into young adults and birthdays reminded us of our own mortality. Dominic continued to improve. Of course, with the dawn of the eighties, medical science romped ahead and miraculous discoveries were almost a daily occurrence. Kit and I took him to our flat in Bourne Street and from there he went into Moorefield's Hospital, perhaps the greatest eye hospital in the world, where he underwent surgery to have further retina transplants. Returning to his bungalow, with almost perfect vision, he managed it's upkeep without assistance. Always hampered by a pronounced limp he had various 'new' legs fitted but, thankfully, the last one, eighth in all, was an unmitigated success so that to watch him walk up the High Street from my vantage point, behind the curtain in the living room, was an absolute pleasure.

Teddy, possessed of a small fortune after the sale of the farm, took to travelling and visited America and Austrailia in the same year. He deserted the Derbyshire Dales and bought a cottage in Henly-in-Arden where, for a time, Michael lived with him. Then Michael fulfilled his childhood dream of becoming an actor. None of us really believed he would ever aspire to a theatrical career but by sheer good luck he obtained an equity card and landed a part in 'The Archers' on radio. The small character part he played was soon 'killed off' but his luck remained and, after auditioning for a role in a West End musical, he got a none singing part in a rehash of the stage version of Camelot. The show packed them in, as the saying goes, which led to even better roles and a substantial part in a television sit-com.

Again I had to accept that a member of our family was gay

Sheila M Barnes

but I found it easier to swallow once the law had changed and people's attitude was kinder. Persuading Teddy to accept the fact was a different matter but he consoled himself in the knowledge that Michael was happy, earning a living and fascinating us all with his show business gossip.

Even into his late sixties, I still fretted that Dominic, also gay, was all alone in the world. All alone that is in the context of not having a lover or a partner but he had all of us and the children adored him. Kit and I were only a stone's throw from his bungalow so we were in constant touch and after the disaster that had been Brian Thorn I consoled myself that Dom was more than content to spend his life with his nephews and nieces, brothers and sister and feel grateful that he had survived the trauma of his, so called, accident.

Even Peter mellowed as middle age turned his wheat blond hair to ash grey and his once ice blue eyes, tired from a life time of fine work, began to blink mildly from behind steel rimmed specs. He never received a knighthood, as Kit had predicted, but he was honoured with an OBE in the nineteen ninety two honours list and that suited him well enough. When I stare at the mural, still intact on my living room wall, I never fail to feel thrilled and still I marvel at the wonders of his illustrious career.

As the century drew to its close he was constantly in demand often by strange young men who performed in the increasingly popular boy bands. John and Phil benefited from Uncle Peter's clientele in so much as invitations to show business parties, occasionally attended by Princes William and Harry, were extended to Peter MacVee and his friends. On one occasion he took Anna to a BAFTA award ceremony where she met a host of stars which resulted in her regaling Kit and I for months on the wonders of her evening on the arm of Peter and, of all people, Cilla Black.

Isabel with Maria always stayed at home. The Taj Mahal suited her and her then grown daughter and, never once, did she show the slightest inclination to accompany her husband or any of us to the glittering parties attended by Peter. Even when Michael sent her tickets to his or Tim's first nights, she thanked him profusely but never set a foot further than Borough Heath town centre.

Our eldest son, John married in the first year of the new millenium and Phil followed suit in the June of 2003. We were less than delighted with Phil's choice of wife, a coloured girl who, at the time, was a high ranking detective with the Metropolitan Police Force. Important enough to warrant her own office at Scotland Yard she had a considerable staff beneath her, so perhaps we should have been proud that such a prominent lady chose to marry our son. Her precise job description was Chief Archive Inspector within the C.I.D. but that, when translated, meant that she researched cold cases.

Even less endearing was her assignment at the time of the marriage which happened to be a renewed investigation into the disappearance of Dorothea Stephens. Kit scowled throughout the wedding service due to his belief that our new daughter in law would spend the next twelve months unearthing our past and constantly quizzing us about the age old mystery. Teddy, possessed of the same opinion, excused himself from the reception which was held at a prestigious golf club near Birmingham. Dominic, however, plainly 'took to her' even embarking on a strange dialogue concerning his accident and, for once, speaking the truth in so much as he 'confessed' that Brian Thorn had wilfully caused his fall from a third story window. Whether because, knowing she was a police officer prompted him towards honesty, or because Brian was long dead, I've no idea but he monopolised the poor girl on her wedding day until, even she, began to look bored.

Peter attended that ceremony only because he happened to be at home with little else to do. When John married he had been in the States painting a mural for a prominent Hollywood film star. Always newsworthy, he had claimed the attention of

Sheila M Barnes

The Sun newspaper who proclaimed him to be her latest lover. To prove their point a centre fold spread was given over to photographs of him wining and dining some extremely pretty woman a quarter of his age. If Isabel read the article or poured over the pictures, we were not privy to her comments or able to share her disinterest, as she avoided both our boys weddings as did Maria.

Kit constantly worried about Maria because, whereas he was quite content to stand by whilst Isabel turned herself into a hermit, he viewed Maria as a virtual prisoner in The Taj Mahal. A situation which we all considered unhealthy and unnatural.

'I've done with interfering,' I told him. 'Isabel and I are on speaking terms and reasonably friendly so I don't want to rock the boat by telling her how to run either her life or Marias'.'

'You should.' Kit said. 'Isabel's growing old like the rest of us and one day she'll die and Maria will be useless. She must get out into the world and have a life of her own. It's criminal keeping her locked away like a pet poodle.'

'She always seems perfectly happy when I visit.'

'Which is what; once a month for an hour? Use your influence Vinnie and persuade Isabel to let her come to one of our family parties.'

But I Failed Kit. Oh, I tried. I practically got down on my knees and begged Isabel to join us for Kit's sixtieth birthday celebrations but she refused point blank. No excuses, no thinking about it, just a plain "No thanks Vinnie, Maria and I don't go out in an evening."

So I tried and Dominic tried. We even discussed our concern with Michael so he and Tim joined in the crusade by visiting the Taj Mahal where they tried to tempt her with tickets for nearby shows but neither man was allowed to put so much as a foot inside the front door.

We never stopped calling the mansion that Peter built, all those years ago, by that absurd name although in reality it's called 'Scots Corner'. Sometimes, in an effort to make Peter appear more family minded and human, I like to think he named it for Pa who was very much a Scot's man. A Highland man in fact. Should I, ever again set eyes on my youngest brother, I must remember to ask him how the name came about but until that kitchen door bursts open and he puts in one of his rare appearances, the question must remain unanswered.

Peter left Borough Heath fifteen years ago when he discovered the truth. The papers said Mr. MacVee had decided to settle in Florence so that he could live amongst the great art treasures of the world. We none of us have an address for him or can tell you where he might be found but I know that even the world's most wondrous collections of art wouldn't have tempted Peter to leave us anymore than a temperate climate would have persuaded him to hide away in the soft mountains of Southern Italy.

Peter, by that time, had learnt that all his money and fame counted for nothing and his affair with Teddy's wife had ruined his life.

He left Borough Heath to be rid of her.

For good.

Chapter Twenty Four

T eddy, five years my senior at the age of almost seventy, surprised us all by forming a romantic attachment with a lady of forty one. A romantic attachment sounds a stuffy expression in this day and age but you will have grasped my meaning. Teddy fell in love or so it seemed with a lady by the name of Kate Tenbury.

He and Kate met on a cruise which Teddy took during the spring of 2004. Out of the blue he decided to treat himself to a world tour on a brand new liner called 'The Mercury.' Strangely enough, when he told us about his intended holiday, I said to Kit what a pity it was that he would travel all alone. Kit said Teddy was born to be alone and I only had to recall his ill fated marriage to acknowledge the truth of that.

'That was hardly his fault,' I pointed out.

'He never loved Isabel,' Kit said. 'She was a help on the farm and a poor substitute for Dorothea but nothing more.'

'Anyway, with his gift for making friends he'll probably be the life and soul of the party,' I tried to sound convincing although, secretly, I doubted his ability to mimic and fascinate at the great age of seventy.

We drove him to Southampton Docks and Dominic came with us. On the bleak waterfront, we all waved goodbye and wished him an enjoyable trip after which the three of us set off for the New Forrest to indulge in our own, compared to Teddy's, very modest holiday.

Three months he sailed the high seas and from every port he sent post cards and, now and again, even rang to tell us more of his traveller's tales. Dominic, then in his mid seventies, expressed a wish to have a similar cruise but we all advised against it. Looking back I think we curbed a great deal of Dom's pleasures by constantly reminding him that he was a semi-invalid. Considering his various disabilities, he lived a normal and happy life but we, well myself in particular, always tended to over protect him. When he spent a few days in London, to promote a new book or visit a hospital to lecture on heart disease, I would fret that he wouldn't be able to cope. Kit used to get cross as it was perfectly clear to us all that Dominic could more than cope with anything and everything. Anyway, as he grew older and a little less steady on his artificial leg, John and Phil were both in town to keep an eye on him. The children adored Uncle Dom and were proud of his achievements, the tragedy was, that if he hadn't been born gay he would never have been involved with a psychopath like Brian Thorn and might have had a loving wife and family as well as an illustrious career. Kit argued that my theory didn't hold water, pointing out that he could well have had the misfortune to marry some bitch of a woman who would have ruined his proffessional chances and been every bit as bad as Thorn.

What did I know?

The day arrived when we were due to meet Teddy at the docks and I for one looked forward to his return. Dominic didn't accompany us on that journey as winter had set in and he had developed arthritis in his remaining knee. Poor Dom suffered most of the ailments associated with old age whereas, up until last year, I have hardly been affected by such indignities. May I say that ommision has now been corrected and I am plagued by a new infirmity or illness almost every day.

Teddy was one of the last passengers to disembark by which time Kit was tired and fractious from hanging onto a rail in the barn of a place that served as a reception lounge for home coming passengers. The wind was howling through two great double doors that opened directly onto the mooring where 'The Mercury' was anchored. In our view, Southampton Water had never looked more unappetising.

Eventually we spotted him and we both heaved a sigh of relief. Two hours standing on aching feet, feeling dizzy staring into unknown faces surging towards you does not make for a pleasant afternoon. But Teddy was not alone, neither was he particularly apologetic for the length of time he had kept us waiting on a Novemeber day when boredom and freezing conditions had practically floored both Kit and I. So it was that we first met and were introduced to Miss Kate Tenbury.

Kate was the owner of a thriving taxi company based in Worthing, West Sussex. She was quite small, somewhere between five foot three and five foot five and she can't have weiged more than eight stone. I suppose I should use metric measurments when describing Teddy's lady love but, and I'm almost proud to admit it, I never came to grips with anything other than pounds and ounces, shillings and pence.

We took to Kate.

The drive back to Borough Heath, for she had agreed to come home with Teddy, was much enhanced by her presence. In other words she made us laugh which, to some extent, compensated for our gruelling wait on the perishing docks. We could plainly see that Teddy was besotted and, apart from our whispered comments regarding the age gap, we were thrilled that he had found a friend on his travels.

Actually, Kate looked even younger than her forty one years and I recall putting her at no more than thirty five. Her complexion was fresh and her movements, particularly when compared to ours, were brisk and agile. For Teddy she showed obvious affection so the age disparity quickly ceased to be an issue.

Teddy had elected to stay with us until the new year as his cottage was in the throws of yet more building work. A conservatory was being added and so was a second bathroom which made me wonder if had prior knowledge that the cottage was to house more than just himself in the near future.

In the following weeks, Kit and I learnt a great deal about Kate and the more we knew, the more we liked her. Dominic was equally enamoured and so was Michael when he visted to welcome his father home from the cruise. Poor Michael seldom saw his mother as Isabel had eyes only for Maria so a new and attractive woman in Teddy's life provided quite an interest particularly as Kate was keen on the theatre. During his frequent visits the two of them spent many happy hours discussing plays and actors and even made trips to see shows as far away as Chichester and Leeds. Teddy, I might add, was more than content to let them go as, still very much the farmer, play acting bored him silly.

'Why can't he get a proper job, Vin?' Is a question he asks to this day and I always laugh and tell him that acting is a proper job always adding that it pays a damn sight better than getting up at five every morning to milk a hundred cows. Actually Teddy secretly adores Michael even though his way of life and chosen profession are beyond his understanding.

Although Teddy always referred to Kate as 'a good business woman,' she seemed to pay very little attention to her taxi firm. Now and again she would phone her manager in Worthing and make, what sounded to Kit and I, like disinterested comments regarding the state of trade.

'It's an unusual business for a lady to run,' Kit remarked over dinner one evening.

'Why?' she asked.

'Oh, I don't know. I mean taxis or cars in general I assosiate with men but then I'm an old age pensioner so what can you expect?'

'My father started it in the early sixties,' she told him. 'Mum and Dad ran it for years and I drove for them until Dad had a stroke in nineteen eighty seven. After he died Mum decided to go and live with my aunt in Hastings and I took over. So, you see, the business was all set up and waiting for me but I gave up the driving side of it some three years ago.'

'So you could take cruises on luxury liners and meet fascinating old fossils like me,' said Teddy.

'You actually drove a cab?' I asked. My question giving the impression I understood her to imply she had been the pilot of a space ship.

'Oh yes, for years. I did the airport runs and most of the long distance trips. I adored driving but when the traffic got manic I was glad to give up and manage the firm from afar but we are one of the biggest operators on the south coast.'

'You see, Vin,' Teddy helped himself to three more roast potatoes. 'When I pick a lady friend I make sure she's rich as well as beautiful.'

I think Kate probably was quite well off but money for money's sake never particularly interested Kit or I so that aspect of her life didn't appeal to either one of us. Teddy, on the other hand, having spent the greater part of his share in the farm, was undoubtedly aware of the financial attraction that came with Kate Tenbury and would have seen it as a bonus.

One afternoon I took Kate to the Taj Mahal to visit Isabel and Maria. It was my afternoon to go to tea and since both Teddy and Kit were away from home I decided to take Kate with me. Knowing Isabel was not fond of visitors I warned her that she might receive a less than enthusiastic welcome from Teddy's estranged wife. Naturally Kate was interested to see Isabel as, by this time, we had all accepted the fact that she was Teddy's girl friend. Can a man of seventy have girl friends: I suppose he can and why not? Teddy was in better health since his retirement from all that gruelling farm work and his appearance was enhanced by a mop of soft white hair framing a face which showed little sign of the passing years.

Isabel, unexpectedly, appeared pleased to meet Kate and Maria was positively charming. (At that time Maria's one claim to fame in our family history lay in her parentage. Since we had all believed her to be Teddy's daughter and then discovered otherwise she claimed our attention more on that score than on any other.)

So hospitable were they towards Kate that I took the opportunity to invite them to join us at a Christmas Eve party which Dominic was holding at his bungalow. Miraculously Isabel instantly agreed a decision which, when I told Kit, thrilled him no end as he constantly worried about Maria's isolated state

'How did you manage to coax the old girl out of her crystal palace?' he asked me.

'She's taken a shine to Kate. I got the impression she only agreed because Kate's going to come back from Worthing specially for the party.'

'Not turned into a lesbian, has she?'

'Shut up,' I laughed. 'One more sexually challenged person in this family and I shall become one myself.'

Teddy appeared and disappeared as his cottage was still in the hands of the builders and his interest in its progress had turned into something of a hobby. We all wondered if he and Kate would announce their intention to move in together once the Christmas holidays were over but, my daughter Anna said, if Uncle Teddy wanted someone to share his bed this side of the grave he better move her in right away. John and Phil found the situation hilarious as, still only in their twenties, Teddy's age and romantic notions had them roaring with laughter. I used to point out that it was not just the young who had a monopoly on sex and people over the age of thirty five, although they would find it hard to believe, still took a healthy interest in love making.

Kate, having settled her affairs in sunny Worthing, returned to Borough Heath and began spending a great deal time with Dominic. At first she stayed with Kit and I but devoted her afternoons to helping him clean silver or put up festive decorations at the bungalow. One evening she rang us, at about nine o'clock, to say that Dom's washing machine had developed some kind of fault which in turn had caused a minor flood in his kitchen. As she described the chaos we gathered that the flood must have been quite severe especially as she added that since it would take hours to mop up, she would stay put, sleep over and return later the next day. Kit took the call and thanked her profusely for helping Dominic but reminded her not to work too hard as the old boy was quite capable of mopping up his own flood.

Kate didn't come back the next day or the day after that but we spoke to her on the phone and none of us, including Teddy, gave the matter of her absence any serious thought. It was Isabel, of all unlikely people, who reacted to the news. Making one of her rare visits to our house she talked of little else.

'She shouldn't be staying with Dominic if she's supposed to be all in all with Teddy,' she announced, quite fiercely during one teatime.

'Why ever not?' I enquired.

'It will upset Teddy.'

Considering the major upset she had caused in her estranged husband's life we thought her remark ludicrous. Even Maria, who usually said very little, reminded her that Kate Tenbury had every right to do exactly as she pleased.

'It's very strange all the same,' Isabel said, adding an outraged sniff.

'I don't see why,' I retorted. 'Dom's absolutely marvellous but extra help is always welcome. Remember he's in his mid seventies now and his arthritis has been playing him up dreadfully.'

'Can't Kit give him anything for that?'

'Not really,' said Kit. 'It's called old age and after all he's been through he can cope with a few twinges.'

'Twinges,' Isabel snapped. 'According to Vinnie, he's practically crippled.'

And so it was that an argument of gigantic proportions flared up during what should have been a pleasant afternoon get together. The simple matter of Kate spending a few days with Dominic seemed the most natural thing in the world to Kit and I. Teddy was away supervising improvements to his cottage and we were busy with plans for the coming Christmas. Both the boys, their wives and Anna were expected home for the holidays, so bed making and grocery buying were occupying my thoughts as was the choosing of presents. Kit, tearing round in an effort to see as many patients as possible so that he would not be over burdened during Christmas week, I doubt gave Kate's absence a second thought.

'You've always told me not to fuss Dominic,' she persisted. 'Both you and Kit have laid down the law to such an extent that I'm terrified to bend down and pick something off the floor which he might have dropped. Now you're more than happy to provide him with a full time maid just to mop up a few drops of water.'

'Does it matter, Isabel?' Kit was tired of the tantrum and wanted her to go, that I could plainly see.

'I hate it when one set of rules applies to one person and then quite a different set to someone else.'

'Listen,' Kit raised his voice, 'with Teddy flouncing off to interfere with his builders every other day, Kate's at a loose end. Dom's trying his best to give us all a super party so what's more natural than her going over to his place to give him a hand?'

'Maria and I could have seen to all that,' she said, irrationally. Bearing in mind that she and her devoted daughter hardly ever set foot out of the Taj Mahal the idea of any of us summoning her to assist Dom with his party plans was farcical.

'Perhaps you and Maria should visit Dom,' I suggested, lamely. 'See if you can find anything worthwhile to do which would help him and Kate out.'

'Are you trying to be sarcastic?'

'Not at all. I just thought you sounded miffed that Kate was putting her oar in.'

'I'm sure Dominic could manage perfectly well without her interference.'

On that sour note, Isabel and Maria left us and, strange to say, Kit and I burst out laughing. Well, it was funny if you think about it. As I've told you, they were living the lives of almost total recluses and any suggestion that we call upon either of them to help organise a festive party would normally have been dismissed as a non starter. Suddenly, Isabel was throwing a tantrum over what she apparently saw as an unnecessary intrusion on the part of Kate and giving the impression of wanting to take her place.

'If she wants to help old Dom,' Kit said, 'let her. At least it would get her away from that mausoleum for an hour or so and allow poor Maria a rare view of the outside world.'

'Tell you what,' I said, supportively, 'I'll ring Dom and tell him she's having a jealous fit or whatever it is we think she's having and suggest that he invites her over to dress his Christmas Tree. How about that?'

'Sound good to me.'

And that was the start of a surprising twist in this saga of a family who had suffered twists enough but it was a very gradual journey and much was to occur before any of us began to understand Isabel's motives for wanting to monopolise Dominic.

Chapter Twenty Five

W hen the new millenium dawned I was seventy years old, Teddy seventy five and Dominic eighty. How hard it was for any of us to believe we had attained such ages!

On Dom's eightieth birthday, Kit and I decided to throw a really elaboarte party. We all considered it a miricle he had lived so long considering what had happened all those years ago in Tettenhall but he was in good health and his coming party was the most talked about event of the year.

A cold wet February morning had warned us that, at our respective ages, future birthdays may be at a premium so Dom's eightieth was considered both a triumph as well as a milestone. I recall Anna telling me that our plans were 'over the top' and that none of her friends would consider them cool. Considering she was no longer in the first flush of youth herself Kit advised her to give the glittering occasion a miss particularly if she continued to criticize using out dated American expressions. The next time it was mentioned I noticed that she applauded our efforts and spoke only of the gift she intended to buy Uncle Dom to mark his special day.

Dwelling on gifts for Dom or anyone else couldn't have

been further from my mind. Somewhat depressed by acknowledging the truth of Anna's comments, I agreed that our preparations for the party were, indeed, over the top as an eightieth birthday diminishes the prospects of future anniversaries or, at least, limits them.

Both boys were at home as was Anna. That fact alone should have roused my flagging spirits but, on that damp and dreary morning, I cooked and arranged tables without the slightest enthusiasum. The usual crowd of our contempories were arriving at seven thirty to join us in, what I hoped, would be a splendid dinner. Kit, I might add, had done everything in his power to persuade me to hold the party at a hotel and avoid all the tedious preparations but I felt that Dom would prefer an informal celebration at our house with just his closest friends.

As I fretted and fussed over the limitations of our dinning room, entertaining doubts as to whether the menu was as wonderful as it had seemed when first I planned it some weeks ago, the kitchen door opened and Peter, tanned from an Italian sun and looking years younger for his fifty seven years, walked into the kitchen.

'I hope this isn't a home coming feast for me?' he commented.

I kissed him and for once he didn't draw back or push me away. Seeing him so unexpectedly filled me with joy and instantly banished my sombre mood. Standing some few feet away from him I exclaimed on his healthy appearance and praised everything from his haircut to his impeccable light blue suit and silver tie.

'Oh, Peter,' I hugged him again. 'It's so good to see you, I thought I might die without ever setting eyes on you again.'

'What a morbid thought.'

'Yes isn't it, but don't forget I'm thirteen years older than you.'

'Are you done with life then, Vinnie, or did you really think I'd disappeared for ever?'

'I never know with you,' I answered, which was the simple truth for seldom had he bothered to write or even phone during all his years abroad. 'You must be longing to go to that palace of yours and see your daughter and Isabel?'

'No hurry.'

'She's quite a lady now.'

'Who's quite a lady?'

'Maria.'

'What an old fashioned expression. Quite a lady!' He laughed and placed a ring on my little finger.

'It's Dominic's birthday not mine,' I said as I stared at the diamond sparkling on my hand. 'I hope you've got some more of these for Isabel and Maria.'

'Nope.'

'Well, I trust you've got something for them.'

'Why, they've got everything they could possibly want?'

The preparations for the party temporaly dismissed I told him all about the reclusive state of Isabel and Maria. I seemed to constantly repeat Isabel's name as Peter, never having bothered to divorce Laura or insist that Isabel did likewise with Teddy, precluded me from referring to her as his wife and any other name would have been inappropriate.

'I'm surprised you and Isabel never married,' I said, voicing my thoughts, 'After all you had Maria to consider. Didn't you love her enough?'

'Can't remember.'

'I know you never loved Laura.'

'You know many things, Vinnie.'

'Do you ever hear from Larua?'

'Nope.'

So you see I might just as well have spoken to the wall or the side of beef that awaited the oven for the coming party. Peter pranced into the living room to check that his mural remained intact. At least, that was my guess as anything he did was usually a mystery.

In the hall he met Phil's wife, Lydia and I heard her greet him; probably wondering who on earth he was. Hurriedly I went to rescue my daughter in law for Peter was not exactly known for his gracious manners and easy conversation. Not that Lydia would make any attempt to charm him. Kit and I had always thought her somewhat boyish and matter of fact so the fame or genius of Peter MacVee would hardly hold her in thrall.

Kit arrived home early that afternoon. Almost completely retired, he still conducted the occasional surgery for one of the young doctors in the town. The day of Dom's party he had been locuming for a Doctor Hamilton who was on paternity leave, celebrating the birth of twin sons. When I told him that Peter had returned he groaned, predicting that his presence would ruin the party and complicate things all round.

'What makes you say that ?' I asked

'Because that's what always happens,' Kit sighed. 'He damages things. Look what he did to Teddy and Laura Bonnington. He might be Peter the Painter as far as the world's concerned but he's a damn nuisance to his family.'

'He's in his fifties now, he's calmed down and he's very rich.'

'What his blasted bank balance got to with anything?'

'It proves his enormous success.'

'Ours proves we've got three demanding children still begging for loans. You might advise our daughter that a job in Sainsburys would help pay her rent and save my pocket.'

Anna's never settled to hard work or been remotely interested in a profession I must admit but to stir up an argument on the day of Dom's birthday and Peter's home coming was not on my agenda. I kissed Kit on the cheek and sent him to the cloakroom to wash his hands.

If I had thought Lydia disinterested in art then I had been mistaken. My next view of her and Peter was some half an hour later when I visited the sitting room to check on my flower arrangements and found them huddled together discussing the mural which Peter had painted over fifty years ago.

Peter was proudly explaining that, due to the special paint he always used, his work hadn't faded despite the years and it's exposure to strong sunlight. Lydia was full of admiration for the animals, laughing at two rabbits peeping out from behind a willow tree.

'Did you paint when you were a little boy?' she asked.

'Yes, in my playroom.'

I pictured that playroom with its vast aray of toys and wondered why none of us had been aware, that amongst the rocking horses and armies of soldiers which littered the floor, we housed a genius.

'It's all I care about,' he told her.

'Do you remember Dorothea?' Lydia asked. I thought her tone as flat as if she were enquiring whether his playroom had been draughty or not.

'Yes.'

'How old were you when she disappeared?'

'About four.'

'Very small.'

'Very young but never small,' Peter smiled.

'Did you ever wonder what happened to her?'

'No.'

'Never curious, not even slightly?'

'I thought they found her under Ma's old goat shed. I read something about it when I was in Italy.'

'The body was too decomposed for identification,' she said.

'Surely you lot could have done something ingenious now you've got DNA tests to help out?'

'Not always.'

'But her mother's still alive, she could have supplied a match.'

'Not my department.'

So Lydia had aready told Peter her occupation but the

subject under discussion was hardly fitting for the day of
Dominic's birthday party so I stepped in and interrupted the
conversation.

'Most of the time that mural's all I have to remind me I
possess a younger brother.' I slipped my arm through his in an
effort to divert her interest.

'You must be very proud of him,' she said, 'but as a family
you must all wonder what really happened to that girl.'

'Of course, but you can't spend you life wondering, Lydia.'
I hoped she would interpret the sharp rise in my voice as a sign
that I wished the subject dropped.

'And then there was the awful tragedy of the baby
drowning.'

'Rose.' I repeated the name and wished with all my heart
that Lydia had remained at her desk at Scotland Yard and was
not pestering me with talk of past tragedies that were best
forgotten.

'Did her mother, Isabel wasn't it, ever come to terms with it
or does she still grieve?'

'What do you think?'

'I think she must be an exceptionally strong woman. It
would have killed me.'

'We never talk about it,' I warned. 'Please don't mention it
tonight of all nights.'

'But she has a grown daughter now?'

'My daughter.' Peter chipped in and, for once, I detected a
note of pride in his voice,

'But she married your brother?'

'Another topic best left out of the birthday chatter,' he
answered.

'And Dominic never married?'

'His tastes lie elsewhere.' Peter rubbed a tiny speck of dust
from the mural but both he and I exchanged glances as he did
so. This woman was asking far too many questions for our
liking and I could see his irritation.

'Yes, so Phil told me. He had a boy friend once didn't he?'

'For God's sake woman,' Peter was angry and I didn't blame him, 'you're not at Scotland bloody Yard now so drop the third degree.'

'I'll leave you two alone,' she said. 'You must have lots to talk about.'

Once she had left the room we did, indeed, have much to talk about. I thought her insufferable and Peter was shaking with rage.

'Bloody creature,' he spat. 'What business was all that of hers?'

'Part of her job I suppose,' I told him, 'but we can do without old history.'

'I'll say.'

Then we talked of his life in Italy and he told me all about his little house that was tucked away behind a mountain. I laughed when he explained the difficulties of obtaining constant running water and how he had to bribe the locals to bring him supplies. At one point I wanted to ask him why he had deserted Isabel but since he appeared relaxed, I decided to hold my tongue. Knowing how much she disliked leaving the Taj Mahal it occurred to me that he may have suggested she went with him but she would have refused.

'Isabel and Maria will be here this evening,' I said.

'I'll see her before then. I want to take a look at my place so I might run into them.'

His statement was ambiguous but then Peter was always strange. The idea that he might just 'run into' the mother of his child and the child herself seemed odd to say the least but I knew better than to comment.

Teddy, carrying a pile of logs, trotted into the sitting room and appeared delighted to see him. He spent quite five minutes shaking his hand and asking him how he was. The three of us chatted for a quarter of an hour or even longer and I was thrilled that Peter was with us once again. Teddy was equally out of humour where Lydia was concerned, telling us that she had also pestered him with questions about the old days and the disppearance of Dorothea.

'You don't think she's still involved with the case, do you Vin?'

'I don't think so, Teddy. She's probably just fascinated since she's married into a family who have a ready made mystery to absorb her. Then there's always some bright spark busy writing a play or a book on the subject so it never really goes away, does it?'

'For me it never will.'

He wore his special sad expression to which I had grown accustomed over the years. Teddy might have married Isabel and sired a son but I knew his heart would forever be with Dorothea. Peter pressed his hand once more into Teddy's and told us he was going to see his house but that he would return in time for the party.

'Will you be bringing Isabel and Maria with you?' Teddy asked.

'Why, are they invited?'

'Of coures they bloody are,' Teddy snorted. 'It's a family party. The fact that the woman still ranks as my wife not to mention the small matter of her being the mother of your child qualifies her for a cup of soup at least.'

'I'll bear it in mind.'

Peter departed leaving Teddy and I to comment on his unexpected appearance and the fact that he seemed more relaxed than usual.

'Kate will bring Dom, won't she Teddy?'

'Course she will. Old Dom will be the talk of the town now everyone knows he's had a woman staying in that draughty bungalow of his.'

'She's taken to him.'

'Women love queers,' he said, but not offensively. 'S'pose they feel at ease with them although at his age any female would feel safe.'

'You're happy with her, aren't you Ted?'

'Very.'

'What about the age difference?'

'As Bernard Shaw said, "What's 25 years between friends?"'

'And Kate, do you think she's genuinely fond of you?'

'More bloody questions.'

'Sorry.'

'No, it's all right Vin. I think she's reached an age when an old fool like me would suit her quite well. That damn cabbie business is very wearing and her folks are gone so she's quite happy to settle for a ancient farmer and enjoy my money when I peg it.'

'What money? The way you spend I doubt there will be anything left except debts.'

After that it was back to the grind stone for me. During what was left of the afternoon I wondered why I hadn't taken Kit up on his offer to pay for a meal at a hotel or, at least, consented to employ caterers. Twenty six people were invited to that party and the task of perfecting the arrangements was exhausting.

Eventually, and with a lot of help, I relaxed and watched Kit set the wine to breath and stack bottles of fine champagne on the sideboard. Phil and John finished setting the table and Anna arranged flowers or, I should say, rearranged my efforts at arranging them.

Kate rang once or twice to ask if there was anything she could do but I told her to concentrate on Dominic. I wanted her to make sure he was properly dressed and ready to receive his guests but, at just gone five she rang again, sounding anything but happy.

'Your sister in law's arrived,' she told me.

'Isabel? What's she doing at Doms?'

'Fussing and upsetting my plans.'

'In what way?'

'Well it may sound petty but I wanted him to wear his new grey suit and so did he but Isabel says it's too formal so she's got him decked out in a coloured shirt, which he wears in the summer, and some green trousers that are very thin and not particularly clean.'

'Tell her to mind her own business.'

'I'm really not in a position to tell her anything, Vinnie. I thought it wiser to leave it to you. I mean we want him to look his best; it's a big occasion for him.'

'Strange,' I said out loud, without intending to do so. 'I thought she'd be occupied with Peter.'

'Peter?'

'Oh sorry, Kate. Our younger brother's turned up from Italy. We haven't seen him for some years and he's at their house now. I would have thought Isabel and he would have plenty to say to each other.'

'Apparently not.'

I looked at my watch and, although time was getting on, I decided to go over to the bungalow and iron out any problems. If Isabel was interfering obviously Kate didn't feel in a position to argue since she still qualified as an outsider.

'Give me half an hour Kate,' I told her, 'and I'll come and put my oar in.'

When I told Kit that Isabel, of all people, was causing an upset with Kate and Dom he laughed and said they had better sort it out for themselves as I was far too tired to go waltzing over there to act as a peacemaker.

But I did go.

I took the car to save my legs and made up my mind that I wouldn't stay for more than a few minutes. I too wanted Dominic to look his best and if Isabel thought she had the right to overrule Kate, I was going to tell her otherwise.

Using my own key, I opened the front door and walked into the bungalow where I found Dominic sitting, looking miserable, in a little room just off the hall which he used as a study.

'Never had so many women in my humble abode for years,' he said.

'What's she doing here?'

'Who, Kate?'

'No not Kate, Isabel?'

'Don't ask me. She just appeared and made me change my clothes. I'm a bit put out about that Vin, I wanted to wear my new suit but she says it makes me look like a city banker.'

'It makes you look like the smart gentleman you are, Dom. I want you to look your very best because this is your special day.'

'Eighty, I can't belive it.' He shook his head in amazment but pottered off to once again change his clothes.

That's when all the trouble began. I went into the sitting room where I found Kate and Isabel silently staring each other out. Isabel was standing stiffly beside the french windows and Kate was at the other end of the large room looking, as they say, daggers drawn.

'Have you seen Peter?' I ignored Kate, directing my question at Isabel.

'The wanderer returns,' she smiled but not happily.

'But he's gone to the house especially to see you and Maria.'

'No he hasn't. He's just checking his property; weighing up its worth. He will propably sell it over our heads if the mood takes him. Maria's about anyway.'

'What made you come down here?'

'Why shouldn't I?'

Keeping a firm hold on, what remained of my patience, I pointed out that since she seldom went anywhere, I found it curious that, today of all days, she sould visit Dominic and tell him what to wear. Isabel then reminded me that she was a member of the family, unlike some, which was said with a nod of her head towards Kate, and that she had every right to visit Dominic whenever she pleased.

I agreed but explained that we all wanted him to look his absolute best as the spotlight would fall on him and an old garden shirt and grubby trousers were not the best choice for a formal party.

Isabel said some spiteful things that afternoon. She accused us of never liking or accepting her but always viewing her as the servant girl who came to nurse Pa when none of us could be bothered to do so ourselves. Marrying Teddy, she insisted, had been nothing more than a sacrifice on her part simply because she felt sorry for him and saw it as an act of kindness. Most hurtful of all she added that Teddy was a rotten husband who, because of his own coldness and cruelty, had forced her into the arms of Peter. I came under the heading of a vindictive snob who used my position as Kit's wife and daughter of the manor as an excuse to ride roughshod over everyone else.

Dominic, listening in the doorway, limped to my side in an effort to protect me from further insults and Kate, hurriedly, excused herself on the grounds that she had no wish to be involved in a family row. The upshot of all the unpleasantness resulted in my bundling, a now well suited Dominic, into my car and driving him to my house. Isabel was abandoned in the, then deserted, bungalow in the hope that she would simmer down and preferably remain there for the duration of the party.

'Don't let her upset you, Vin,' Dominic put his hand on my shoulder.' It's been my opinion for some time now that she's unbalanced and I say that as a doctor.'

'She's certainly acts that way.'

'Shutting herself away from the world hasn't helped either.'

'But why now, Dom? Why wait for your birthday to cause trouble?'

'Could be because I'm eighty and she's finally grasped that, not only am I a dyed in the wool old queer who'll never fall for her charms but because, at my vast age, I'll probably die in the next year or so.'

'Oh, darling, don't ever die.' I took his hand from my

shoulder and held it firmly in my own as I drove.

Dominic replaced it on the steering wheel.

'Pay attention to the road Vin, or we'll both be dead by tea time.'

Chapter Twenty Six

E ventually the case was officially re-opened but I, for one, hardly bothered to read the newspapers or follow the reports which appeared on the news bulletins. Sky News had a field day regaling its viewers with the details on the hour every hour throughout the day and most of the night. It did cross my mind that newscastors and reporters alike must be extremely grateful when an intriguing story breaks; especially a really gripping mystery remembered by, and handed down, by hundreds of people who have longed, perhaps all their lives, for a conclusion.

When Teddy sold the farm, all those years ago, and discovered the remains under the floor of the goat shed, we all believed the mystery partially solved. The body was female and believed to be young therefore we were quite certain that it must have belonged to Dorothea Stephens. Disappointment lay in the fact that no such deduction was reached, the remains re-buried and the case closed once again. But in the final weeks of 2005 advanced technology enabled a team of forensic scientists to re-examine the once more unearthed remains and prove conclusively that Teddy's grim find was, indeed,

Dorothea.

Lydia travelled up to Borough Heath from Scotland Yard to tell us the details long before the media pounded on our doors. Phil was with her and so solemn were their expressions that we feared they had brought news of a recent bereavement. Kit said he couldn't have cared less and I agreed. We weren't being callous; we were being realistic. The whole saga had strangely intruded on all our lives and it had rolled on and on like a giant snowball gathering more and more intrigue as the years had progressed. Now the snow had melted and we had all grown old.

Could we keep caring?

'I wonder the public are still remotely interested,' I sighed.

'You shouldn't have belonged to such a prestigious family.' Lydia told me.

'Big fish in little ponds comes to mind,' I replied.

'Your mother was related to the Duke of Somerset, wasn't she?'

'Yes, but none of us ever met him or any of her side of the family come to that,' I added.

'And then Peter became world famous.'

'As a dauber of walls,' Kit sneered.

'Nevertheless a family who can boast members of the nobility amongst their relations complete with a brother who numbers the Queen and the President of the United States amongst his patrons is bound to make headlines whereas the local fishmonger and his brood would have faded from memory a month after it happened.'

Her lengthy and preposterous explanation of our renewed claim to the front pages annoyed Kit who wanted to know on what evidence the scientists had agreed that the remains were those of Teddy's long lost girlfriend? Lydia said Dorothea's family had never ceased to pester the home office to resume the investigation; a fact of which I was fully aware.

'Mrs. Stephens gave further samples of her DNA, didn't

she?' I asked Ldyia.

'Yes and so did two of her nieces.'

'Which proved their point?' Kit said. 'Well, they can all rest content now that they know a hand full of bones was once their aunt.'

'The results have given them closure, you see'

'Can't see what difference it's made,' Kit grumbled.

'Families are obsessed with finding the body of a loved one. It closes the case, not happily but the very fact that they can arrange a funeral and openly grieve brings peace of mind.'

'But it all happened over half a century ago for God's sake,' Kit snorted.

'At least they'll have a grave to visit which will stop them wondering where she is for ever more,' Phil added, lamely.

'Oh, God,' I put my head in my hands. 'You're not about to tell us we've got to face a public funeral, are you.?'

'Uncle Teddy might want one,' Lydia said.

'Uncle Teddy ought to be left in peace,' answered Kit. 'He's had years of misery over that woman. Let the men in the white suits and her own family give her a quiet burial and leave the rest of us out of it.'

Dominic came over later that day and so did Teddy and Michael. Later still Peter arrived but we were spared further visits from Isabel and Maria. Phil and Lydia, tired of our whining, went to Birmingham but promised to be back for in time for dinner as John and his wife, Samantha, were also expected. John, like his father before him, was completing his internship at The Chelsea and Westminster Hospital. As it happened Anna had recently returned from Canada, where she had been holidaying with a school friend so, on the day that we received Lydia's news, all three of our children were at home.

A family reunited by a ghost from the past!

If the news hungry public craved a final curtain to our mystifying story, they were to be disappointed. Teddy was emphatic that he would not attend some half baked ceremony involving nothing more than a bag of bones which he said had no bearing on the girl he had once loved. Dominic, pleading old age, also decided to give the funeral a miss. Kit and I both felt it incongruous to put in an appearance for someone who had died before we were even married. Our children followed suit with the exception of Michael who quite horrified us by commenting that it might be entertaining and therefore he would go if only to see what happened. Teddy rolled up The Times and swatted him like a fly which brought a smile to our lips for the first time that day.

'Will the police be there?' he asked.

'No idea but I should think it'll just be a private affair for the Stephens family,' Teddy answered. 'Remember, we haven't been officially alerted, I mean no one except Lydia has told us anything.'

After dinner, when Kit was serving drinks and I was handing round cheese and biscuits Michael asked the question which, up until that point, we had all carefully avoided.

'What do the police think happened to her; does anyone know?'

Everyone looked towards Lydia. If anyone in that room had the slightest inkling, obviously it would be her. Working out of Scotland Yard it was reasonable to suppose she would have information which the press and we, as a family, were denied.

Lydia shook her head which indicated that either she had nothing to add or else that additional information was classified and could not be divulged. As the evening wore on an awkward silence prevailed. Considering Dorothea had meant so much to us and was on the verge of becoming Teddy's wife, I felt we were treating the news with appalling apathy. Actually that was not the case as, in our hearts, we had all believed her dead and consequently grieved for years but human sorrow lasts just so long otherwise none of us would survive a loss.

Peter, who had been the last member of the family to arrive, was also the first one to make a move. He announced that, as there was nothing more to discuss, he was going home and my sons agreed, saying they too, would call it a night. Anna told me not to dwell on the news but to be thankful that we now had a clear idea of what had befallen her.

Which was absurd.

None of us had the slightest idea what had befallen her. To know her remains had been positively identified was one thing but to understand how they happened to be found under the floor of a goat shed was quite another. My thoughts ran haywire but I thought it best to smile and wish everyone a pleasant night's sleep. Kissing Teddy, after helping him to fasten his overcoat, we were interrupted by a bang on the front door.

'If that's a patient I shall scream,' said an overwrought Kit.

'It won't be,' I assured him. The days of patients calling at the door were long gone as were the days of doctors rushing to their bedsides.

It was John who opened the door, causing a draught of icy air to lift the edge of the beige Wilton carpet which lay across the square hall. No sick person or worried parent stood on our step that night but a woman who was as familier and yet as strange as it was possible to be at one and the same time, rushed into the house.

'Isabel, what the hell are you doing here?' Teddy asked, while everyone else just stared mutely at the soaking figure who resembled the woman portrayed in Munche's painting, 'Scream.'

'Raining harder than I thought,' Kit said, ambiguously.

It was Phil who made the first move; he walked towards her and placed an arm around her shoulders. 'Come into the warm,' he said.

His gesture broke the ice, shattering the silence and making it easier for us all to mutter a few kindly words or remark on the unexpected downpour. Isabel, white and speechless, reminded me of an actress made up to play the part of a dying woman in one of those vampire films that my children used to watch.

We all trooped back to the sitting room and sat down in a circle; our attention riveted on Isabel. I told Kit to stoke the fire. We still had coal fires but the old collieries had long ceased to deliver coal to our doors from waggons stacked at the pit heads.

'They took their time' she said.

'What?' said Teddy, who either couldn't hear or was too bemused to grasp her words.

'Identifying her body. They took their time,' Isabel repeated.

'Oh yes. They have to be one hundred percent certain,' I explained.

Kit offered her some brandy and even Peter made a hurried suggestion that he drive her home so that she could change her clothes and get some rest.

'No I want to tell you something,' she said, directing her remark, strangely enough, to me.

'What is it?' I whispered.

'I killed Dorothea,' she said.

When none of us spoke or even moved she clasped her hands tightly around her knees and began a speech which was as presice and to the point as if a script writer had penned it in readiness for a public hearing.

'I killed Dorothea,' she repeated.

Chapter Twenty Seven

M r. Lawrence has returned.
Of course I knew he would. He is determined to add an epilogue to his wretched play and his curiosity will not be denied. He is young and sees a means to make money out of our misfortune. Perhaps he plans a title along the lines of, "The Final Solution" or "The Body Under the Goat Shed." A gullible public will be intrigued and the lure of fame encourages him to pester me.

Only yesterday Pan, watching me take my seat at the writing desk, asked why I didn't publish such a work myself. I told her I was writing a short history of Borough Heath and the mining community in general but, for some reason, I decided to keep quiet as to the subject of this present saga. John and Phil know of my scribblings but Anna doesn't because she would fuss. During her last visit she gave me a protracted lecture on the good sense of keeping silent should a discussion concerning skeletons in our cupboards arise. Her criticism is always more than I can bear.

When Isabel died, she threw one red rose onto her coffin then turned away and left us standing at the open grave. Later she wrote to me from Thailand, of all places, and said she had met some man and intended to marry him. I very much doubt she will, our history has always blighted her plans although most of what happened occurred long before she was born.

'Your collection is remarkable.' Mr. Lawrence is telling me. Unable to summon the courage to begin his inquisition he stares at my vast collection of porcelain figurines.

'My husband and I first started buying them in antique shops and later in auctions. It was quite a hobby.' I think of Kit and his love of fine china and wish he were here to escort this young man to the door for I am tired.

'Your husband must have had an eye for beauty.'

'An eye for many things, Mr. Lawrence.'

Kit adored Royal Worcester and Dresden china. Phil's wife, Lydia is busy cataloguing our collection at the moment as, ever practical, she says I'm under insured. After everything died down she quietly left the police force and now works for a large firm of auctioneers in Birmingham. Although she says she enjoys her new found occupation and is relieved to be free of the pressures which accompanied police work, it is my belief that she found our old tale of murder and mystery an embarassment given that she worked for Scotland Yard. By assosiation she might have thought herself notorious!

'When did he die?' Mr. Lawrence is studying a small figure of a boy with a parrot on his arm: I do hope he won't take it into his head to pick it up. Teddy broke a hand painted loving cup last time he was here and I almost cried.

'Three years ago,' I tell him. 'He was amost eighty six.'

Life without my beloved Kit is meaningless. I have no loving companion to sooth my soul, no partner to pass these years of my old age and no one to make me laugh. But we had fifty eight years together and many have less or none at all so I must be grateful and count myself lucky.

'Your children must be a comfort, Mrs. Barry. I belive you have two sons, one daughter and four grandchildren?'

So I tell this stranger, who is probably not in the least interested, all about John who is now a distinguished doctor in Wimpole Street. Phil and Anna are discussed and so are both my daughters in law. John's son Alexander and Phil's three daughters smile at him from behind their silver frames on the mantelpiece. I am a proud grandmother and he must endure my catalogue of their accomplishments.

'And your nephew Michael MacVee, he is to make a film in America, I'm told.'

'Not his first, Mr. Lawrence. He played Max De Winter in Rebbeca for Warners two years ago.'

'Ah yes, I remember.'

I doubt he does; the film was a pale shadow of the Lawrence Olivia version but this young man would be too polite to say so. Naturally anything Michael does is of interest to me and a delight to Teddy. These days of our dottage are lived in the past but lived also through the lives of our children so news of Michael or my sons and especially of Anna are the highlight of our existence.

'Your sister in law left a daughter, Maria I believe?'

He believes! Incredulous man; he will have researched the smallest detail of our family history. Maria is probably as familiar to him as his own sister but he thinks to prise information from me by pretending his knowledge is scant.

'My niece inherited my late brother's bungalow. She lives alone but I see her regularly.'

'A blessing no doubt?'

'Yes.'

I fight an urge to talk at length of Maria, whose close proximity is indeed a blessing, but decide against it on the grounds that I have no wish for this man to know more than is absolutely necessary. Pan brings tea and our trite conversation ceases as his eyes wander back to the Worcester figurines. Sitting stiffly, he remains silent and I imagine that if Kit were here he would whisper that French phrase about not speaking in front of the servants.

'And so you never suspected Isabel MacVee?' He clears his throat before asking the vital question.

'Of course not. Why would we?'

My mind drifts back to a time in the sun. When Borough Heath was little more than a mining village; when the forest was clothed in a rusty brown hue every autumn and green and gold in the summer. I see again the cow yard and Ma sitting under the ceder tree. Pictures of Pa strutting around the farm roll across my mind like tape through a video machine. Clearly I recall the day when Teddy declared his intention of managing the farm and spending his life tending the land. Of course, memories of Dominic before the accident are always with me for he was the most handsome man in the Midlands.

The most attractive man in the world.

Isabel was young then, just a girl. A little mouse who followed her aunt from room to room almost unnoticed by we who owned the rooms and reigned over the great house. When Kit was alive I used to ask him if he thought us unkind in employing a stranger to tend Pa rather than do so ourselves? Kit always shrugged and said we were very lucky that we could afford such help as the care of a sick man is draining on the rest of the family. Sometimes I would ask him if we were remiss in not realising that Isabel was madly in love with Dominic?

Mr. Lawrence notices that my eyes are riveted to a large black and white photograph of Dominic taken when he was in his early twenties.

'A handsome young man, your brother,' he comments.

'Very,' is all I say.

Many girls fell for Dom with his light blue eyes and fine chiselled features. Teddy once told me that, on summer nights, girls would cycle miles from the surrounding villages just to catch a glimpse of him. He said it used to make him jealous because for all his humour and skills with mimicry he was never favoured with so much as a glance from any one of them.

Sheila M Barnes

But Dominic had no interest in pretty girls, although the age and the law forbade him to say so, whereas poor Teddy adored them and would have given all he had to attract just one; any one.

In the winter months, Isabel used to watch Dominic from behind the steamed up windows of Pa's sitting room and, as the year mellowed, she watched us all. How privileged she must have thought the children of her aunt's employer!

'She made something of a friend of your brother, Peter I believe?' Mr. Lawrence asks.

I nod and think of poor little Peter. The cuckoo in the nest, the last born whom we shunned. We, the established trio who commanded only each other's attention, were far too occupied to pay attention to a small boy who had little to say for himself and nothing to say to us.

'Peter and Isabel, although years apart in age, were both lonely,' I tell him. 'They clung to each other probably because they had no one else and, that, I regret.'

'And it was about this time that Dominic went away to university?'

'A little later if I remember correctly. Teddy took over from Pa and became farm manager.'

'And you took care of the house and your mother?'

'Oh, we had staff for all that but I was certainly at home. I never went out to work.'

Although the events of the past are forever etched in my mind the years and months of their occurrence are fused so dates and sequences are beyond recall. I remember the feeling of emptiness when Dominic went to university and Teddy was away from home. An image of Dorothea Stephens comes to me as clearly now as it did in those summer days when I thought her soon to be my sister in law. The little dog, Raq, I can almost touch, so vivid are my memories when I dare to think back to the time which this man is so painstakingly researching.

When visions of a young Peter and a little Rose enter my

field of remembered vision, I shudder and dismiss their images as soon as possible. But in my dreams they are unbearably clear and then I have no power to banish them. Worst of all are the nightmares that lead me to the shed where Rose drowned or the balcony where Brian Thorn caused Dominic to fall to the flagstones far below.

'Does the mural require restoration?' Mr. Lawrence asks stiffly.

'No.'

Sometimes, in strange moods, I think the mural has a life of its own. For well over half a century it has graced that wall and, despite extensive redecoration everywhere else, it remains untouched. Hardly a painted leaf has faded and each tree and blade of grass are as fresh today as when Peter toiled over them in a time long gone.

'And that was the first you knew of his talent, Mrs. Barry?'

'Indeed it was.'

'You must have been delighted when your brother, Teddy, brought Dorothea to the farm.' Mr. Lawrence has an infuriating habit of flying from one topic to another. I find it unnerving.

He is correct of course because she was a joy to us all. Some brothers might have brought girls whom we disliked or thought unsuitable but she was perfect and how well she blended into our lives and the farm in general. Pa and Ma liked and approved of her; in fact Teddy could not have bettered his choice.

'And, Isabel, she took to her as well?'

I have to think back. He speaks of a time so long ago that I pause before I answer. Isabel was a servant or the niece of a servant so her opinion, good or otherwise, would have been of no consequence but I can not recall any ill will between her and Dorothea.

'She liked her well enough I think,' I tell him.

'Until she thought her interested in Dominic?'

'She may have sought an explanation. Isabel was never a pretty girl although she was what was termed, attractive. She took great pains to please us all and was constantly vying for Dominic's attention. Her failure must have been puzzling especially since she saw no rival.'

'So she began to imagine he coveted Dorothea?'

'That is what she said in her statement.'

'But obviously that was not the case?'

'I wished it had of been.' I want to explain my reasoning but Dom is no longer with me to require defence or explanation so I drink Pan's tea and hope Mr. Lawrence will curtail his questions and soon depart.

'You understood his preferences shall we say?'

'He was homosexual. Gay we would call him now and, of course I understood but Isabel would have had no idea.'

'Because such things were not spoken of?'

'They were illegal.'

'Poor Dominic.'

'Yes.'

Pan has a habit of switching on my television set when she serves my supper. It is part of her ritual although I tell her that I prefer to eat in silence. Unless a rare program takes my fancy, I tend to stare blankly at the screen and think of other things. I sometimes wonder if Dom was attracted to any of the young farm hands with their fine sinewy bodies and tanned complexions? After all I fell in love with Kit and Teddy with Dorothea so, maybe, there were other men before the wretched Brian Thorn claimed his attention.

In a different age Ma and Pa might have worried about the absence of female company in the life of their eldest son but Ma was self absorbed and Pa uninterested in his children so it's my belief that they never even noticed. But, when I think of those evenings spent in the garden or walking the paths of the forest, I vividly recall Isabel tagging along; never obviously pushing herself into our tight knit little group but there all the same. Even now I remember Dominic's interest in Dorothea; his engaging manner and apparent devotion. Poor Isabel must have interpreted his attention as something more than good manners and a natural fondness for his brother's girlfriend.

'No one ever discovered who fathered her child?'

'No one ever asked.' I reply for, with hindsight, I don't think we cared or thought it important. We were just overjoyed that Teddy had found happiness with someone else so, the fact that his bride to be came complete with a ready made family, seemed irrelevant.

'I would have thought it a disgrace given the attitude of the day.'

'In any other circumstances it would have been but after what had happened we felt only relief that he had a renewed chance of happiness.'

'How did Teddy react to Rose's death?'

'You had better ask him, Mr. Lawrence, for it was all a very long time ago and my head is beginning to ache.'

Teddy won't give him the time of day but, thankfully, he takes the hint and stands up. His brief case bulges with papers which I suppose are copious notes concerning our family history. Perhaps he will see fit to occupy himself with a lengthy enquiry into the mystery of Isabel's pregnancy but what information could come to light after all this time? I doubt even Peter would have any idea and poor Maria knows so little of her mother's life that questioning her would prove useless.

My guess, and that's all it is, would be that in desperation she turned to a local lad in the hope that he would marry and provide a home for her. Penniless and dependent on her aunt and our employment, she must have become frantic. The welfare state was hardly the treasure chest it has now become and a homeless girl could have starved.

'She was lucky that Teddy even considered her,' Mr. Lawrence voices my own opinion.

'He was vulnerable,' I tell him. 'Grief does that to you.

Believe me, I speak from experience; it takes your reason and sometimes your common sense as well.'

'So Dominic was never aware of her romantic feelings towards him?'

'I think towards the end of his life, when she started to interfere and pester him, he began to realise but by then it was too late and, if anything, he probably found it amusing.'

'But it hardly mattered then?'

'Only as a nuisance value.'

'And obviously he never felt anything for her?'

'Perhaps, as a sister in law, he felt a sense of loyalty but her behaviour made things difficult all round as you can imagine?'

'Only too well.'

There our discourse or his inquisition has to cease. Pan senses my need to be alone and escorts Mr. Lawrence to the door. He mutters something about visiting Teddy and is profuse in his thanks for this interview with me. I shake his hand but remain sitting as the memories he has evoked have added to my exhaustion.

'Oh, Mr. Lawrence,' I remember a point of extreme importance. 'The copy of Isabel's statement. I would like it back as soon as possible.'

'Let me give it to you now. I no longer require it,' he adds.

From the depths of his briefcase he produces a folder containing a thick sheaf of papers. 'I have taken the liberty of copying it,' he says as he hands it to me.

'I suppose it will figure dramatically in your play?'

'If my backers think fit.' With a slight bow he follows Pan to the front door.

I am left staring at dozens of type-written pages which were found after she died. Maria brought them to this house and Teddy and I read through them together. We needn't have gone to the police but Anna said it was a duty which we owed to the Stephens family. Six weeks after we'd read them I gave the entire collection to Lydia and she took them to Scotland Yard.

The case is now closed.

Chapter Twenty Eight

T he Statement of Isabel MacVee.

For the past forty five years I have lived with the artist Peter MacVee. I carry the same surname but not through marriage to Peter. Before I gave birth to his daughter and took up residence in his house, I was married, and remain so, to his brother Edward MacVee.

In this, the seventy fifth year of my life, my doctor tells me I have contracted an incurable form of Leukaemia and can not expect to survive beyond six months. It is therefore important that I document the events of my life for the sake of those who have a right to the truth.

I was born near Borough Heath in nineteen thirty three, the only child of a miner and his wife, Nellie. No brothers or sisters would follow my entrance into the world as, before the anniversary of my first birthday, both my parents were dead. Mother, from a virulent strain of influenza and father as a result of a mining accident which claimed not only his life but those of twenty six other miners who fell victim to a gas explosion at the Mid Borough Heath Colliery.

My mother had very few relatives and my father none at all.

However my plight was treated sympathetically by the kind people of the parish who sought to find someone who would care for me thus preventing a prolonged stay in the local orphanage and subsequent adoption. To this end a search was instigated and, within the space of less than two weeks, a distant cousin, by the name of Doris Haywood, was located. Miss Haywood, although poor herself and adamant that she would never legally adopt me, eventually agreed to take responsibility for my existence provided any trouble I was likely to cause was kept to a minimum.

Assurances of my saintly conduct being given and accepted, I was dispatched, post haste to her less than loving care in nearby Walsall. My new accommodation, although only of a temporary nature, was in the home of her current employer, a wealthy industrialist of advanced years. Had I been old enough to admire my surroundings I would have marvelled at the new found splendour to which my unfortunate circumstances had led. The house, where I shared a large room with Miss Haywood, was as luxurious as it was cavernous and, by the time I attained the age of six and three quarters, I considered myself exceedingly privileged to be living in such dazzling resplendence.

My gratification was to be short lived as, one week short of my seventh birthday, all aspirations of grandeur were dissolved over night owing to the somewhat trying death of the rich industrialist. Miss Haywood, being merely his nurse, was dismissed before noon the following day.

Having no home of her own and possessed only of two crumpled pound notes, reluctantly donated by the dead man's wife in appreciation of her untiring services, she introduced me to the dubious hospitality of the Salvation Army. A worthy and charitable association who, then as now, overflowed with the milk of Christian kindness. Adapting to life in a seven foot square cubicle complete with a creaking bed and two red blankets plus a breakfast of stale bread and margarine, presented an unbearable deprivation.

Doris Haywood, whom I was instructed to call, 'Aunt Doris,' was a nurse without benefit of qualifications. Lacking not a morsel of formal training, her patients generally fell into the category of aged invalids, unwanted relatives or the mentally unstable for whom treatment let alone cures were no longer an option. Her wages amounted to little more than a pittance and the work was usually unsavoury, heavy and unrewarding. But, for all the disadvantages, the houses where she scivvied, often for sixteen hours a day, were warm and comfortable. Food was plentiful and we were never begrudged ample supplies.

My aunt made little impact on her employees as her personality and presence discouraged friendship let alone fondness. Looking back it seems reasonable to suppose that her services gave satisfaction as return visits to the Salvation Army were rare and seldom exceeded a period of more than one month at the most.

Usually, after committing to an engagement, the term of her employment would be lengthy as elderly invalids have a habit of surviving almost indefinitely. Those tending towards wealth and property are particularly adept in the art of longevity as they believe it their duty to severely try the patience of anxious benefactors. During these prolonged life spans, I was dispatched to nearby schools where I made it my business to excel in as many subjects as possible. It has always been my opinion that bettering one's self is the sole purpose of existence and as I had no intention of following my inherited aunt to the bedsides of the incontinent dying, I became a assiduous student.

In due course her vocation, and sole means of income, led us to Borough Heath and the farm belonging to the MacVee family. My aunt, being deemed a suitable applicant for the position of nurse companion to Mr. MacVee, was duly appointed and, as in previous cases, no objection was offered with regard to my presence as her unpaid assistant. Since I might have been classed as an encumbrance, I was schooled in the twin arts of silence and obedience thus preventing embarrassing comments regarding the extra cost of keeping two people instead of the expected one.

My position was both invidious and demeaning as almost all my youthful instincts had to be suppressed in an effort to disguise the fact that I was there at all. On reflection I can honestly say that my entire childhood and early youth were lived in anonymity and a concerted effort to be overlooked by all and sundry.

Survival became a matter of dwelling in the shadows, silent and unobtrusive.

It is difficult to remember at what point or during which particular humiliation, I first began to rebel. During the early years I accepted my inferior status, even showing gratitude to my aunt for her care and attention. Unfortunately, having never experienced an atom of affection, it wasn't long before I woke up to the fact that a gulf of monstrous proportions existed between myself and the rest of the human race. A circumstance which, I realised, was in desperate need of rectification.

Once the chasm became apparent, a jealous awareness began to take root. Obsessed by the grand lifestyle of the MacVee children I began to make odious comparisons between their world of luxury and wealth and my own dismal existence. Laughter, comfort, confidence, indulgence, all words which had no bearing or place in my own life, figured largely in theirs.

Lavinia MacVee I particularly envied. How carefree and fine she was. Only a few years younger than I but blessed with everything which I lacked or was ever likely to possess. Her brothers, both appealing and cultured young men, ignored me completely and, occasional civil greetings apart, I doubted they noticed me at all. Dominic I compared to a Greek God, although never having seen such a being the comparison was probably rooted in the fact that, lonely and bored, I had read far too many of Aunt Doris's cheap novels. My imaginary love affair with him began from the very first moment I watched him stride across the fields and smile his striking smile at either Lavinia or his brother Teddy.

Teddy MacVee, less appealing but still possessed of the easy manner of one accustomed to wealth and all its attributes, was blessed with both a talent for amusing and a compassionate disposition. Often, during the long winter evenings, it would be he who would spend his time reading novels to his father. If my aunt permitted such an indulgence, I would sit quietly in the shadows and admire his fortitude but I never found him particularly engaging or even interesting. Sometimes, when he deigned to glance in my direction, I would attempt what I hoped might be interpreted as a flirtatious smile but, meeting Dominic in any corner or corridor of the vast house, I would suffer a nervous reaction which resulted in an embarrassing inability to do or say anything which might engage his attention. Since I was never rewarded with the merest flicker of interest, I resigned myself to the depressing fact that the lives of the MacVee family and that of my own would never cross.

But there was another brother and, although barely removed from the nursery, I was able to identify and emphasise with him. Peter MacVee, although some ten years my junior, was the baby of the family. Lacking even an atom of charisma but blessed with the features of an angel, his existence was barely acknowledged by Lavinia and the elder boys. Treating their little brother as they would a farm hand's son or a gypsy lad they managed to ignore him in much the same way as they ignored me. Even Aunt Doris, who seldom voiced an opinion regarding the families for whom she worked, said their treatment of him was nothing short of a disgrace. On one occasion she even added that she thought it an act of criminal negligence to disregard one so young. Agreeing with her sentiments and having all the time in the world and little to do with any hour of it, I took to seeking him out and taking him for walks. Sometimes I read out loud to him or took his hand and led him to the forest where I taught him the names of the various trees and plants. Gradually, and possibly because I had the good grace to acknowledge his existence, he displayed a modicum of affection towards me which, almost accidentally, led to my discovering his amazing talent. Receiving a privileged invitation to a locked room adjoining his playroom, I was allowed to view his paintings which, although my knowledge of art was scant, I recognised as works of genius.

Because he suffered a heart disorder, Mr. MacVee handed over the responsibility of the farm to Teddy many years earlier than would have been the case had he been a fit man. Dominic, I understood, was set on becoming a doctor and although I admired his dedication, I grieved for his loss when he eventually left home to go to university.

Mrs. MacVee, usually surrounded by a host of servants, seemingly spent her time doing very little and gave the impression of being quite indifferent to both her husband's health and the welfare of her beautiful children. The luxury and ease of her life I attributed to her wealth for it had freed her from the usual restraints and enabled her to marry the husband of her choice. I, possessed of nothing, could hardly expect to capture a wealthy or handsome man and would have to consider myself lucky if a poor labourer was kind enough to offer marriage in exchange for a life of drudgery. Needless to say, Dominic, good-looking and heir to a fortune, already had my heart but, sadly, remained completely oblivious to the few charms of which I was possessed.

The years of my youth seemed destined to melt away without a glimmer of hope for anything vaguely approaching a joyous future. Peter remained at my side and so did my aging aunt but other than the meagre comfort of knowing that I was unlikely to starve or perish in the cold Midland winters my prospects for a happy life diminished even before I reached the milestone age of twenty one.

Dominic came and went. Sometimes he would condescend to smile and very occasionally he would briefly pause and enquire as to my welfare. Once he thanked me for my devotion to his sick father and praised the loyalty and patience of Aunt Doris.

Other than that I came to the conclusion that he positively disliked me.

Three years into our involvement with the family, Mr. MacVee showed distinct signs of improvement and I feared that he might recover his health sufficiently to dismiss my aunt altogether. Luckily his wife, showing sparse interest in his wellbeing, either failed to notice or totally ignored the sudden upturn in his health. Even Aunt Doris heaved a sigh of relief as, had she been a devoted wife, Mrs. MacVee would have celebrated his improvement and felt able to tend him herself.

The change in his condition coincided or was brought about by a young woman who came to stay at the farm. Her name was Dorothea Stephens and, at not quite eighteen, she was pretty enough to provoke my instant jealousy. With her brilliant brown hair and bright hazel eyes she outshone the likes of me a thousand fold. Not only in looks did she excel but in personality and intelligence as well. Soon I gathered that her interest lay with Teddy which was amazing when surely, with all her attributes, I would have supposed Dominic to be her choice.

But Dominic was not immune to her charms, that I painfully saw. During the late spring and early summer, the young people took to spending their evenings picnicking under the cedar tree on the vast lawn which lay to the rear of the farm. Night after night, Lavinia, Dominic, Teddy and Dorothea enjoyed hours of late evening sunshine and good food in that rich garden whilst Peter and I watched from afar. Just now and again I would summon enough courage to approach them and, I must admit, I was never turned away. Teddy always offered food and invited us to sit on one of the many seats which were scattered around the great walled garden. Tongue tied, I would smile and study my feet whilst they chatted and laughed or else I would hold Peter's little hand until someone spotted him and ordered him to bed.

As the summer wore on, old Mr. MacVee became fully occupied. The west wing of the farm house took his attention as plans were afoot to turn it into a self contained apartment for Teddy and Dorothea as it appeared they were to marry. The conversion held little appeal for me as it bore no impact on my own dull life whereas both Lavinia and Dominic, possessed of a vested interest in Teddy's future happiness, thrilled to the idea. The usual tranquil atmosphere which encompassed the farm house became charged with excitement.

Of course I envied Dorothea. She would never want for a comfortable home or a diamond ring to enhance her beautiful fingers but her choice of brother I still found puzzling. Once, when we came across the two of them kissing in a shady part of the forest, I said to Peter that for the life of me I couldn't kiss Teddy as I found him quite repulsive. Peter, as was usual with him, made no comment.

So curious did I consider her choice that I even mentioned it to Aunt Doris who, strange to say, told me that all men were not alike and women, even beautiful ones such as Dorothea, would fail to attract a man like Dominic MacVee.

But, as high summer heralded the coming harvest, I had reason to doubt her words.

Dominic was at home for long periods during that particular year and having little or no interest in the farm he devoted his time to entertaining Dorothea. Enviously, I would watch them link arms and take walks in the early afternoon whilst Teddy laboured away in the cowshed or in the fields. Sometimes they would be gone for two or more hours and, although I was too young to suffer raised blood pressure, their absence enraged me. It was my fervent opinion that no girl could walk or be alone with Dominic without falling for his charms and I feared it would only be a matter of days before she transferred her affections from the ugly brother to the dashing and beautiful one.

Lavinia seemed oblivious to this new found friendship and, even more strangely, so did Teddy. Had I been in his shoes, I would have been alerted to the danger of losing my beloved for there was no doubt the poor creature was besotted. Neither Mr. nor Mrs. MacVee paid any attention to Dominic and Dorothea's intimacy and, at times, it seemed as though I was the only person living in that house who cottoned on to the fact that if a wedding was to take place at all then it would not be between Teddy and Dorothea but between Dominic and Dorothea.

Mr. MacVee, so improved in health, would totter out into the late evening sunshine and take his place under the cedar tree to eat the lavish supper which the maids brought to the garden. His wife, sewing on a cane chair, would add little to the conversations but her children were full of animation and laughter; only Peter remained silent and disinterested. Aunt Doris would sporadically remind me that my place should be beside her in the chill room off the hall where she folded linen and darned socks. But what dull enterprises such chores presented when I could mingle, however remotely, with such vibrant youngsters.

A spaniel puppy was bought for Dorothea and he became her constant companion. She and Dominic would take him to the forest or train him to heel in the vast grounds of the farm. Watching and dwelling on their happiness caused a bitterness as acrid as vinegar to rise in my throat. Surely, I thought, Teddy must begin to see for himself the threat posed by her proximity to his handsome brother. But every member of the family appeared blinded to their growing friendship; even showing delight that Dorothea was so thoroughly entertained.

Towards the end of July, the weather broke.

The hot sunny days that had enabled the young people to

cavort into the late hours of evening were suddenly ended by a massive thunder storm. I had watched the storm clouds gather since tea time and worried that pouring rain would spoil my usual hours of pleasure. Although only able to watch and long for their friendship there was a certain joy in being close to the family and fancying myself a member of it.

By seven o'clock it was obvious that any plans for a picnic under the cedar tree that particular evening would have to be abandoned. In the distant forest deer scuttled towards the safety of the undergrowth, rabbits ran as though chased by hounds and birds flew from their usual perches on the old brick walls and circled the trees. Sighs of disappointment were to be heard as everyone fretted over their deprivation. Lavinia and Dominic, realising that there was nothing for it but to indulge in indoor occupations, erected a green baize card table in a corner of the sitting room whilst Teddy set about stacking honey jars in the back kitchen. Mr. and Mrs. MacVee, probably the least put out of the entire family, contented themselves with simple tasks such as reading and, in her case, the inevitable sewing.

Peter took my hand and led me to the locked room area beyond his playroom where he proudly showed me his latest painting which depicted a lily pond complete with a mass of dew dropped water lilies and two superb green frogs. It was whilst I was admiring his latest masterpiece and marvelling that one so young could achieve such perfection that I saw Dorothea's dog wandering, as if lost, on the long landing. Whether a sudden impulse or a real desire to create mischief assailed me, I cannot say but I left Peter and grabbed the dog. Knowing that he meant so much to Dorothea I deliberately sought to cause distress. My jealousy matching the threatening storm, I ran from the house just as the first drops of heavy rain began to splash onto the cow yard. The dog tucked under my arm, I raced for the far field where I knew he could escape the confines of the farm and scurry to the forest where his instinct would incline him to chase the wild life.

No one saw my departure or noticed that the dog was missing. The usual laughter and happiness of the young people was petulantly subdued by the weather which made me smile. To see them thwarted gave me pleasure and I imagined their further distress when Dorothea started to fret for her puppy.

Lavinia, deserting Dominic and the proposed card game, arrived in the kitchen and began wiping raindrops from some apples in a wicker basket. Speaking to Teddy she complained that Dorothea had declined an earlier invitation to accompany her to the orchard. All those well heeled children fussed and fretted if they imagined themselves snubbed by anyone bar each other. As the first few claps of thunder rumbled in the distance, they fretted even more declaring their evening ruined. Old Mr. MacVee made one of his rare appearances below stairs and ordered everyone to leave the vicinity of the windows declaring it unsafe to be near glass.

Dorothea was no where to be seen and I personally wondered where she had gone but the others seemed oblivious as to her absence. Peter had descended from his playroom but, as usual, he was ignored so I took his hand and led him to the kitchen table where we began a game of snakes and ladders. As we played he told me that one day he intended to paint huge pictures which would cover entire walls. Becoming, for him, quite loquacious he added that he would be famous and very rich before he was twenty five. Two maids and Matty the housekeeper, busy preparing a supper more suited to indoors than the usual garden fare, laughed and commented on the strangeness of the little boy who they said would only aspire to farming like his father and brother before him.

The storm worsened and Dominic strolled into the kitchen to ask if any of us had seen Dorothea as he said Teddy was worried about her. I know I said nothing but Peter, recalling the little dog, started to mutter something about it wandering about on the landing. For, whatever reason, I nudged him to keep silent and my unspoken command was instantly obeyed.

Within half an hour the entire household were alerted to the fact that Dorothea was missing and an almighty search began to take place. Not being remotely interested I took Peter to the back porch where we watched as forks of lightening flashed across the cow yard, illuminating the forest like a million watt searchlight.

By ten o'clock the search had reached panic proportions so much so that no one noticed that Peter had not been put to bed. He and I clung to each other aware of the clammy heat and the charged atmosphere. Aunt Doris appeared and told us she intended to go to bed as there was nothing she could do. She advised me to do the same but the prevailing excitement prompted me to decline and continue my watch from the kitchen steps.

From within the house, I could hear Lavinia and Teddy rushing from room to room calling Dorothea's name, an enterprise which I found laughable. Did they really think that the usually sociable girl had gone into hiding or locked herself in a dark room to sulk on account of the weather spoiling yet another party? Peter and I took an avid interest in their escapades but neither of us bothered to join in the search. At some point he yawned and just when I was thinking it cruel to keep him from his bed any longer Dominic arrived on the steps and asked me to hand him a towel so that he could dry his drenched hair.

It grieved me to see my idol soaked to the skin and beside himself with worry all over a silly girl who was probably sheltering with her wretched dog in one of the barns. Peter asked him what all the fuss was about and he explained that Dorothea had gone to look for her puppy and must have got lost so everyone was busy searching for her.

Handing back the soaking towel, Dominic then asked if I would take his torch and go down to the lower fields as all the available searchers were still occupied with the immediate vicinity and the out-houses. Delighted that he should seek my involvement, I took his offered flashlight, followed him down the kitchen steps and out into the yard.

There we parted company as, like a man possessed, he dashed away towards the perimeter of the forest itself. Still clinging onto Peter I decided to go the other way and head for the beech grotto behind the goat shed. Puddles and slippery cobbles hampered our journey and Peter, being so young, had difficulty keeping his balance. Strange for such a stoic child he began to whimper and complain. To comfort him I lifted him into my arms and took him inside the shed where Mrs. MacVee kept her two goats.

Deciding to rest for a short while and then take him indoors, I looked out across the rain lashed heath and saw Dominic racing across the hundred acre field where Teddy kept his breeding bulls.

All of us, from the boot boy to Dominic himself, had been warned time and again concerning the dangers of approaching the bulls and no one, except Teddy and two experienced farm hands, ever entered their field. To this day, I can instantly recall my feelings of terror as I watched him darting about hardly bothering to dodge the dangerous beasts.

And all for a stupid bitch who had decided to go carousing all alone during a monumental thunder storm!

A temper, I scarcely knew I possessed, flared as I continued to gaze at Dominic who persisted in his precarious chase between the two bulls and I prayed they wouldn't take it into their shaggy heads to charge him. Luckily, their interest lay in huddling together under the oak trees in an attempt to avoid the worst of the weather. Just as I'd satisfied myself that Dominic wasn't in quite the danger I had feared, Dorothea Stephens walked leisurely into the goat shed. To quote her actual words after all these years would be beyond me but I remember she greeted us in the manner of someone who has just wandered in to seek shelter from a casual shower. Since she appeared totally oblivious to the turmoil her absence was causing, I placed Peter on the ground and berated her for her indifferent attitude. Particularly, I pointed out, in no uncertain terms, the dangers faced by Dominic as he leapt about the bull run searching hedgerows and undergrowth in an effort to find her. Dorothea laughed, clapping her hands in glee as she watched him cavorting between the bulls even adding comments concerning his madness in exposing himself to such danger.

'He's looking for you,' I screamed.

'Then he's a bigger fool then I thought,' she said.

Those were her words. Clearly, although more than half a century has passed I can still, in my mind, hear her calling Dominic a fool and, just as clearly, I can remember my reaction. Almost hysterical with rage and disbelief I grabbed her by the shoulders and shook her violently.

'He's risking his life for you,' I shouted.

'Take your hands off me,' she screamed back.

In that moment she ceased to be the good humoured and pretty girl who everyone, including me, thought sweet and inoffensive. Jealous of her and her position I might have been but never had I regarded her as selfish or arrogant. In ordering me to take my hands from her shoulders I believed her to be inferring that my touch was demeaning; that I was beneath her, unworthy of sharing the ground on which she stood. Dominic's brave efforts to rescue her, she thought pathetic as she did those of the whole family and the farm labourers, all of whom she branded as lunatics.

'They're all mad' she snorted. 'I was merely looking for Raq and had to shelter for a while. What a fuss!'

I hit her.

She hit me back.

Whether maliciously or merely in her own defence I cannot say, but her slap caught my left eye and lower lip. I remember blood poured from the lip and the taste of it enraged me even more. Suddenly I was the poor servant girl. The hanger on. Nothing more than an impediment belonging to the old nurse who was facing redundancy herself due to the resurgence of the master of the house.

Peter must have reacted either to the sight of blood or to my distress because, before either of us could stop him, he grabbed a large stone from the floor of the shed and hurled it at Dorothea. It caught her a hefty blow to the right side of her head which instantly knocked her to the ground. A mere glance at the ensuing wound persuaded me that urgent attention was required.

My heart sank as I visualised a dozen or more people rushing to her aid. Doctors and even an ambulance, I suspected, would have to be summoned. Recriminations and police enquiries would follow and my aunt and I would be dismissed instantaneously. Poor little Peter, young as he was, I feared would be placed in a house of correction and all because a worthless girl had taken it into her head to shelter from a rain storm.

Oh yes, I killed her.

I grabbed a shovel, with a cast iron base, and I struck her more than a dozen times. There was little sound. No screams just soft murmurs more of amazement than pain followed by silence. Peter watched but, being Peter, he remained speechless and unmoved. During his brief life span he had learnt that whatever he did or said he was always ignored so silence was his best option.

I knew she was dead and the knowledge was something of a relief. I had seen off my enemy; my rival. Beyond the partition, where the goats were housed, lay a deep pit or trench, for quite what purpose I had no idea, but it served me well for I pushed her body deep into it and piled a quantity of wooden planks on top. My work was far from finished but, provided the search was either called off or diverted, I considered myself safe for the hours of darkness which lay ahead.

Clutching Peter, I made my way back to the house. All the servants were either in bed or out searching for Dorothea. Mr. and Mrs. MacVee, I knew would be somewhere behind locked doors so, on my way to Peter's nursery, I saw no one and certainly no one saw me. There was blood on my dress but not as much as you might imagine and not a spot of it had fallen on Peter. Hastily, I put him in his bed where he fell asleep instantly, leaving me with all the time in the world to discard my clothes. The quietness was eerie, only a few far away sounds made by the army of searchers managed to filter fitfully through my semi-opened window. Undisturbed, I had a leisurely bath and then made my way down to the kitchens where I flung all my garments into the roaring range that burned like a furnace both day and night.

Returning to my room I slid onto my bed and slept for perhaps two hours but no more because when next I woke, darkness was still shrouding the farm and the forest. The rain had slackened but streaks of it lingered on my window panes and the air was chill. Donning a coal black jumper and a pair of the cumbersome slacks, which had reached popularity just after the war, I hurried downstairs and back towards the goat shed. All around people were still milling about flashing their torches in every direction and calling the name of Dorothea. Mostly, thank goodness, the body of the search had moved away from the immediate sheds and out-buildings and neither Teddy nor Dominic were anywhere to be seen. Had anyone noticed my presence it would not have been thought unusual or memorable for dozens of women were out that night and, because of the darkness, unless a torch was shone directly in someone's face, identification was impossible.

During my long life, until very recently that is, hard work has never presented any problems. My body has stood me in good stead but that night I laboured almost beyond my own capabilities as covering Dorothea's body was a major task. When you recall the intensive search carried out by the police and the multitude of helpers who toiled day and night for over a week, you will acknowledge the brilliance of my efforts for no one ever discovered her body or suspected where it lay. The planks, which had conveniently been to hand and served as a temporary cover when first I dumped her in the pit, I laid symmetrically so that they resembled a floor, long laid. Making sure that my grave blended with the rest of the shabby hut, I covered it with builder's sand, broken tiles and bricks, upturned plant pots, half empty sacks of animal feel and long abandoned garden and farm implements.

And my labour was rewarded for she lay there for over fifty years undisturbed and almost forgotten until my fool of a husband decided to destroy the goat shed and alert the authorities of his find.

But much was to happen before he unearthed my old enemy and some will say I suffered retribution for my act although, when you think of the luxury in which I have lived this past thirty years, I doubt you will think me too hard done by.

Teddy was distraught when the search was finally called off and the case closed. Thin and ill from grief occasioned by the long hours of searching, I thought him weak and a mere shadow of his usual vibrant self. Dominic returned to university, Lavinia, quiet and lonely, remained with her parents. For myself, I might just as well have expired with Dorothea as, ignored by everyone, I took on the aspect of a ghost forever doomed to journey, unseen, along the corridors and staircases of the old house.

Aunt Doris, herself affected by the mysterious disappearance of Dorothea Stephens, began to show distinct signs of aging and, apart from serving the odd meal to her master, she kept to her room. Mrs. MacVee spoke of dispensing with her services and I worried for our future as, not being proficient in either farm or house work, I feared a lengthy stint in a Salvation Army Hostel was inevitable.

Blind panic set in.

Once the war was over the farm labourers returned. Those cheery girls who had worked the land during their absence were free to search for better paid and more suitable employment but many of the so called war heroes were lonely and restless. They sought girlfriends and some sought wives. Many a plain and poor girl I saw hastening to the altar where the promise of a protected life raising babies and enduring drudgery, seemed a better prospect than spinsterhood and deprivation.

Teddy, burying his grief in his work, I seldom saw. Lavinia remained distant. Dominic appeared and disappeared but any hopes of a future which included him, I had long abandoned. The once happy farm house was burdened with the gloom of its recent past and even Peter showed more interest in his hallowed painting than accompanying me on my solitary sojourns to the forest. For consolation, or for safety, I allowed a rough farm hand to befriend me thinking that, dislike him as I may, he presented some sort of insurance against the poor house. Unfortunately, for I was as they say an innocent abroad, I quickly found myself pregnant and deserted by my boorish companion.

The worst possible scenario presented itself. Not only did life in some run down hostel seem inevitable but total isolation loomed. Even Aunt Doris would banish me, for to be pregnant and unwed was considered a sin equivalent, in many people's eyes, to the crime I had already committed on the hapless Dorothea Stephens. Just as I was wondering if a noose tied to an oak tree in the nearby forest would best absolve my disgrace Teddy, realising the ever faithful Matty was soon to leave, offered me the position of housekeeper.

I turned him down.

What else could I do?

Some say there is a God or a guardian angel who tends our needs as we struggle through life. Maybe there is for when, finally, the family learnt of my predicament they dismissed it as nothing more than a casual inconvenience. Not only was I allowed to remain but the job of housekeeper plus a generous wage and accommodation for both myself and Aunt Doris were offered as part of the bargain. My gratitude and determination to please were paramount and I knuckled down, preparing for a lifetime of servitude. When my baby was born, the MacVee's celebrated her birth with the same enthusiasm they would have expressed had she been one of their own.

Strangely enough, for all my new found blessings, happiness eluded me for I desired much more out of life than a kitchen and a cookery book. My daughter, perfect as she was, only served to remind me of the rough brute who had fathered her and, more and more, I envied the family their position and their wealth.

But watching Teddy become increasingly restless and unwell, there were moments when I regretted my part in the disappearance of his beloved Dorothea and I softened in my treatment of him. Instead of silently passing by when we met in corridors or the cow yard I took to asking him how he felt and enquiring as to whether he was sleeping and eating well? These small tokens of interest seemed to appeal so I increased my attention and brewed fresh tea whenever I saw him approaching the kitchen. Extending my efforts, I researched cookery books and became inventive with his meals added to which I studied agricultural manuals and learnt how best to converse with a dedicated farmer for whom other subjects proved irksome. His somewhat unlikely fondness for my baby was an added bonus and although, I cared not a jot for Teddy himself, I saw possibilities in winning his approval.

You all know the outcome of my small endeavours for we were married in the spring of nineteen sixty one. As husbands go Teddy was a disaster but, since my interest in him was nil, such a boring trifle was easily dismissed. The fact that I came complete with a five month old infant, who would bear his name but not his bloodline, seemed of no consequence to either Teddy or any other member of the MacVee clan. So delighted were they that their beloved son and sorely deprived brother had found happiness with another woman that her sins were as nothing compared to her benefits!

My daughter, whom I named Rose, turned Teddy into an instant father over night. Had my feelings for him been of a genuine nature I would have suffered envy for there was no doubt he loved her dearly. Even Peter, for whom the word love was merely a four letter combination in his red leather dictionary, delighted in my child and Lavinia and Dominic appeared equally infatuated. As she grew from tiny baby to endearing toddler, her popularity with each and every one of them reached mammoth proportions, all of which I viewed as threatening. Obsessively, I worried that her constant presence would deprive me of Teddy's undivided attention and, more importantly, I had my heart set on giving him a child of his own.

Only too aware of the MacVee correctness and devotion to family, I thought it only a matter of time before they tired of my bastard and began questioning her parentage. Rose, I feared, represented no more than a novelty who would outwear her welcome as she grew older and the unique charms of babyhood faded. Without her I thought to win back Peter's attention and also claim Teddy's sole affection. Our marriage had thus far been almost sexless, an omission which I put down to his continued fretting for Dorothea and later to his contentment in the fact that, because of his devotion to Rose, he already fancied himself a parent.

But babies and very young children are fragile and a farm in those days was a minefield of danger. Everywhere lethal machines were left unsupervised as were infants who were allowed to wander the fields and collect buttercups from the water meadows where the cows protected their calves. For myself, I harboured little sentiment for my daughter as memories of her conception and the foul man who had fathered her negated any natural feelings of motherhood. Desperately needing my marriage to be a success, I decided to start my life anew but to attain my goal, most unfortunately, it became clear that Rose would have to go. In my own defence, allow me to say, that the prospect of her exit caused me some regret even though I felt my future dependant upon it.

Should this narrative sicken your hearts you will be relieved to know that it was not I who drowned Rose. Her sad death ranked only as a common accident unless my neglect can be brought to book. Fascinated by her newly acquired achievements in the walking stakes, she took to tottering to the cow yard and wandering into the partially restored buildings. One particular barn, still incomplete, was normally made secure when the day's work was finished, but due to heavy rain, the builders had abandoned their task early and forgotten to install the safety gates which prevented accidental entry.

Rose, who at the time was playing with Peter, must have trotted inside the unprotected shed and fallen into the collected rain water which lay below the foundations. Peter, too far away to steady her, screamed for help and I ran out to see what was happening. Together we watched as she floundered in the sandy waters far below ground level. Whether Peter expected me to rescue his small companion or whether she was still conscious, I cannot say as my memory holds only the briefest record of the moment. Turning quickly from the scene, I hurried Peter back to the house for, as with Dorothea, I feared he would shoulder the blame and be sent away. One day, I knew, he would be hailed as a genius and for that he must be protected.

Tragedies in common with triumphs gradually diminish and after weeks and months of heartbreak, even some on my part, the grief of Rose's death faded. Lavinia, whom I now had the privilege of calling Vinnie, married Kit Barry and Dominic qualified first as a doctor and then as a heart specialist. By this time I had acknowledged the truth of my Aunt's prediction that not all men are attracted to beautiful women. Dominic certainly was not as, being privy to family information, I had learnt that he was homosexual. Grieving for my knowledge, I contented myself that my marriage had placed me in a position where I was able to play a major part in his life and call him Dom as did the others. I also believe that I was the only member of the family who discovered that his moody and prolonged stay at the farm, after he had quit his job in Surrey, was due to the fact that he had fallen in love with a fellow heart surgeon and was lavishing both time and money in an effort to capture his attention. Such knowledge saddened me intensely but my love remained as strong as ever.

When, through the vile action of this man, whose name I learnt was Brian Thorn, he was so dreadfully hurt and disfigured, I was convinced he faced imminent death and my thoughts, once again, returned to the prospect of a noose hanging from a great tree in the forest.

For what would my life be worth if I were never to see him again?

But the family, aided by the then affluent Peter and a collection of foreign doctors, saved him and he was returned to Borough Heath thus saving both our lives for I knew no further rivals for my love would pursue him after that.

Eventually, and not without an epic struggle to overcome the indifference of my cold and distant husband, Michael was born: the true son of a MacVee. Once he was safely delivered I considered my position in the family both secure and respected. Romance and excitement were replaced by motherhood and hard work. Helping Teddy on the farm, managing the accounts and visiting my new found relatives for Sunday afternoon tea parties, became the substance of my weekly routine.

But Dominic's struggle for survival continued to incense me and I swore vengeance on Brian Thorn. Not one member of my acquired family showed the slightest inclination to seek retribution. His near death experience was always referred to as, 'the accident'. I thought them a bunch of milk sops but where they were weak, I was stalwart and my love was stronger than any of theirs for all their well bred cooing and kissing.

My hours of toil on the farm had equipped me with driving skills so, persuading Teddy to invest in a second car, I felt I had the means to hunt Thorn down. Diligently, I trawled the towns and cities of The Black Country, later completing a mile by mile exploration of the whole of the Midlands. But I learnt nothing. Since the practise in Tettenhall had been sold there were times when I feared he had disappeared for good but I remained relentless in my pursuit.

London became my next target as I knew that Thorn, like Dominic, had trained in Chelsea and had, in all probability, returned to the anonymity of the capitol.

Leaving Teddy and Michael for any length of time presented a problem as venturing far from the farm or Borough Heath was frowned upon. As luck would have it, during the most exacting period of my search, Aunt Doris was conveniently taken ill and hospitalised. Her illness provided the perfect excuse to cover my, all too frequent absences, and my devotion to her sick bed was applauded by the family as a whole!

Finding Thorn was not as difficult as you might think for he was a well known heart surgeon; even a famous one. Tracking him down proved less arduous than would have been the case had he been an ordinary working man. Just four days short of a month it took to discover his whereabouts. Due to my exhaustive endeavours, I eventually located his whereabouts. His home, which I learnt was rented, was a large Victorian villa surrounded by willow trees and dense bushes. Suiting my purpose to perfection, it stood in its own grounds some distance from the road and his car, a blue and white Standard Vanguard, was usually parked in the gravel driveway during the evening. Using the knowledge I had gleaned from my labours on the farm, severing the hydraulic brake hose presented little difficulty although the prospect of such an action actually killing him, I thought unlikely.

However, having observed Brian Thorn's driving habits I knew him to be fond of exceeding speed limits so the odds were not entirely unfavourable. Unfortunately I had to face the fact that, whereas a sudden brake failure might result in some kind of accident, the severity of such an occurrence was obviously unpredictable. Gloomily, I accepted the fact that a slight scare may rank as my only achievement and the risk of causing injury or even death to an innocent road user did not entirely pass me by.

Should this narrative have been written in praise of some worthy endeavour I could have penned the phrase, 'God was with me,' for within twelve hours of my tampering, Brian Thorn suffered a major car crash on the North Circular Road near Hendon Way and was killed outright.

In today's climate of police expertise and forensic scrutiny, I doubt his death would have been dismissed as simply as it was over half a century ago but, as no one else and no other vehicle was involved, the press reports merely stated that a prominent heart surgeon had been killed during a fatal motoring accident in North London.

Justice, I have always believed, was duly served and I had every reason to suppose the MacVee family were suitably pleased but I shall never hear their praise nor receive their thanks for they will be appalled to read of my part in their silent celebration. Years later I discovered that Dominic actually expressed regret on hearing of Thorn's death despite the fact that he was the author of such devastation to his own life.

Which just goes to show what splendid people they all are!

Now I must face my own judgement for the days of my life are few. Having read the above account of my assorted sins it will come as no surprise to learn that my belief in the existence of either a deity or a life yet to come are non existent. My only regret and deeply felt sorrow lie in the thought of parting from my beloved daughter, Maria.

Perhaps Peter will show her just a little of the kindness he was unable to show to me.

Dominic has been the love of my life but I married Teddy and have spent my life protecting Peter. Three brothers and each one so different from the other that you would be forgiven for thinking them unrelated or inhabitants of another galaxy altogether.

When, as a young woman, I understood that I would never be loved by Dominic and equally that I would never love Teddy, I thought to find happiness with Peter and for a very short time I did. Lying in his arms one night I told him how I had feared he would shoulder the blame for my part in Dorothea's disappearance and Rose's death. When I told him I had tried with all my heart to prevent his marriage to Laura he merely laughed and said he had tried to avoid it himself but equally had failed.

His attraction to Laura Bonnington was almost inevitable. Fret and worry over it as I did, it was understandable for Laura was a very pretty girl and Peter had long been deprived of anything approaching affection. Also she presented a challenge in so much as Samuel Bonnington had sought to ruin him so it pleased Peter to seek revenge. Each time the old man thought himself and his daughter rid of the hated MacVee boy, back he came and claimed her attention all over again. The last straw was her pregnancy but that was a mistake which rebounded on Peter and brought only misery to Laura.

Perhaps, if I have any regrets, they also concern Peter. As you will have gathered, my determination to protect him became feverish. The years progressed and, as each one passed, I marvelled anew. Believing his genius to be unique, I also realised that a concerted effort to gain the required recognition was paramount. Fame and fortune were within in his grasp but

I knew no obstacle must thwart his progress.

Laura's sister, Rose, (an ill fated name I will agree,) began to dominate his life. A poor crippled dwarf, whom I feared would present a hindrance to a man possessed of Peter's genius, seemed set to claim his complete attention. After a childhood of deprivation, her fondness for him stirred his emotions and, in her physical disfigurement, he recognised his own isolation. As his family had shunned him people equally shunned her. For very different reasons both believed themselves to be outcasts and Peter, identifying with her loneliness, viewed them as similar souls.

There was no question of a romantic attachment between the two, either then or in the future, but my fears were founded on something much deeper than physical attraction. Perhaps, because of my own insecure youth, I conjured images that wiser heads would have dismissed for I lived in trepidation that they would run away together. Aware that he cared not a jot for his family and little even for me I truly believed that they would quit Borough Heath in an effort to find a happier life.

Rose might have offered the affection he lacked but I saw her as an obstacle; an impediment to his talent and a drag on his genius. Laying his brushes aside, I imagined a future where he would squander his youth tending her frailty and, just as I had believed Brian Thorn deserved retribution, I convinced myself that I must free Peter from the restrains of Rose Bonnington. No member of the MacVee family were likely to move a finger to intervene. Hands were wrung and tongues wagged behind lace curtains but no action was taken to part the pair.

That was their style but it wasn't mine!

Kit Barry, my brother in law, was a good but careless doctor who allowed his house to be littered with medical samples. Over a period of not more than six tea times I collected enough pills and potions to kill half the population of Borough Heath. Perceiving myself to be the sole agent of Peter's liberation, I invited the ill starred couple to lunch at the farm where I doctored Rose's parsnip wine with a liberal dose of hyoscine. Unfortunately, although my efforts in advanced pharmacy lacked little in the way of expertise, Kit and Stafford Infirmary thwarted my efforts and restored her to her usual uncertain health. Never shy to complete a task I was forced to repeat my efforts twice more before a tempting slice of chocolate fudge cake finally claimed her life. As with Brian Thorn before her, no inquest took place and her death was attributed to gastroenteritis.

Grieving for my action would have been out of place. It has always been my belief, that should we meet in some cloudy beyond, Rose will thank me, for who would wish to grow old in the form of a dependant dwarf?

From then on my life centred upon Peter. His success became my success and I thrilled for his achievements. How dull everyone else seemed to be. Watching Teddy fight his cancer and Lavinia raise her precious children even my beloved Dominic, disfigured and spoilt, began to lose some of his appeal.

My remaining stash of Kit's pills saved Eleanor Bonnington from the inconvenience of old age and Peter, posing as a modern day Mr Rochester, seized the opportunity to banish a grief stricken Laura to a mental institution. The shy and silent Venetia he dispatched to another country altogether after which he was easy prey as he floundered round the farm trying to help his stricken brother.

I represented a diversion, a measure of fun on a sunny afternoon but when I told him I was to bear his child, his interest lapsed and he deserted me completely. But what luxury he bestowed upon the woman who thought to spend her years in a Salvation Army Hostel!

You all call my home The Taj Mahal.

I have always called it Heaven on earth.

Without Dominic my life has meant little and the years pall so I thank each and every MacVee for dubious favours and hope my saga entertains you in the quiet evening of your own old age.

Maria knows nothing of my various missions but she will miss me and your care will sustain her more than the millions that Peter will, one day, bestow upon her.

For what are riches if a life is lived without love?

Isabel MacVee.